Forever

Lost Souls MC Series
Book One

Blue Saffire

Perceptive Illusions Publishing, Inc.
BAYSHORE, NEW YORK

Blue Saffire/Perceptive Illusions Publishing, Inc.
PO BOX 5253
Bay Shore, New York 11706
www.BlueSaffire.com

Publisher's Note: This is a work of fiction. Names, characters, places, and incidents are a product of the author's imagination. Locales and public names are sometimes used for atmospheric purposes. Any resemblance to actual people, living or dead, or to businesses, companies, events, institutions, or locales is completely coincidental.

Ordering Information:
Quantity sales. Special discounts are available on quantity purchases by corporations, associations, and others. For details, contact the "Special Sales Department" at the address above.

Forever/ Blue Saffire. -- 1st ed.
ISBN 978-1-941924-05-1

Love can be right under your nose. It's all in how you see it.

—Blue Saffire

Star Gazing

Eva Kennedy

I look up at the stars that start to come out. I've graduated high school. It should be a big day, but all I can think about are the people who aren't here to celebrate this with me. The sun shined all day, not a cloud in sight.

Yet, I feel them like weights in my heart. The gloominess is there even if no one can see it. I look around the backyard of the Lost Souls clubhouse and take in all the laughing and smiling faces. I see them, but I wonder if they see me. Really see me.

I've tried not to let anyone catch me moping, but this is a hard day for me. At one point, a slight wind kissed my cheek and I almost burst into tears. My gaze lands on *him* for the millionth time, the only reason I've had a real smile at all today.

He came to my graduation BBQ. He even brought me a gift.

Music fills the air nearby, grabbing my attention. I look to see my little sister, Sal, has brought out a small radio just for our little group around our small bonfire. In the background some rock music plays, but Sal turns on some R&B and I know she's done it for me and my best friend, Misty.

Misty isn't just my best friend, she's the daughter of the Lost Souls' VP, Mix. That's a long story there, for another time.

"Ugh, I'm going to kill Colin one of these days," Erica says as she comes over with four beers in hand.

"Oh please, you'll be glued to his side in five minutes," Misty teases. "You two can't stay mad at each other for longer than two seconds. It's only the fact that you're both stubborn as fuck that you'll take a whole five minutes."

I laugh at Reap's pretty pouts. Erica or Reap as we all call her is gorgeous. It's hard not to notice even through her rough biker exterior.

Which is what draws your attention to the gorgeous best friends. Their friendship is almost as stunning as the sight of the two of them together. The pair are indeed inseparable.

"She's right, you know. He's going to say something he thinks is funny and he'll come looking for you to tell you about it and the next thing you know, you both are going to take off laughing," I say.

"Y'all don't know what you're talking about," Reap mumbles, handing over the beers.

Sal looks around before she takes one. No doubt looking for our big brother. I know exactly where King is. He's with *him*.

I steal another peek in their direction. How does a man his size make jeans and a cut look so good? His thighs are a thing to marvel at as are his arms. The rips in the jeans only make him look that much more sexy.

The white T-shirt beneath his cut stretches across his chest, showing off all his muscles as it molds to his abs. I bite my lip and sigh. If only I were older and had a little more confidence.

I push up my glasses and turn away. Taking a sip of my beer, I tune back into the conversation. A frown comes to my lips as the bitter taste registers on my tongue.

This stuff is gross.

"What are you talking about?" Sal laughs.

"Right," Misty exclaims. "You two are saying the exact same thing. Why are you so mad at him?"

"Never mind. You guys don't understand," Reap huffs.

"I think I do," Misty says.

I tilt my head at the way Misty says that. I know my best friend. She's hinting at something. Before I can lock in on what, Sal gets my attention.

"Hey, so you guys are going to school in Georgia. Are you ready for that?"

I think on the question for a bit. Sal has gone away to school for longer than I can remember. Me, I don't know how I feel.

I know King wants me and Misty to go to Georgia. I've been accepted into a great program. I've never really fit in around here, so...

"Yeah, I'm excited, I think. Something new. Maybe I can reinvent myself," I say and laugh.

"I don't think you need to change anything about you. I love that you love books and you're in your own world most of the time. Just because we've grown up around bikers doesn't mean we have to be just like them. I think Mom and Dad would be really proud of you."

I take in a sharp breath. I don't think Sal even knows how much I needed those words. I wrap an arm around her shoulders and tug her close.

"They'd be proud of you too. King and I both are." I kiss her forehead and give her a squeeze. "We just have to keep pushing. We'll make them proud."

Owen Mason aka Brick

I glance across the yard and catch her sitting with her friends and sister. I have to take a pull from my beer and shake my head clear. Where's the girl with pigtails and that chubby-faced smile?

Fuck.

I wasn't expecting any of this when I arrived. It's the dress. She's not in her baggy jeans and T-shirt. Damn. Eva is a grown woman now.

Not grown enough, asshole. She's eighteen, you're twenty-seven. King would kill your ass.

I swallow and turn away. My thoughts are so confusing. My gaze has landed on her so many times today. Something is off. She doesn't look as happy as she should.

I muse on that. Cage and Rose aren't here for this. King has thrown a hell of a BBQ, but their absence has to have a weight to it.

"What's the deal with your cousin and that chick she's been bringing around? You haven't mentioned that shit since you've been here," King says, drawing my attention.

I frown as I think of Jemma and Mags. I don't know what to think of the situation. Honestly, from the moment Eva walked out of the clubhouse when I arrived, I haven't thought about either of them.

I shrug. "I'm not sure. It's been fun," I reply.

King narrows his eyes at me. "Listen, be careful with that shit. Something ain't right about them two. I know she's your cousin. I get your history. You know I understand you, brother. Just a word of caution," he warns.

I nod and take a sip of my beer. A peal of laughter followed by a round of curses makes me turn to look in Eva's direction. Grim and Reap are roughhousing and cursing each other out.

I smile. I've never seen closer friends. I know for a fact the two would die for each other. You don't see one without the other for long.

"Those two are nuts," King says, jutting his chin in their direction.

"We all are, brother." I smile.

"Nah, Eva and Sal still have a shot." His tone has become more serious.

I scan his face. Yeah, Eva's not for me. I could never taint her with the lost soul I am. King wants different for his girls. I get it.

You do realize he didn't mention Misty?

Probably because she's seen fucked-up shit like the rest of us. I reel it in. All thoughts of Eva are pushed from my mind. Maybe I shouldn't come around this summer.

CHAPTER ONE

Not Again

Eva

Four years later…

"Hey, you coming out of there anytime soon?" my drunken "date" growls on the other side of the bathroom door.

I roll my eyes. Just my freaking luck. I can't believe I've found my way into trouble again.

King is going to kill me. I've been a pain in his ass since my mother became his dad's old lady. I became an even bigger pain when King's dad and my mom went for a ride they would never return home from.

King is nine years older than me. He was twenty-five when our parents died. He took me in without question. I'm sure he has regretted that every day since.

You probably think I was one of those sixteen-year-olds who spiraled out of control after losing the only father figure she had ever known and the mother she loved so dearly, but that isn't the case.

I never gave King any real trouble when it came to my behavior, still don't. Nope, that King could deal with. He would set my ass straight and send me on my way. No, the type of trouble I get into is the type I don't even go looking for and still can't understand how I keep finding it.

Just a few months ago, King stripped one of his brothers of his patch for getting piss drunk and grabbing me from behind. He sucked on my neck and groped my breasts when Misty ran to get King for help. King came storming out of his office, his voice rumbling like thunder.

"Have you lost your fucking mind?" he had roared.

Striker, the drunk brother who was pawing me, released me right away. "Brother, I—" Striker never finished his sentence. King knocked him out cold.

All the Lost Souls know not to put their hands on me. King goes straight ballistic if anyone even looks at me or Misty for that matter. Touching one of us is like committing suicide.

However, when it comes to me a lot of guys have a death wish. Some guy is always getting his ass handed to him because of me. Since I was sixteen, I've had a double-D cup, with hips and ass to match.

I'm five feet, four and a half inches tall. Yes, I am going to count my half. Every inch counts for this little mama here.

At twenty-two, you would think I have learned a thing or two. It's not my fault. It's not like I try to bring on the attention.

Hell, I go out of my way to avoid it. I wear baggy T-shirts and loose jeans in hopes to hide my curves. I even try to hide behind the mass of my curly bush of hair.

It doesn't work. For some reason, guys like to see if they can get the chubby little nerd to drop her panties for them. It's a wonder King even lets me out the house these days. I've packed on a few pounds that have gone straight to my hips and ass.

"Hey, you all right in there?" This guy doesn't know when to quit. He scratches at the door like a puppy begging to get in. "I'm telling you, you're in for a good time. Come on out."

I groan and pout at the door. King is going to lose his shit when he finds out what I've gotten into this time. I bet he wishes I were more like my sister, Sal.

She never gives him any trouble, but I think that's because she isn't around. Sal may have everyone else fooled, but not me.

I guess that's why King made sure I picked a college a state over. Not too far away, but far enough. I know he thought sending me and Misty away to college would be for the best, but it hasn't worked out that way so far. We're home more than we're on campus and when we're on campus, shit like this happens.

"Come on, Eva, open the door," my "date" slurs from the other side of the door.

He's such a jerk. He said he forgot his wallet in his apartment, and we would only need to stop here for a few seconds to get it. A few seconds turned into him having a few beers, which turned him into Mr. Touchy Feely.

The only reason I'm even on this date is because of Misty. She asked me to tag along on a double date with her and some guy she has been seeing. Well, my dear friend, Misty happened to get a stomach virus, which certainly stopped any plans she had to go out. She has been no good to the world for the last two days, held up in the bathroom with her phone and the toilet.

She cancelled on her date, but insisted I still go. I'm so pissed at her right now. I never date and I mean, *never*. King would have a coronary if he knew this is how my first date turned out.

A date with a douchebag. King has such big dreams for me. He wants his little sister to have it all.

Yup, I'm his little sister no matter who our parents are. He has always looked out for me. Now that he's the president of the Lost Souls, he takes his role even more seriously. I think, to King, taking care of me is one of the duties he inherited from the former president, his dad.

"I should be studying for my architecture exam, not on a date with this douche," I mumble to myself.

Then there's the fact that I also have an interview King set up for me tomorrow morning. It's for an internship at one of the brother's firms.

Oh, yeah, the Lost Souls may be a bunch of down and dirty, red-blooded bikers, but there are some really wealthy ones among the ranks. You wouldn't know it when at the club. They all blend in, rough, dirty, and as raw as they come. However, there are those among the brotherhood who have placed themselves in the right social circles to run shit.

I sigh heavily as I stare at my phone. There's only one way out of this apartment, if I want out of here anytime soon.

I plan to kill Misty.

Brick

"I've got you, brother. I'll take care of it," I say to King on the other end of the line as I sit on the edge of my bed.

"Never doubted it. Take care of my girl and make sure you get in and out without unnecessary problems, you feel me?"

"You're not talking to a rookie, King. It's been a long time since I've been a prospect. I did more than earn my patch." I chuckle. "I'll handle this like a pro."

"Thanks, brother. Good to know I can still rely on a good few."

"Call you later," I say before disconnecting the call.

It's the middle of the fucking night, but when my brothers call, I'm wide awake and ready to roll. The Lost Souls saved my life. When I was a kid, my dad used to beat my ass for fun. Cage Kennedy, the former prez of the Lost Souls, took me in like I was his son and raised me alongside his own boy, King.

I'd always been good with my hands and I loved to draw. I was also a wiz in school. Cage knew people in high places, so when he spotted my talents, he pulled some strings and sent me off to school. I didn't have to worry about a thing. From the time I was seventeen, I'd been groomed to start Soul Deep Architecture and Construction.

I have made the club a lot of money, not to mention, greasing the hands of those friends who pulled those strings for Cage. It gutted me when Cage and his old lady, Rose wrecked, killing them both on impact. I was stunned, Cage was an excellent rider. He taught me.

When I wasn't away at school, I spent all my time on the back of a bike. King and I are like brothers. As tight as can be. He's a stand-up guy and as great a prez as his father.

I sigh into my tired hands. I'd decided to help out on one of the worksites today and I'm paying for it now. Standing, I let my body crack and creak before walking into my closet. I move past my expensive suits. This call is going to require me to get down and dirty.

Someone is fucking with one of the club's princesses and that shit just won't do. A smile teases my lips as I think of the little nerdy girl who followed King around during my summers home. The last time I saw Eva was during the huge cookout King threw for her high school graduation.

Gone was the adorable little girl with the long plaits in her hair. Eva is a straight knockout and she doesn't even know it. I had to remind myself then she was only eighteen. King would have my balls if he knew the things that cross my mind every time I see Eva. She's had my attention for a long time.

"Fuck," I mutter and shake the thoughts away.

I should feel like a perv, but when it comes to her, I simply don't give a fuck. Eva will do that to a man. It's that silky smooth, chocolate, cocoa brown skin and those large brown eyes. Her eyes remind me of fine whiskey, dark and glowing. Doesn't hurt she has big fucking tits and a big juicy ass to match.

I snort at my thoughts. That's probably what the asshole who has her locked in his bathroom is thinking. I'm going to hang him by his fucking balls.

Rage and possessiveness take over as I think about what King relayed to me. Eva called him to say she went on a date and the jerk now has her hiding in the bathroom after she locked herself in there.

King has his hands tied with club business and needs someone he trusts to handle Eva's situation. I don't envy King at all. His daddy married Rose and King gained not one, but two sisters out of it.

Sal is the youngest. She's a super genius with computers. Sal has been in boarding school since before Cage and Rose's accident.

King didn't see any reason to bring her home out of the environment she had known most her life. Eva, on the other hand, became King's priority, whether she knows it or not. Everything King does has Eva's best interest in mind. He truly sees both girls as his little sisters, but having had Eva around for so many years, he favors her.

I, on the other hand, have watched Eva from afar. Eva may be a part of the club life, but she's still in her own world. It's like watching her live in her own little bubble. I haven't had real interaction with her since the summer before we lost Cage and Rose. Hell, I don't know if she even remembers me or knows who I am anymore.

I tug on a pair of jeans, a black T-shirt, and my Lost Souls cut. I shove my feet into my heavy boots and head down to the garage. I have a few cars and bikes. Like I said, I've done well for myself and the club.

At the thought of having Eva on the back of my bike, wrapped tightly around me, I head for the Harley. I start for the address King sent me in a text. Leave it to him to have a tracker on Eva's phone. I'm sure Sal was the one to put it on there too.

When I pull up outside the student apartments, I cut off my bike and climb off. Several people are hanging out of their doors, staring in the direction of the apartment I'm heading toward. As I get closer, the commotion that has their attention floats to me.

"Oh shit," one guy gasps as I walk by. His eyes grow wide and he stumbles out of the way. As I move forward, all eyes are torn from the door the yelling is coming from.

Oh, yeah, I'm one big motherfucker. You can see that whether I'm in my suits or cut. However, when I'm wearing this cut, I look a hell of a lot scarier. Some of the onlookers tuck back into their apartments, others take a step back, but are still too nosy to close their doors.

Not one of these assholes have tried to do a thing to help. They are just watching and listening. Well, I'm here to help.

I send my boot right into the door Eva's GPS signal and the raised voice of the douche she's hiding from have led me to. The door splinters off the hinges and I move right into the apartment. I follow the voice further inside, my anger growing the further I move in.

I need to make this quick, the last thing I need is the press getting wind of me having been a part of something shady, especially with my club affiliation. There are some people who would love to throw some dirt on my name and to see my company go down in flames. Nevertheless, I will never deny my brothers.

We don't usually allow me next to the trouble is all. That's the way it is for most of my brothers who conduct legit business for the club. Most people associate bikers with bad news and crime.

Sure, we may have our hands in some illegal shit, but most of the brothers run some type of legit business that brings money into the club, big money.

We also have targets on our backs because of the cuts we wear on them when not in the office. So, the cleaner we can stay, the better. Well, tonight is different. This is Eva.

"Come on, baby." The lanky punk comes into view. He's now whining at the door Eva must be behind. "You came here to have a good time. Come on out of the bathroom. Let me show you that good time."

"If she's hiding in the bathroom, I don't think she's having much of a good time," I drawl as I stand behind him with my arms folded across my chest.

The punk turns toward me, and I swear he's about to piss his pants. A grin touches the corner of my lips. He flaps his mouth open, but nothing comes out. He roams his wide gaze over me to take in my size.

It's pathetic. How did a little shit like him get a date with Eva? It pisses me off the more I think about it.

"Would you mind stepping aside. Something in that bathroom belongs to me," I say, cocking my head to the side as I point at the door in question. "Eva, get your ass out here."

CHAPTER TWO

Time to Go

Eva

"Oh. My. God," I breathe.

This night cannot get any worse. I would know that voice anywhere. I have dreams about that voice.

He probably didn't even know I existed until King called in this favor tonight. King told me he was on club business and he wouldn't be able to get to me.

When he said he was sending someone he trusts, I had a feeling he was talking about Brick, but I prayed it would be anyone else. Owen "Brick" Mason is what dreams are made of. Six five, two-hundred-plus pounds of pure controlled muscle.

When you watch Brick move, you can see every move is intentional. Oh, I should know. I watch him every chance I get. He doesn't come around the club as often as others, but when he's there, I notice.

Brick was one of Dad's special kids. Cage had a way with people. He found what made you tick and then he made you see the best in you.

I've been around the MC life for as long as I can remember, and I know for a fact Cage was a phenomenal prez. King is following in his footsteps. I guess it's in his blood.

Cage saw something in Brick and sent him off to be someone. I'm not entirely sure what it is Brick does, but I know it has made him wealthy. On a few occasions he has come to the club in a fancy car or slipped inside King's office dressed in an expensive suit. God, what that man does for a suit.

I stand and rush to the mirror, looking over my reflection. I look a mess. That usually never bothers me, but in this moment, I'm cursing myself for not following all of Misty's suggestions.

"Oh man," I groan-whisper at my appearance.

I left my hair free and wild. My bush of bangs hangs in my face, instead of pulled back into a bun like Misty ordered. I wore the tight red dress she gave me, but instead of the red pumps she wanted me to wear, I put on my black wedge heeled sneakers. Eyeliner was as far as I went with the makeup, because I almost put an eye out doing that.

Thankfully, I stopped wearing my glasses freshman year of college. That decision too was courtesy of Misty suggesting and pleading. The things I let my best friend talk me into. I don't know who's crazier—her, or me for listening.

"Eva."

I groan again, giving up on trying to push my hair out of my face as Brick growls out for me to come out once more. I love that sexy growl. His southern accent doesn't hurt at all either.

It's funny how I know his accent from anyone else's. His family moved down from Tennessee years ago, but he has never lost that drawl. It's distinct from the South Carolina and Georgia twangs I am used to hearing around the club.

"Eva, I'm not gonna say it again, darlin'. Get that ass of yours out here, now," Brick demands, causing my body to tingle all over.

"Shit," I mutter.

I'm totally going to embarrass myself. I move to the door and turn the lock, when I peek out, Brick is standing right there with his arms folded across his large muscled chest. His arms are nearly busting through the sleeves of his T-shirt.

I don't know how he pulls off those thick muscles, but still somehow manages to look lean, yet powerful. Those thighs, someone help me please. I would love to be just one leg of those jeans.

Brick has a gorgeous face to match the rest of him. He has a sharp jaw he keeps framed by the well-groomed beard he wears, but it does nothing to hide those full sexy lips of his. His green gaze seems as if it can melt through you.

I love his hair. It's shorter on the right side and a bit longish on the top, which you notice when he sometimes blows the top out. Other times, like now, he combs it over to the left side. I have always wanted to run my fingers through it. The thought alone makes my fingers itch to take action. Oh, to see my brown fingers run through his copper blond locks.

I may not have a lot of interest in the opposite sex, but that's probably because all of my interest is in this being of the opposite sex.

"He's not going to hurt you, baby girl. Let's go. I need to get you out of here, now," Brick says with a slight frown.

I nod my head in understanding. Brick doesn't get his hands dirty unnecessarily. That much I do know.

I don't get much into club business, but I do know some of the brothers are responsible for representing the Lost Souls in a better light. This has disaster written all over it if we don't get out of here.

I step fully from behind the door and out of the bathroom. I swear I hear the sharp intake of air Brick takes. He moves toward me in an instant. He nearly pulls me from the apartment after grabbing me by the hand.

I'm confused about what's happening, but I let him lead the way anyway. We're outside at his bike in no time. I'm glad my dark skin can hide the blush that takes over my face as people watch us leave the apartment.

Brick takes my purse and tucks it away for me. He then gently places his helmet on my head before he swings his leg over and onto his bike. He holds out his hand for me, to help me climb on behind him. I wrap my arms around his slim taut waist as best I can, and we're off.

Brick

If I valued my life at all I wouldn't be doing what I'm about to do. I would take Eva straight home to the apartment right off campus that King had me set up for her before she and Misty moved here. If I had any sense, that would be exactly what I would do, but my sense flew out the window the moment Eva walked her sexy ass out of that bathroom.

I thought she was a knockout the last time I saw her. Hell, she is a stunner now. All woman, all curves. She's fucking gorgeous. No kid sister left in that body for me to see. All I see is a woman I need to fuck.

I want her and I want her bad. I can tell she has no fucking clue how amazing she looks. That wild hair and those sexy as hell shapely brown legs. I've heard some of the jealous club whores calling her fat behind her back.

Eva isn't fat at all. She's pleasantly plump. She has the kind of body you want pinned up on your wall. Fuck, I want to pin her to a wall, butt naked with her legs wrapped around me. I'm out of my mind for what I'm about to do, but at this point I'm beyond caring. She's a grown ass woman now.

I pull into the garage of the old warehouse I've converted into my home. The place was a Georgia dump when I got my hands on it. Now, let's just say I have been offered millions on more than one occasion for it.

I cut the engine on my bike and hold out my hand to help Eva off first. She reluctantly places her tiny hand in mine and swings her leg off. I watch her hungrily as she removes the helmet I placed on her head. She hands it to me before she rearranges her dress and smooths a hand over her hair.

She looks up from the ground and her brown eyes meet mine. I don't know what she sees in my green ones, but whatever it is, makes her part her lips and her nipples hardened beneath the thin fabric of her dress.

I shoot my hand out and wrap it around her waist, tugging her back toward me as I remain seated on my bike. She lifts one of her hands to my chest, the other to my bicep. Her sweet breath fans across my lips as it puffs out of her mouth.

"Do you know how fucking gorgeous you are?" I say only inches from her parted lips.

"N-n-no," she stutters out.

I slide my hand down to her plump ass and give it a gentle squeeze. She moans softly and melts into my chest. Fuck, she is going to be the death of me.

"I want to taste your lips, Eva," I say huskily. "You going to let me taste you, baby?"

"Y-y-yes," she moans.

I need no further invitation. I bend my head and seize her lips the way I have wanted to for longer than I care to admit. I'm not expecting the fire, passion, and electricity that sparks between us. When she parts her lips wider to allow me access to her mouth, I growl as I plunge into the depths of her warmth. Eva wraps her arms tightly behind my head as she locks her fingers in my hair.

It's the last tug at my fraying restraint. I slide back on the seat and lift her from her feet, bringing her small, lush body across my lap. I cup one of her full breasts over her dress and start to play with her nipple. She feels so damn good in my arms.

I release her lips to trail hot kisses down her neck. Releasing her breast, I reach up and run my hand down her throat before tracing her collarbone with my rough fingertips. She shivers in my arms. I'm so turned on; I can't see straight.

Pushing the strap of her dress from her arm, I chase its descent with my lips. I then tug the dress and her bra under her breast, capturing her nipple between my teeth. Eva cries out but tugs my head closer to her heated flesh. The sounds coming from her lips are driving me to the edge.

I suck on her nipple hard before letting it pop free from my mouth. "I need to fuck you, baby. Tasting you isn't going to be enough for me."

"Yes, *please*," she whimpers as I push her dress up over her hips, letting it bunch up at her stomach.

I tear her panties free from her body, needing to get into her sooner and not later. She moves her fingers shakily to my jeans, tugging frantically at the zipper and releasing the button. I reach in for my cock to free it, lifting her up over me by her hips with one arm.

I tease her soaked pussy with the head of my cock and nearly come at the feel of how wet she is for me. I can't hold back any longer. Lining my erection up with her soaked lips, I pull her down onto me with one strong thrust.

The ear-piercing scream that leaves her lips causes me to pause. My eyes grow wide as I realize I've just rammed right through her barrier. She's fucking virgin tight. What the fuck was I thinking?

"Shit, shit, shit," I gruff. I brush her hair back from her damp face. "Baby, are you okay? I'm sorry, I wasn't thinking."

The way she looks into my eyes snatches something from my soul. Right then and there it's sealed. She's mine. Eva Kennedy belongs to me. I don't care who I have to go through to have her.

"Yes, I'm okay. You're just so big and... I wasn't..." She pauses and bites her lip. "I wasn't ready."

"I'm so sorry, baby. If I would have known I would have done this differently," I say sincerely, regretting the way I have done this, but not regretting the claim I'm staking on her.

"No, this is exactly how I have dreamed of it, over and over," she says softly.

I narrow my eyes at her. "What did you say?" I ask in a low rumble.

"I've dreamed of you taking me just like this a million times," she repeats.

I grab her face and devour her lips. Her walls start to become increasingly slick as they squeeze around me. Eva wiggles her hips and bucks forward. I take the hint, wrapping an arm around her lower waist and guiding her up and down on my shaft, slowly at first.

"Yes," she cries out when I release her lips. "Oh God, Brick."

"Owen," I growl. "You call me Owen when I'm fucking you, baby."

"Yes, Owen, yes," she cries as I pick up the pace and start to thrust up into her, hard.

"Fuck, you feel amazing," I grate through my teeth. "Shit Eva, your pussy is so fucking tight, baby. I'm trying to take it easy, but you feel like heaven."

"Please, don't hold back, I want you so much," she whimpers.

I almost lose my shit right there. I tilt her back until she's flush against the bike, shifting my body without breaking our connection I start to pound into her. I press my face between her big tits and nuzzle my bearded cheek between them before placing a kiss to the side of each. I watch as goose bumps break out over her skin. I love the feel of her soft skin against my beard.

"Come for me, baby. Give me that goodness."

I reach to pin her legs over my shoulders then lean in to take her mouth again. As soon as I plunge my tongue into her mouth, she gushes around my cock, causing me to follow right behind her. I keep pumping my hips, not wanting it to end, already feeling my cock isn't spent.

"I need to get you to my bed." I chuckle and kiss her sweaty face. "I'm not done with you yet."

Eva

I can't believe it, I had hot, dirty sex with Brick. Sorry, Owen. None of my dreams measured up to the real thing. He's huge.

Not only in length, but his girth is more than impressive. I know I'm going to be super sore in the morning, but I don't care.

We lie there covered in sweat on his bike for a few minutes, before he pulls out of me and scoops me into his arms. With little effort, he carries me to the elevator that takes us up to the main level of his apartment. He makes me feel much smaller than I am.

He walks us straight into his bedroom, placing me in the center of the bed before he heads into the en suite bathroom. He returns with a wet washcloth and climbs on the bed prying my legs open.

I look away shyly and hear him chuckle. He leans over my body, cupping my face with his free hand. He kisses my lips softly. It's a tenderness I'm not expecting.

"This is mine. Don't be shy with me, darlin'," he says against my lips, gently stroking me clean with the washcloth in his hand.

He pecks my lips one more time before returning to his task. Once satisfied with his job, he tosses the rag and starts to remove my shoes. He then pulls my dress the rest of the way off and unclasps my bra from my torso. I squirm on the bed, feeling exposed and uncomfortable.

I mean, look at him. Brick earned his name from Cage once he started to bulk up as a teen, or at least that's what everyone says. Me, on the other hand, I'm jelly and rolls to compliment.

Owen gives me a knowing look. "You are beautiful. Every inch of you. You don't see yourself like you should. Sexy, curvy, toned, and perfect," he says while punctuating his words with kisses to my lips, belly, thighs, and then he starts his way back up my body.

"If you say so." I snort.

He looks up from my belly, where his lips just finished caressing my skin. Like a panther he climbs up my body. "Darlin', you know the code better than anyone else. I don't lie, so when I say you're perfect, that's the truth," he says as he hovers above me, his nose to my nose.

"Okay," I whisper.

He fists a handful of my hair and tugs my head back. His full lips come down on mine, setting my body ablaze all over again. He groans into my mouth and cups one of my breasts with his free hand. I arch my back, pushing into him. I love the feel of his beard brushing my skin and grazing my lips.

He plays my nipple with his thumb like his favorite instrument. I'm so hot for him, I feel like my skin is burning. His heated body hovering above mine does nothing to help the situation. He's only scorching me with his masculine heat and power.

His kiss is hungry and commanding. I don't realize I'm fisting the sheets until my fingers start to hurt from the death grip I have on the fabric. Owen breaks the kiss only long enough to tear his own T-shirt over his head. I try to give as good as I'm getting. Releasing the sheets, I reach for his back and dig my nails in.

He growls and shifts his big body to shove his jeans off. He moves again until he's lined up with my entrance, his thick shaft pushing at my folds. I'm so wet. He slides easily up and down my drenched lips. I rock my hips in frustration, needing him to penetrate me now.

"You want my cock, baby girl?" He chuckles against my lips.

"Yes," I whimper.

"Tell me how much you want me," he says, and I feel myself gush at the sound of his husky voice.

"Please, I need you."

"How much, baby?" he replies, looking me in my eyes. His green stare burns through my soul.

"Please, Owen, I need you so much it hurts," I moan.

"Mmm," he grunts, but he doesn't slide into me the way I need him to.

Instead, he moves down my body and settles between my legs. I shoot my hands into his hair. He grips my thighs and takes his first lick of my inner thigh, only to follow with a lick on the opposite one as well.

The brush of his beard and tongue on my skin has me keening for more. When he takes his first stroke against my puffy, wet lips with his tongue, I lose it. I tug at his hair and bow my back off the bed. His lips curl into a smile against my skin, right before he dives in like he's starting a feast.

He licks, sucks, and nibbles on my clit, overwhelming my body with the stimulation. I squeeze my thighs around his ears and cry out his name. Misty is always telling me what I'm missing by not having sex. God, was she right.

I ride Owen's face as I tug his hair while he devours my pussy. I'm already mourning the loss of this type of loving. Where will I find a man who can satisfy me like this after tonight?

I'm not fooling myself with thoughts that I can have this ever again. Tomorrow morning, I'll be a distant memory to Brick.

He'll go back to his life and I'll go back to mine. With that thought, I ride his face harder. I want to soak up all this pleasure for my future memories.

"Owen, I'm… Oh God… I'm… yes, I'm coming," I pant.

I'm breathless as my orgasm shatters me into a million pieces. I'm still clutching his hair when he crawls up my body and plants a kiss on my lips. I moan into his mouth when he seeks my tongue with his and I taste myself on his lips.

I gasp when he slides into me finally. It's not hard, but it's not slow either. I'm so slick, my body allows his large shaft to move into me smoothly as he stretches my walls to accommodate his girth. I bury my face in his neck and muffle my cries of pleasure as he starts to move his hips in and out.

"This is my pussy, Eva," he grunts.

It's the second time he has spoken those possessive words. He has no idea how much I want them to be true. I would be in heaven if Brick would make me his old lady. I'd let him brand me in a heartbeat. Just the thought has me so wet and needy.

"Fuck, Eva," he calls out as I start to rock my hips to the steady rhythm he has set.

Owen shifts to his knees and really starts to work his hips, rolling and thrusting them hard into me. I cry out and he starts to pound into me with earnest. I can feel him swelling even more inside me.

"Ah, Owen, I can't hold on much longer," I moan.

"Don't hold back. Let it go, baby," he groans before tugging my head back so he can cover my lips.

I cry my release into his mouth, and he swallows it whole as he hisses out his own release only moments later. I'm vaguely aware of him pumping his seed deep inside me as his cock twitches with the gush of his release. I smile sleepily as I come down from my heavenly, Owen high.

He kisses my temple. "Sleep, baby, I'm going to want you again," he breathes.

CHAPTER THREE

Consequences & Truth

Brick

My phone is buzzing insistently on the nightstand. All I want is a few moments of sleep, I have to be in the office at nine a.m. I didn't get back to my place after rescuing Eva until after one a.m. We fucked until at least six. Well, I reached for her a few times after she'd fallen asleep with each mind-blowing session.

If I didn't have to get up for work, I probably wouldn't have let her up for air at all. I'm addicted to that warm pussy between her legs. It doesn't help that she lets loose more and more each time I'm inside her.

Eva turned into a real hellcat in the wee hours of the morning. I'm not complaining. I loved every single second of it.

I may be the CEO of the firm, but I take my job seriously. I have a few projects on the table that need my attention. All I want is an hour of sleep.

I would be good if I could get that. At thirty-one, my body doesn't recover the way it used to. Working on site and fucking Eva into oblivion are calling my ass out right about now.

"Fuck," I grumble as my phone starts buzzing again.

This is the best sleep I've gotten in a long time. Its heaven having the weight of Eva's body on top of mine, while I have one arm wrapped around her waist, cupping that lush ass of hers. Her warmth is pulling me under to just sleep and ignore the phone.

Fighting it, I pull my heavy lids open. I reach for my phone, so it doesn't wake her at least. I curse again as I see I'll need to get up in a few anyway. I grit my teeth, preparing for what's on the other line.

Swiping the screen, I answer the call. "Hello," I grumble low into the connection.

Eva stirs on my chest and sighs, not waking, but nuzzling deeper into my heat. I lift my hand from her ass and absently play with the hair at her temple. It's so soft beneath my fingertips. Not like my hair, but still soft to the touch.

"Where the fuck is Eva?" King growls into the phone. "She's not answering her damn phone."

I sigh inwardly. I knew this was coming. Like I said, if I had an ounce of a brain, I would have taken Eva home last night. I sat awake in between our bouts of lovemaking, trying to figure out how to handle this.

I won't lie to my brother. That's not an option. I also won't hide how I feel about Eva any longer. She belongs to me. If I have to go toe to toe with my best friend over this, then that's what I'll have to do. I'm not letting her go.

I think carefully over my next words. I don't want to get into a heated argument with Eva laying here in bed with me. I don't want to wake her if I can help it. I go to slip from beneath her, but she follows me like a magnet. I chuckle inwardly and give up trying to move.

"She's with me. She was shaken up last night, so she came to my place." This isn't a lie that I tell.

Eva was in shock from the moment she stepped out of that bathroom. It was written all over her beautiful face. Whether it was because of the situation or because I had come for her, is something King doesn't need to know right now.

King sighs into the phone, but his next words cause my brows to draw and my chest to tighten. "I need another favor. She can go to the apartment to pack a few things, but I need you to keep her with you until I can smooth some shit over," King says sounding so unlike my brother.

He sounds frustrated, unfocused, and almost desperate. This time I do pull my body from beneath Eva's and swing my legs over the side of the bed. I stand and pad my way into the bathroom. My chest is tight with the need to go to war for my woman's safety.

"What's going on?" I growl into the phone. "Some motherfucker have a death wish?"

King releases another breath. I can see him shaking his head in my own mind. "No brother, this shit is on me. I don't want to involve Eva in my shit. I just need some time. I know this is asking a lot, I need a few weeks. I don't need to complicate this any further. Trust me, when I wrap my head around this shit, we're going to need to have a few beers together," King says.

The turmoil in his voice is clear. I think better of adding to his stress by telling him about me and Eva right at this moment. It can wait, for now. Something tells me King has tipped the scales on something that has been long coming. If it's what I think it is, this could work in my favor.

"You know I have your back, brother," I say. "She's good with me. I'll take her to the apartment before I head into the office. I'll just have to move some things around."

"Thanks, brother," King says sounding relieved. I feel like shit. He's asking this of me, thinking he can trust me. "Make sure she gets her ass up for her interview and gets there on time. I don't want her thinking things are being handed to her. I spoil her and

Sal enough. The women in my life drive me fucking insane. Listen, I gotta go."

Eva

I feel the absence of his warmth instantly. I crack a lid open to see Owen's perfect ass walking into the bathroom before he disappears behind the door. I groggily notice his phone in his hand. As my brain clears and his muffled voice in the other room start to reach me, I become self-conscious and wonder if it's his girlfriend on the other line.

I have seen the women Brick dates. They are the total opposite of me. Tall, thin, once or twice, I have seen him with a Latina woman, but calling her curvy next to me is an understatement of the century. For the most part, he dates classic Barbies.

I huff in frustration with myself. I was so caught up last night. I should have never let this happen.

I've just wanted him for so long. If I really tell the truth, I don't regret it. Not even as my body screams sorely at me.

Owen is insatiable. He reached for me countless times last night, bringing me to the point of blackout with pleasure I never knew was possible. My chest tightens with jealousy as I think of any other woman knowing the pleasure he gave my body.

I mentally prepare myself for the walk of shame I'm about to do. I lift up from his bed and collect my clothes. I put on my bra, remembering my destroyed panties with a shake of my head, before stepping into my dress and sneakers. I look around for my purse and remember it's still with Brick's bike.

I need my phone to call a cab. I look at the bedside table and curse when I see the time. I have to get home and get ready for my interview. I move to leave out of his bedroom when the hairs on the back of my neck stand up, and the room turns frosty cold.

"Where the hell do you think you're going?" Brick demands from behind me.

I turn on my heels slowly and crane my head back as he moves across the room to close the space between us. Even without shoes, he looms over me with his imposing height.

Instinctively, I place my hand on his chest when he's right in front of me. The pissed expression on his face softens a bit as he places his hands on my hips, pulling me into his warm body and hard erection. My own desire pools between my legs and I'm shocked my body can still react after all the times he has taken me already.

"I need to get home and I didn't want to be in your way. I just thought I'd call a cab," I murmur.

Owen snorts, he cups the side of my face before leaning down and capturing my lips in a passionate kiss that buckles my knees. I wrap my arms around his neck, forgetting the fact I haven't freshened up and have morning breath. He doesn't seem to care.

"You're not going anywhere," he commands. "Get your pretty ass back on the bed. Once I shower and dress, I'm taking you to your place to get some things and then I'll drop you at your interview."

"How do you know about my interview?" I ask, drawing down my brows.

"You'll be surprised by what I know about you, sugar," he says with a wicked grin. He releases me and turns back for the bathroom. "You'll need to pack enough for a few days, maybe weeks, baby." He turns his head back in my direction and his hot gaze travels over my body. "If I had more time, you'd be taking a shower with me. *Tomorrow.*"

He says the last word with so much promise before he disappears into the bathroom again, leaving me stunned. I blink a few times before I have no choice but to follow his instructions. I take a seat on the edge of the bed and ponder his words.

When they start to sink in, a smile spreads across my lips. He wants me to stay with him. I bite my fist to stifle my squeal as I fall back on the bed. This can't be happening.

I pop up, sitting up straight once again and frown. One thought runs through my head.

King is going to kill us.

CHAPTER FOUR

In the Shadows

David

Somewhere in New York...

"I need more time. You have to buy me more time," she snaps into the phone. The woman is frantic, and I can't blame her.

The shit is getting ready to hit the fan. I have bought her all the time I can. At this point, I can do no more and I really don't care. I need to get as far away from all of this as I can.

I will not be able to return to Brazil and most of the States are off-limits to me now. I really know how to get myself in the middle of a mess. It's no longer worth the trouble.

I sigh heavily into the phone. I didn't know I was digging myself into such a big hole in the beginning. These two broads are going to be the death of me if I don't walk away now.

"There's nothing I can do. It is already in motion. He knows everything. His new connections already wanted a reason to go after your little boyfriend and his friends." I shrug as if she can see me. "This is on you. I have no more help for you."

"Listen to me, you care for me, don't you? He doesn't even care what happens to me or his own family. I need just a little more time," she whines and purrs as if that will make me change my mind.

I've learned to see through her. The manipulation on this one. *Dios*, I was so stupid.

"I think this is where you keep going wrong, *chica*. You are mistaking the feelings we men have for you. You were fun to play with in my bed. Now you have become an inconvenience. Do not call me again. I have nothing for you," I snap into the phone. I am growing wary of all of this.

She releases a sharp gasp over the phone. I can feel her recalculating her strategies, but I will have none of it. I wave over one of my men, covering the phone, I whisper his instructions. I need to cover my tracks before I disappear. I really have made a true mess of things.

It's not like I have ever really called any one place home, but now I've gotten myself into the deep end in the few places I didn't have to watch my back in the past. I don't want to know what my cousin has planned for me when he finds out of my involvement here.

"David, please," are the words she settles on.

"Jemma is your only hope," I reply and cut the call.

I place the phone to my forehead. My words are true. Jemma *is* her only hope. Whether I have a change of heart or that batshit crazy woman actually comes through for her, is a question of life or death for her as well as me. I just don't think I will be sticking around to find out.

I've been avoiding Jemma. She's the only one who can cause me to change my mind. I was supposed to just have fun with two hot women who showed their gorgeous asses up at my club. If I knew then any of what I know now, I would have left them right on the main dance floor and never would have invited them to the VIP lounge.

Leave it to me to fall in love with one part of a psycho duo and in lust with the other. Their crazy asses have spent the last three years talking me into all types of stupid shit and I have allowed my dick to tell me to say yes, every time.

I need to get my ass out of here before King and Brick realize what's been going on. Dead men don't fuck, so staying to help isn't going to do me any good. No matter how I feel about either of them, this is finished.

What a fucking mess.

CHAPTER FIVE

Must Be a Dream

Eve

As I follow Brick back to the garage, his scent surrounds me and makes my mouth water. We step onto the elevator as Brick pulls out his phone and starts to type out a text with his long fingers.

I bite my lip and squirm beside him. I know I should say something, but I'm afraid anything that comes out of my mouth will sound stupid.

He looks up from his device and searches my face with those probing green eyes. As the elevator slowly lowers, he places his phone in his pocket and starts to crowd my space. My chest heaves in anticipation.

"You keep looking at me like that and you're not making it to change a damn thing," he says.

I lower my lashes and place my hands on his waist, reveling in the fact that I'm touching him so freely. When he wraps his arms around my back, I tremble and melt into him all at once.

The elevator stops right as I think I've found something cool to say. However, I swallow the words as Brick lifts my head to peck my lips before he turns to get off the elevator with my hand wrapped in his.

We make our way to the bike from last night and he retrieves my bag. I'm so lost in images of him pushing inside me, I don't realize he's handing me my purse. I furrow my brows at first. However, when he turns to head for the black pickup truck a few spots over, I understand.

"I'll help you up," he says before opening the door and lifting me by my waist.

Memories if how easily he carried me last night fill my head. His hands are always so warm. My nipples harden as I think of what their warmth felt like throughout the night.

I get nervous as it hits me, he's taking me to my place. Brick is coming to my apartment. You have no idea how many times I've daydreamed of this happening.

"We'll stop for something to eat after you change and we get your things," he says with a smile as my stomach grumbles.

My entire face flushes. How embarrassing. I want to fall into a hole in the floor of the truck. That is until he reaches over and places a hand on my thigh once we're out of the garage and on our way.

"We don't have to stop. I'm sure I can find something in the apartment to grab," I say, finally reconnecting with my body and brain.

"We'll see," he replies.

My belly has bigger problems than hunger as he circles his thumb against the skin on my thigh. Lord, help me. I might need two showers by the time we get to the apartment.

Oh, shit, Misty.

I have no idea what she will say about Brick showing up to the apartment with me. Maybe I should tell Brick we shouldn't let on to anything when we arrive. If he's half as attentive as he's been this morning, she'll have all kinds of questions.

The firm squeeze he places on my leg tells me that's not going to happen. Lost Souls are alpha males. Telling them not to do something is like challenging them to do it.

My mind is consumed with what to say to Brick the whole ride to my place. When Brick parks the truck I turn to him and give a trembling smile. I feel so awkward.

"Brick—"

"Owen, darlin'," he cuts me off giving me a sharp look.

I smile like a goofball and nod. "Owen, I won't take long. You can stay here or if you want to get that breakfast—"

"I'm coming in with you," he says, looking at his watch. "Let's make it quick."

He steps from the truck without another word and rounds it to open my door. I take a deep breath before taking his hand as he helps me out. You can't say Lost Souls don't have manners.

At least the ones raised directly by Cage do. Most of the time.

We make our way up to the apartment in silence. Owen with a protective hand on my back. He has no idea how much it's working to calm me.

"You can have a seat in the living room if you like," I offer as we step into my apartment.

He grunts in response, taking in the living room. I look around the space and wonder what he sees when he looks at it. The apartment is really nice—nothing but the best for King's girls—but nothing like Owen's place.

I tend to be the neat freak out of Misty and me. I'm somewhat relieved when I note the stillness of the place. Misty isn't here. Some of my nervousness leaves. However, as King comes to mind, a chill runs through me. I'm going to have to deal with my actions soon enough.

"Can I get you anything?" I ask as I turn and look up at Owen.

He smiles down at me and reaches for my face. My toes curl in my shoes as he presses his lips to mine, then deepens the kiss. I twist my fingers into the lapels of his suit, grateful for the toothbrush he loaned me before we left his place.

He breaks the kiss and places his forehead to mine. "The clock is ticking. Shower and get ready and then you can pack some things," he replies.

It takes me a second to collect my thoughts and comprehend what he just said. My mind races with a million thoughts. To think, one botched date and here I stand. Brick is in the middle of my apartment, kissing the sense out of me.

Dream ends in five... four... three...

"Come on, baby. Get moving," Owen says with humor in his voice, snapping me from my musing.

This is no dream. I nod and head for my room to strip and get my things to shower. I look around and once again note Misty's absence. I send her a quick text.

She could hardly leave the apartment as of yesterday. I start to become concerned. What if she had to go to urgent care or the hospital and I wasn't here?

My phone chimes with a text.

Misty: Out for breakfast.

Me: With who?

Time ticks by as I wait for a reply. It dawns on me she's not going to answer right away like she normally does. I twist my lips to the side and frown, but catching the time on my phone, I decide not to press. I need to shower and pack. I also need to get into the right state of mind for this interview.

That thought alone sends my nerves through the roof. Today is a big day. It's the first step into my future.

A great internship will open so many doors. Although, I'm not even sure I want this one with this company. I plan to take it seriously because King set it up.

"Shape up, Eva," I mutter to myself as I walk from my bedroom to the bathroom.

I peek down the hall to find Owen pacing the living room as he looks down at his phone. He looks up as if feeling my eyes on him and a smile spreads across his handsome face. My breath whooshes past my lips.

Yup, I change my mind. I must be dreaming.

CHAPTER SIX

A Clearer View

Brick

I pull up outside of the office building and place the truck in park. Eva has looked nervous the entire ride. I know this interview is a big step in her career. Eva has talent.

King talks about it nonstop. I've seen some of her work and he's right. Eva is more than talented. I'd love to see what she does with it when given a chance. Time will certainly tell.

"You'll do just fine," I say to break the silence.

Eva licks her lips and nods her head. She smooths down the front of the black pencil skirt she's wearing with her hands. I involuntarily lick my lips. She's wearing the fuck out of that skirt.

I shift in my seat to get a little relief. I wish I would have called in for the day and had Eva reschedule her interview. At this point, I would have if I didn't know for a fact King will be calling later to check on how things went for Eva—which is so unlike me.

I can't say that I'm not curious as fuck about why King really wants Eva to stay with me. However, I have no complaints. King gave us a forty-five-minute window to get Eva packed up and out of the apartment.

During that time, I watched her pack her things and get ready for her interview. I have to say the thought of her spending time in my space had me giddy like a teenage boy. Only thing that annoyed the fuck out of me was, her seeming not to pack enough.

Eva placed more books and electronics in her bag than anything else. I made a mental note, I would take her shopping this weekend for a few more things. I've never wanted to spoil a woman before Eva, but she has me wanting to do all types of things I've never wanted to do before.

I scowl as she reaches for the door handle to get out of the car. Not about to have that, I place my hand on her thigh and squeeze it gently. She turns those big brown eyes on me, and a part of my soul tugs loose.

I'm thrown by the feeling. I have never been in love and I'm not sure I'm ready to start claiming I am now. Believe me when I say I have no intention of letting Eva go. I'm just thrown by such heavy feelings so early on.

Then she blinks those big eyes at me, and I can't think of anything other than having her heart fully, which of course would mean me giving her mine. Her round orbs seem to suck me in. I'm so drawn to her, it irritates me.

I never have rational thoughts when she's around. I am already playing with my life as it is. I drop my eyes to her lips before returning to her eyes. Eva looks nervously at the clock on the dashboard.

"You still have ten minutes. You weren't going to just leave without giving your man a kiss goodbye, were you?" I ask and tilt my head.

Eva's eyes go wide in her pretty face, causing me to chuckle. I crook the finger on my free hand, beckoning her to me. She licks her lips and leans forward.

I groan inwardly as her full breasts peek out of her silky red blouse. I know Eva doesn't dress with the intent to be sexy. She just can't help it.

Impatience sets in and I cup the back of her neck and drag her to my lips. I trap her full plush mouth with mine and taste what belongs to me. Her lips taste sweet from the pastry I stopped to get for her on the way here.

I deepen the kiss, wanting nothing more than to devour her. This is foolish on my part. I know she has her interview and I need to get into the office.

If I wasn't a greedy, selfish bastard, I would be satisfied with a peck on the lips and allow us both to move on with our day. I suck her bottom lip into my mouth before pulling away. Pressing a kiss to her forehead, I try to reel in my breath.

"That's much better," I breathe.

Eva pulls away with a smile on her lips as she reaches up to touch them. She looks at me with dreamy eyes, then reaches for my lips. When her soft fingers touch me, I want to suck them into my mouth, but I restrain myself.

"Should I take a cab to your place after the interview?" she asks shyly as she wipes her red lipstick from my lips.

I reach up to hold her fingers in place. "No, sugar, I'll get you home. Focus on your interview, I'll take care of the rest." I release her hand as my attention is pulled away by my phone. "Good luck, baby," I say with a wolfish smile.

I glance down at my phone and scowl. It's too early for this bullshit, but if I don't answer, this whole day can turn to shit fast. I give Eva a chance to climb out of my truck before picking up the call as I watch my woman walk into the office building.

I smile, Eva knows damn well the stilettos she has on are too high for her comfort, but she's still working them. Her sexy hips sway as she teeters on her red stilts. I adjust in my seat once again.

"Brick, I hear you breathing," the whiny voice on the other end of the phone fills my truck. I almost forgot I answered the call in the first place.

I sigh and shake my head to clear it as Eva disappears from my view. I shift the truck into drive and prepare for whatever this pain in the ass has for me today.

"How can I help you, Jemma?" I gruff.

"You can help me by not ignoring me. You said you'd help me. Why haven't I seen you in weeks?" Jemma says.

"First, Jemma, I said I would see what I could do. Whatever, this isn't my damn problem, but I'll see what I can do and when I can do it," I growl.

"It *is* your problem, Brick. If you would have paid more attention to your own shit, I wouldn't have gotten fucked over. You could have made things work. You're selfish and always have been. This would never have happened if you thought about someone other than yourself," she shrieks.

"Are you fucking kidding me right now?".

Not a damn thing she's saying makes sense. I think she's finally lost her entire damn mind. I look at the console and pull a face.

"Are you forgetting who you're talking to, Brick? You owe me," she tosses back.

"The hell I do," I bellow. "Your ass ain't gonna keep threatening me. You and that bitch are starting to get on my fucking nerves. How many times are we going to go through this? I'm not the selfish one here. Don't you forget that. I let you into my life and tried to do right by you and you brought that shit storm in with you. Now you need to fucking deal. It's over and she's your problem."

"Fine, Brick. Have it your way. Don't say I didn't warn you," she huffs and hangs up.

Of all the families I could have been born into, I get the one that's batshit crazy. Jemma is my annoying ass cousin. I don't know how I let her drag me into her shit every time, but I have done it one time too many.

Doesn't help that the one time I let my dick make a decision for me, it turned out to be a big fucking mistake. Jemma has used our shitty past against me repeatedly, but that shit stops now.

I need Eva. I need her to calm my ass down. Things just changed.

I pull up the number for Troy, the head of HR and finance, and give him his new instructions. I have already broken every rule I've set, what's one more?

Eva

I can feel his eyes on me as I walk into the large office building. It's doing nothing for my already fried nerves. Oh, my God, that kiss. As if I'm not already struggling to walk in these shoes. I swear, that kiss seared my equilibrium.

I smooth a hand over my tight bun. Again, I question my choice of clothing. Misty picked this outfit out for me a week ago.

Actually, her shirt choice was a bit tighter, but since she wasn't in the apartment when I got ready for my interview this morning, I decided to switch the shirt out. The red satin wrap blouse is a bit more suitable for my large breasts.

Toning these puppies down has always been an issue for me. However, after seeing the way Owen stared at me when I came out of the bathroom at my apartment, I feel kind of sexy and new. I know it sound silly, but the way Owen looks at me is different from the way other men look at me.

It's not the same predatory look I'm used to getting. When Owen looks at me, I feel wanted on a different level. I was stunned when he asked if I was going to just leave without giving my man a kiss goodbye.

I'm still trying to process that I slept with Brick last night and well into the morning. I should be exhausted, but I feel energized and ready to take on the world. I think that's what made me bold enough to wear the outfit… well, most of the outfit Misty laid out for me.

Speaking of Misty. I pull out my phone and check to see if she's replied to my last text. There's a text, but it's from my interview. They've changed the floor I need to report to.

I frown, wondering what that's about. Whatever, I shrug it off as I turn my thoughts to Misty and questions start to pop up. I wasn't expecting her to be gone so early in the morning. Misty likes to sleep in, especially lately.

When I texted her the first time, she gave a quick response that she was out for breakfast. When I asked who with—wanting to know if it was the friend of that prick from last night—she never replied. I have to fill her in on her boyfriend's best friend's behavior. They say birds of a feather...

I've never seen what Misty sees in Joe, Jordan, oh, whatever his name is. He doesn't seem her type at all and I haven't dismissed the eye rolls she gives when he's around. Then again, Misty hasn't been herself lately.

I've just been so consumed with school and finals that I haven't called her on it. I intend to now though. That date last night was totally her fault. I guess I can't be too mad at her for it. It did lead to my night with Owen.

Sigh. I love getting to call him by his real name. I stutter a step when I realize I didn't get his number to text him when my interview is over.

Oh, just great.

I turn to look out of the glass front doors, craning my neck to see if I can spot him, but I no longer see his truck. I backtrack a few steps to make sure he's gone and to my disappointment, he is. I look down at my phone and groan at the time.

I'll just have to figure this out after my interview. I don't have time now. I turn back around and rush for the elevator. I have nervous butterflies in my belly as the car starts to move up to the thirty-fifth floor.

When I step out of the elevator, I can feel the sweat dripping from my fingertips. I am so freaking nervous. I am grateful for the black fabric of my skirt as I rub my fingers against it.

I step up to the receptionist's desk and wait patiently for her to hang up the call she's on. I try not to squirm when her blue eyes lock on me. Once again, I smooth a hand over my bun.

Brushing my thick hair back seemed like the most reasonable and sensible thing to do. I went with red lipstick to match my shirt and shoes. Maybe that was a little too much.

The way she's eyeballing me, I feel like I'm lacking something. I slyly wipe at my nose to make sure nothing is hanging. From the stare she's giving me, I feel like something is.

She hangs up the phone and looks up at me with a fake smile. I shake myself from my self-deprecating thoughts. I try not to let my frustration show through and give a fake smile of my own.

"How can I help you?" she asks with another underwhelmed once-over.

"My name is Eva Kennedy, I am here for an interview with Mr. Reynolds," I reply as pleasantly as I can. I don't want to piss anyone off before I even get the internship.

Her eyes narrow as she looks me over again. Okay, now she's just pissing *me* off. *Internship or not I am about to let her have it... is she really glaring at me? What the...*

"Eva?" a man questions nervously from behind me.

I turn to find a medium height guy who seems to be in his late thirties or early forties standing behind me. "Yes," I reply as I look at him questioningly. I'm starting to get a bit uneasy with these two. "I'm Eva."

"Great, great," he says giving me a broad grin. "I'm Mr. Reynolds, Troy Reynolds. You have to forgive me. I'm a little thrown off my game. The big boss has never asked to sit in on an intern's interview. I just called Beth here to let her know I would come to greet you personally."

I wrinkle my brows, trying to understand what all he's babbling about. I know King set this all up. Maybe the brother he arranged this through wants to oversee things. King is quite particular when it comes to me.

I lick my suddenly dry lips, feeling the pressure mounting. King may want to see me happy, but I know him. I am sure he has told them not to just give me this internship. Knowing I now have to answer to the higher powers that be has my stomach twisted in knots.

"Okay, I hope I'm not late. I'd hate to have held your boss up," I say softly.

Reynolds throws his head back and laughs. "No, no, you are just fine. Actually, I was instructed to wait with you in his office. He's on the way up. You and I can get to know each other while we wait," he replies, but I'm not too sure I like the way he looks at me when he says it.

I shift on my heels, then on second thought, I straighten my shoulders and lift my head. I will not cower and make a fool out of myself or King. I was raised by a bunch of bikers. This guy is not going to intimidate me.

I vowed last night I wouldn't find myself in one more crazy situation. Enough is enough already. I nod my head at my thoughts, but Reynolds takes it as my reply to him.

"Come on, Eva," he says, holding out a hand to show the way. "Let's head over to the boss's office. Can Beth get you something to drink… coffee, water perhaps?"

"No, thank you," I murmur.

"Excuse me for saying this, but we don't usually get interns as pretty as you around here. Not just pretty, but impressive. I have seen some of your work, you are very talented. I have been looking forward to this interview. We haven't taken on new interns in a while," Reynolds rambles on.

"Thank you, I think," I utter the last part under my breath.

"You're welcome. So, like I said, I usually don't have the big boss sitting in on these things, but with your talent, I don't blame him. I believe you will actually be working as his assistant *if* you are offered the internship. Which is a great opportunity, by the way. You will get on-site and in-office experience." Reynolds continues to talk as we enter a large office with windows that open to the city.

He waves for me to take a seat next to him in front of the large mahogany desk. I take in the magnificent office space. The office is large but designed on a curve.

The desk we sit in front of is in the center of the curve, placed in front of an amazing view. The office branches into two sides that anchor the desk. On the right side, is where a drafting table sits with blueprints open on it. It too has a gorgeous view. I would give anything to have an office view like this.

On the other side, not too far from the desk is a comfortable-looking sofa. It's flanked by two accent chairs and in front of it is a coffee table. Instead of a view, there are pictures on the shelves, but there are a few.

I sit, listening to Troy's rambling, praying for his boss to arrive. When the double doors we came through finally open, I sigh in relief. Only to suck the air back in as I stare at the man that has just walked in.

CHAPTER SEVEN

Who I Am

Brick

I smirk at the shocked look on her gorgeous little face. Initially, I had planned to stay far away from Eva and her internship. I was going to let her work with April, one of our designers on a lower level in the building.

That all changed this morning. When I called Troy, I let him know I want Eva as my assistant and I would be a part of her interview process. I know he was thrown off, but what I say goes around here.

Besides, I know Troy and I wouldn't put it past him to hit on my woman. That shit isn't happening on my watch. From the look on Eva's face when I first entered the room, I could tell he has probably already said something that has made her uncomfortable. The guy just can't help it.

"Good morning, Mr. Mason," he says.

I glare at his dumbass as I walk to my desk. I told him to wait in the reception area until I arrived. Not in my office. I'm going to have to make some shit clear to him real soon.

I unfasten the button to my suit jacket and run my hand down my beard, all while keeping my eyes on Troy. I see he gets the point, when he squirms in his seat and turns bright red. He's fucked up.

I sit and glare at him a few seconds longer for good measure, before pulling my eyes away from him and turning to Eva. When my gaze lands on her surprised face, my scowl fades and a smirk forms on my lips.

Eva groans out loud and smacks the palm of her hand to her forehead. "Owen Mason, *the* Owen Mason, how could I be so stupid. I never put it together," she whispers almost to herself.

"Not your fault, darlin'. That's the way I've made it." I chuckle and wink at her, giving her a knowing smile. "You're just proving I'm doing my job."

Like I said before. I don't deny my connection to the Lost Souls, but it isn't something I broadcast either. When you're a man as large and wealthy as I am, people are already intimidated. There's no need to throw my club affiliation on top of that, not unless it's needed. In some circles, it is a fact best unknown.

Troy gives a nervous smile. "I'm sorry, do you two know each other?" he asks, awarding him my glare once again.

I ignore him and turn back to Eva. "I was impressed when your file came across my desk. Your transcripts are impressive, and your portfolio is amazing. I like that you sent it over as a video presentation, rather than bringing it in the old fashion way. It shows your initiative and innovation."

I sit back in my chair and stroke my beard again as I watch a stunned Eva process all of this. "What are you looking to get out of this internship, Ms. Kennedy?" I ask trying to keep this as professional as possible.

Eva licks her lips and straightens her back. I can see her mentally pulling herself together, after the initial shock. She's the sweetest thing ever. I love watching her find her bearings.

"I know that Soul Deep Architecture and Construction is one of the top firms in Georgia." She pauses and winces. I think it's once again hitting her, she has missed a big piece to the puzzle here. I try not to laugh at her. It's really an easy miss.

Besides, while in her apartment, I found her lecture notes on a discussion about my firm. Eva had doodles, scrolls, and sketches all over the sheet. It was clear she paid little attention that day.

She clears her throat and starts again. "I think this will be an opportunity for me to gain some real-life, hands-on experience and to hone my skills."

"I think this would be the perfect place for you. I plan to give you as much hands-on experience as I can," I say with a sly smile and innuendo laden throughout my words.

Troy clears his throat. He's starting to annoy me, and I can't for the life of me remember why I wanted him here in this meeting. *If he wasn't here you would be fucking her, not interviewing her.* I have to remind myself.

I cut my eyes at Troy and suck my teeth, like something nasty is in them. Troy smooths down his tie, before looking between Eva and me. I don't like the way his eyes linger on her breasts and legs. I have to stifle the growl that tries to rise up in my throat.

"Eva, I think there's great potential for growth for you here," Troy starts with a smug smile. "Working with Mr. Mason will set your career off in the right direction."

I grunt in response to his interruption. I'm sure he thinks he's doing his job, but his welcome has just run out. I'm not interested in having company any longer.

"Troy, I would appreciate if you would get Ms. Kennedy squared away to start her first day. You can leave the package she needs to sign with Beth, and I will take care of the rest," I say and wave a dismissive hand.

Troy blinks at me a few times. This isn't how things are normally done, but Eva had the internship well before today. I really was impressed with the email she sent with a full presentation on her and her skills. It was cute and brilliant at the same time.

"Oh… well… it was a pleasure meeting you and welcome, Ms. Kennedy. I look forward to seeing you around the office," Troy says as he comes out of his shock. "I'll get right to it, boss."

I refrain from rolling my eyes at the little kiss ass. I just want him out of my office. Eva mutters her thanks and Troy finally takes my glare for what it is. He hurries from my office, leaving me alone with a stunned Eva. I sit for a few moments waiting for her to speak up.

"What happened, baby? Cat got your tongue." I laugh when she says nothing.

Eva

Yes, a cat has my tongue. So many things are running through my head. Granted, I know more about the architecture firms in South Carolina than the ones in Georgia, because I had always planned to go back home after graduation. I wanted to do my internship in South Carolina as well, but King set this interview up here.

I've heard a lot about Soul Deep Architecture and Construction in my classes, but as I said, I gave it little attention because my heart has been set on going back home. Last semester, Professor James ranted on and on and on about the genius behind the Soul Deep Architecture and Construction company.

He spoke of how young the CEO and his team are. He went on about how great their ideas and designs have been in the last few years, gaining them multiple high-paying contracts. That's why I was so excited when King said he got me the interview.

I have never known what Brick does for a living and for all intents and purposes, until last night, I have only ever addressed him as Brick. The bells never went off in class when his last name was mentioned.

Our professor mentioned the CEO of Soul Deep Architecture and Construction isn't really big on photos. A Tony Tracey is the face of the company. Now him, I remember, he's gorgeous and his face is always on the cover of a magazine. Where Brick is rough, but well-groomed, Tony is the clean-cut all-American boy. I was expecting him to walk through those doors, not Brick, freaking Owen Mason.

"Why didn't you tell me?" I finally push out.

"I had no intention of interfering originally," Brick rumbles in that deep sexy voice. Everything about him is sexy.

His voice drives me nuts and each time he strokes his beard, I want to run my fingers through it. I love that while his hair on his head is a copper blond his beard leans more on the side of being a true red. His lips are full enough not to be consumed by his facial hair.

He's killing the tailor-made charcoal suit he has on. The gray tie around his neck is doing something fierce to his green eyes. I feel a shiver run through me as his gaze pierces me.

"What changed your mind?" I murmur.

He lifts to his full height and moves around the desk, until he's standing before me. He leans against the desk and looks down at me. I fight not to squirm in my seat.

"You," he says and holds his hand out. I place mine in his without further thought. He pulls me into his arms. "I would much rather have you with me each day. I think I have become addicted to you, Eva."

His words are breathed into the crook of my neck. I shiver and wrap my arms around his neck. He tightens his embrace around me, slipping his hands down to cup my ass. When I wiggle my behind in his hold, he growls into my heated skin.

"Owen," I whimper when he sucks my skin into his mouth.

"I have a full hour to indulge in your delicious body, Eva. I'm not going to make it through the day without being inside you at least once," he says huskily.

"Yes, please," I beg.

Just as fast as the words leave my mouth, I'm flat on my back. A gasp leaves my lips as I hit the desk and look up into blazing green eyes. Owen is so large looming over me.

"I love that begging, darlin'. Think you can keep that up for me while I eat this pussy? Will you do that for your man?" Owen says. His drawl is heavy and sexy as hell.

And there he goes calling himself my man again. Is that who he is now?

"Owen," I say softly. My gaze pleading with him not to make me feel like shit for asking with whatever answer he gives. "What is this? What are we doing?" I bite my bottom lip, but I refuse to take my eyes off of him.

He wrinkles his brows and pauses his hands that were pushing up my skirt. "I thought I made that clear already," he says with a scowl on his handsome face. He leans into me and takes my lips with his. I grab onto his suit jacket to keep from drowning.

I whimper his name when he breaks the kiss. Breathless, I cup his face as he stares into my eyes. Suddenly, all lightness leaves the room and I know his next words are going to be heavy.

"You belong to me, Eva. You're my woman and I'm your man. I know I owe my pound of flesh for taking you the way I did, without going to King first, but it's done. I will pay whatever price is owed. I'm not letting you go. Now come here, I want you even more," he commands.

His lips meet mine with impatience and a passion I have never known. I push his suit jacket from his shoulders. He tosses it behind him. In a flash he has his hands under my skirt, tearing my panties down my thighs.

Owen breaks the kiss to drop to his knees. Pushing my skirt up over my hips to my belly, he releases a groan. He hooks my legs over his broad shoulders. I cry out when he places his large hand on my belly and flicks his tongue out over my slit.

He hums a throaty sound but doesn't pause in his full-on assault. I lock my fingers in his copper locks and hold on tight. His beard only adds to the pleasure as it brushes my soft skin.

I sort of forget we're even in his office as I sing his name and pant for more. I beg just like he asked me to. I only remember where we are when both his office and cell phones start to ring.

I clamp my mouth shut, but Owen doesn't seem to care as he doesn't stop for a single second. He actually shoves his face further into my folds. I hold my cries in as my legs begin to quiver. I'm dripping all over his desk.

"Eva," he growls into me.

"Yes," I whisper.

"I can't hear you, baby," he groans. "I feel you about to come, but I don't hear you. What's the fucking problem?"

"Owen," I moan. "I can't, we're in your office. Someone might hear."

He lifts to his feet, unfastens his belt, and shoves his suit pants down his hips. His thick cock springs free, looking swollen and angry—if that's even possible. He pushes my thighs further apart and shoves his rock hard length into me. We both cry out as my channel sucks him in and tightens around him.

"Mmm, ah, shit," he grunts and leans to kiss me with my juices clinging to his lips and beard. "Do you think I give a shit?" he grinds out as he pounds into me. "I own this pussy and I want to hear you say it. Don't ever hold back from me."

"Oh God, yes," I cry out loudly, so loudly, I nearly miss the shouting and pounding outside the office door.

Owen, however, seems to totally miss the noise as he continues to thrust into me. "My Eva," he breathes as he gives me hard long strokes, then follows with hard short ones.

My toes curl in my heels and I grab a hold of the back of his sweat-drenched dress shirt. I'm in a cross between ecstasy and confusion. He feels so good, but the shouting and pounding outside the door is getting louder.

As if he can tell my focus isn't solely on him, he pushes his fingers into the back of my bun and pulls my head back until I have no choice but to look into his eyes. With his other hand, he grabs a hold of my butt cheek and squeezes hard. He drills into me without mercy, rolling his hips at just the right angle.

He looks so sexy as his nostrils flare, he bites down on his lip, and his eyes roll back. I think I'm coming just over the beauty of watching him enjoy being inside me. The grunts and groans are just the perfect complement to the perfect meal. Owen is just that delicious.

"I'm coming," I gasp in awe.

"Fuck, I know, baby. Shit, I'm right with you," he bellows.

His hot seed bursts into me as my walls quiver and contract around him. It is then when the air in the room changes, I become aware the banging has stopped. Owen is quick to pull me into his chest before he turns his head to look over his shoulder.

His body tenses against mine. "I know I locked that fucking door from my desk, so why the fuck is she standing in my office?" he demands.

"I'm so sorry, Mr. Mason," comes the voice of a female. I think it's that receptionist.

I peek around Owen's large body and sure enough, it's her, standing there with a smug, disgusted look on her face. The bitch's smile soon fades with Owen's next words.

"I told you she's never allowed in my office without my say so," he bellows. "You're fired, get the fuck out and take her with you."

I look to see who the *her* is and next to the receptionist, Beth— *was that her name*—stands a tall thin but shapely woman. She's brown, but not as dark as me. She has a Latina look about her. She has on a tight white dress and nude heels. The outfit is completed with a pissed off expression.

"I'm not going anywhere until I talk to you. You won't listen to Jemma, well now you can deal with me," she says heatedly.

"Get the fuck out of my building, Magdalena," Owen says with a deadly calm that hits harder than if he had yelled it.

I duck back to see his face. I can only see his profile as he scowls at the women at the door. A vein pops out the side of his forehead as one throbs in his neck. His grip on me tightens as he holds me closer. He is still inside me, so I remain still.

"Fuck you, Brick. Tell that whore to leave so we can take care of business," Magdalena says.

Owen slips from my body and tugs up his pants in a flash. He fixes my skirt enough to cover me and then storms over to the stunned women at the door.

"What the fuck did you just call her?" he sneers into Magdalena's face.

"What does it matter? You fuck them then leave them. Why is this one any different?" she replies and lifts her chin.

"*This* one is very different, Mags, so different that if you ever, and I mean, ever, disrespect her again, I will make your miserable existence even worse," Owen says darkly.

Magdalena goes pale and takes a step back. Her gaze travels over me and she narrows her eyes in my direction. I fidget with my clothes, feeling embarrassed to have had them walk in on us.

"Oh please, how much worse can my life get, Brick?" she says as she keeps her eyes on me. A chill runs through me when she smirks in my direction. "After all, I did just walk in on my husband fucking another woman."

What the fuck did she just say?

CHAPTER EIGHT

Wrong Man

Brick

I nearly vibrate out of my skin. If looks could kill, Magdalena would be dead on the spot. I look at the evil bitch as if I could burn her to a crisp right where she stands. I don't even turn to look for Eva's reaction. I can feel her and I'm ready to lose my shit right here and now.

"Eva, don't you move, keep your ass right there. She's my ex-wife and it's a lot deeper than the shit rolling around in your head, baby. Don't. Fucking. Move," I growl out, still not turning to face Eva.

I look into Magdalena's eyes and see the soulless bitch for who she is. "You were the biggest mistake of my life. I let you and that little vindictive, manipulative cousin of mine talk me into marrying you and I have regretted it every fucking day since.

"Whatever shit you've gotten yourself into now, it's on you. I don't give a shit and I'm not helping. You fuck with my woman, now you pay the price," I say and fold my arms over my chest.

"Your woman," Magdalena seethes. "She's nothing but some little girl you're chasing time away with. You haven't known a woman since the last time we fucked."

"Unbelievable," I hear Eva breathe from the desk behind me.

I close my eyes and my nostrils flare. I can't believe this shit is happening after the amazing sex I just had with Eva only moments ago. I open my eyes and address Beth first.

"Why are you still here?"

"I... I... I, you're really firing me?" Beth asks with a look of complete confusion on her face.

"I've never minced words around here, Beth. So, I'm having a hard time figuring out why you're suddenly having such a hard time comprehending."

Beth nods as tears fill her eyes. She looks at Magdalena as if she can offer some help or comfort. Magdalena looks at her in disgust and rolls her eyes. "You're no good to me now," Mags scoffs.

I tighten my jaw as I think of how long Beth has been helping my bitch of an ex-wife. It's taking everything in me not to explode right here on the spot. I pull my cell from my pocket.

"I need security up here in my office. Beth Rogers is not to leave this building until Diggs gets here and talks to her," I speak into the phone as I watch both Beth and Mags' reaction. They both pale and look nervous.

Diggs works for an outside security firm I hire, and yes, he's a Lost Soul. Both Beth and Magdalena have run across him before. He's one scary sight. Gruff, huge, and tattooed, Diggs is just intimidating. He has a young face that matches his age, but the front of his hair is gray and adds something sinister to his aura.

There's a squad within the Lost Souls who you just know not to fuck with. Diggs happens to be a part of that squad. Magdalena knows this to be a fact. Beth, I can tell, has assumed as much from the vibes that come off of Diggs when he has come by my office.

I shoot a text to him, so I can find out what has been going on behind my back. Magdalena looks like she's contemplating running. She just can't manage to pull her attention from the woman behind me long enough to try.

I know exactly where Eva is. My body is attuned to hers. I feel as she walks up behind me. I reach behind my back for her waist and pull her against me. She won't be bolting around me for the door.

I smirk to myself when I hear her gasp for air as I pull her close. Her breasts crush against me and I swear my cock twitches for her. I don't know if I will ever get enough of her.

I look over my shoulder. "I can explain it all. You're not leaving this building without me," I murmur to her.

She just looks up at me with her big brown eyes. I can see the sadness in them, and it tightens my chest. I shift to kiss her forehead but keep her pinned to my back.

"Learn to trust me," I whisper.

She nods, but I see the mistrust written on her gorgeous face. I bite my lip in hopes to reel in my anger. Unfortunately, Mags has never learned when to shut the fuck up.

"Where'd you find this one? What makes her so special?" she says as if disgusted.

I snap my head back toward Mags, but to my surprise, I'm not the one who gets to respond. I'm stunned as Eva shoves me aside. She steps right into Magdalena's face and points her finger.

"Let's get one thing clear. I don't give a fuck if you are his present or past wife. That's between the two of you. What you're not going to do is disrespect me, like I'm not in this room," Eva fumes in Mags' face. She moves in closer, still pointing.

"What I do know right now is that he belongs to me until you can prove otherwise. So far, you haven't done shit that has. So, fuck with what's mine and I'll show you what's so special about me," Eva warns.

A smirk reaches my lips. I'm so turned on. *Now that's how you handle being my old lady.* Hearing those words in my own head swells my chest with pride and want.

Not want for pussy, but a want I've never had before. Eva is fast becoming something I hadn't even known I wanted. I lick my lips and close the space to wrap my arms around my woman's waist. I pull her back into my chest and kiss the top of her head.

"What makes her so special is that she's mine. Don't test that, Mags. I mean that shit. Don't come for my woman," I confirm. "I've told you. I'm not helping you. We're done."

I watch as fire and fear ignite in Magdalena's eyes. For the first time, I don't think I'm the sole source of this fear. She has really gotten herself into some deep shit. I shouldn't care, but my instincts cause me to pause for a moment.

Then my commonsense kicks back in, this is Mags. She and Jemma live to stir shit up. I'm not getting dragged into her manipulation. Not this time.

Eva may have stood up for her place as my woman, but I can still feel she's questioning everything in her pretty little head. Straightening that shit out is more important to me at the present time. I need her to know she's the only one who matters. I don't give a shit what Magdalena has to say at the moment, because with each second that passes, I can feel I'm losing my woman.

Eva is slipping right through my fingers, even as I hold her. I can't have that. I tighten my hold on her waist. I've already made up my mind, the rest of this day is going to be run remotely.

I'm going home and taking Eva with me. We need to talk. I need to clear all of this up. Mags has the wrong man if she thinks she's going to barge in here and demand shit from me.

"This isn't over," Magdalena says as she tears her eyes off of Eva to glare at me. "We will be talking, like it or not."

Mags turns and storms from my office, leaving a stunned and nervous-looking Beth in her wake. I snort. Mags is right about one thing, this isn't over. Once I have things cleared up with Eva, I'm going to get to the bottom of what Mags and that trifling cousin of mine have gotten themselves into this time.

As security enters my office to retrieve Beth, I loosen my hold on Eva. I turn her in my arms and look down at her. The disconnected look in her eyes flays my insides.

"Let's get you cleaned up and I will explain." I sigh and plant a soft kiss on her lips.

I nearly growl when she doesn't return the kiss with even a small gesture of receiving my touch. I hold on to my restraint and place a hand on the small of her back. I know my cum has to be running down her legs. It's the only thing that has me holding on to my sanity.

The simple fact that I know I've branded her as mine several times since last night. Despite the conversation I'm having in the back of my mind about whether or not Eva is on any type of birth control, I refuse to ask her because I will never enter her body with anything between us.

I have never slept with another woman without protection. Not even my ex-wife, for as long as I was bewitched by her. Eva is the first and I plan to make her the last.

I lead Eva over to the bookshelves in my office. I reach into the shelf where the hidden switch is and pop the lock with my thumb print. I make a mental note. I need to get Eva printed so she will have access to my hidden apartment over my office.

There are few who know of the hidden panel or my apartment. I look down at Eva, watching her reaction to me opening the hidden door. I smirk at the look of appreciation only an architect at heart could have.

I can't wait for her to see the apartment itself. I know she'll love it. I'm hoping to defuse some of her uncertainty with something I know she will appreciate.

Fingers crossed, Mason.

Eva

I'm burning with anger and most of it is anger toward myself. I can't believe what just happened. Just after Brick said he belongs to me, his wife walks in on us having sex.

He says it's not what I think, but I'm not sure I believe that. Now that the shock has worn off, I remember the woman he called Magdalena. She's the Latina woman I've seen Brick with more than once.

She's not like the other Barbies I've seen him bring around only once. No, I've seen her a few times before. I just never knew she was his wife.

I feel an ache in my chest as Owen leads me over to the bookshelves. I furrow my brows at first. I have no idea why we are going to the gorgeous shelving. He just said we were going to clean me up.

I kick myself mentally as our mixed essence rolls down my thighs. I feel stupid and cheap. The soreness between my legs earlier had felt like a delicious reminder of last night. Now, it just feels like the sting of my stupidity.

Once again, I've gotten myself into a mess. King is going to kill us both when he finds out. I don't know what I was thinking.

My eyes widen and I'm pulled from my mental chastising. Owen sticks his hand in the bookshelf and a panel pops open. As the door widens a staircase comes into view.

I'm floored. The staircase leading up to the next level is made of glass. Each step is backlit by soft blue lighting that illuminates the landing.

Owen lightly nudges me forward with his hand on my back. I begin to climb the stairs one at a time on heels I'm already teetering on. I gasp as the stairs glow brighter with each step I take. I reach for the banister and make my way to the top.

If I was impressed with the staircase, I'm in awe of the apartment. From the breathtaking wall of floor to ceiling windows to the seemingly open floor plan that reveals a kitchen and living space.

I say seemingly because there actually are walls, they're just made of panels of glass. I have to blink when I notice the glass has been fashioned to separate the space without actually looking like it's there. It's simply breathtaking.

"The glass is designed to frost over when privacy is desired in any one area. Each panel can frost into a range of four different colors," Brick says close to my ear, reminding me he's behind me.

"It's... wow, this is mind-blowing," I murmur.

"I like a little variety in my space," he says with a smile in his voice.

I turn to look at him. "Yeah, it seems you're like that with more than your space." I frown up at him. I didn't mean for it to come out as bitchy as it does, but my feelings are still a little raw and confused.

I watch his jaw tic under his bearded skin. It's like his green eyes blaze as he seems to reel in his temper. I don't flinch away like most would do around him or men like King and the other brothers. I've learned to stand my ground around bikers, or they'll run you right over.

Brick nods at his own thoughts. He reaches to lace his fingers with mine, then leads me up the hallway that has a view into the kitchen on one side and a gorgeous dining room on the other. As we move further up the hallway, I notice the glass panels in this area start to take on a gray frosted hue, making them no longer see-through on either side.

"I usually keep the bedrooms blocked off," Brick grumbles beside me as if by way of explanation.

I can still tell his words are tight and measured. As if he wants to show me the apartment, but there's something else pressing on his thoughts.

He pulls me to a mahogany door that has frosted glass inlays and pushes it open. When I step into the master suite behind him, my mouth falls open. The attention to detail is amazing.

However, I don't get to take it all in. Brick pulls me into the bathroom. It's just as amazing as the master suite. The walls in here are constructed of the same thick glass panels, but what makes the bathroom outstanding is the mix of glass and brush metal finishes. Even the shower walls have an intricate design of blue glass and gorgeous brush nickel basket weave tiles.

Brick leans over the huge tub and presses a few buttons with his free hand. Water begins to fill the tub on both ends from what appears to be thin air. I lean in and see there are slits in the walls on each side and the water is pouring from them.

My imagination takes off on different designs and my fingers itch for a pad and pencil. I'm in such awe, I don't even feel when Brick releases the zipper at the back of my skirt.

When it falls to my ankles, I turn and look up at him. He strokes my cheek with his fingertips as his eyes lock on mine. I'm brought back to my present dilemma once again.

I reach for his hand when he goes to release my shirt from its wrap. "Brick, I—" I start, but he cuts me off with a growl.

Cupping my face in one of his large hands, he places his thumb under my chin and tips my head back. His eyes are fierce as he locks them with mine. I can see his ears are red. I remember from when we were younger, they turn red when he's angry.

"You're mine, Eva. There is nothing and no one who can or will change that. You're angry, but you need to reel that shit in. You're gonna let me explain that shitstorm I used to call a wife and then we're going to move on," he says.

"You don't have to explain anything to me. I think this was all a mistake," I say softly.

He places his hand on the back of my neck and tugs me into his body. He crushes my lips with his own and consumes every part of my being. When he releases me, I don't even know what I was trying to say to him.

He searches my face before he reaches to complete his task of releasing my blouse. I bite my lips and shift on my heels. He slides his hands into my shirt, pushing the blouse from my shoulders to the floor.

"I'm laying it all out, Eva. We're going to get to know everything about each other. The way I should have done this in the first place," he mumbles and pulls a face.

I nod and allow him to remove my bra. He then reaches for his tie and tugs it loose and over his head. I watch as he starts to unbutton his shirt before dropping it onto the pile at our feet.

Once his pants are unfastened, he drops them to the floor. I turn away, folding my arms around my middle. Brick reaches for my chin, bringing my head back to face him. A smile traces the corners of his mouth.

"Don't be shy." He winks at me. "I know you like what you see."

I bite my lip, trying not to smile back at him. He turns and walks over to the vanity. He opens the mahogany cabinet door and reaches inside. He pulls out a tub of what looks like bath salts or something.

It's brand new. I allow my smile to surface as I watch him concentrate on taking the packaging off. He fumbles to peel the plastic from the container with his big fingers. When a giggle bursts from my lips, he lifts his green eyes to look at me through his lashes.

I'm shocked when he sticks his tongue out at me. It's the last gesture I expect to come from this giant biker. It's adorable and playful all at once, melting my heart.

I reach out a hand. He walks over, placing the jar in my palm. I proceed to open it as he places his hands on my hips. As I peel the plastic away, he dips his head to lick and nip at my neck.

He moves his lips to my ear. "I'll do better," he whispers.

When he pulls back, I look up into his eyes and hand him the jar. He takes it from my hold, making sure to graze my wrist with his fingertips. A shiver runs through me.

I wrap my middle again as he moves to shake the pink and white contents of the jar into the tub. When the scent of vanilla and strawberry reaches my nose and bubbles begin to form, I realize it's bubble bath. Brick closes the jar and turns off the water by pressing more buttons.

He moves to return the bubble bath to where he got it. This time I watch from under my lashes as his manhood points straight at me. He stops right in front of me and scoops me into his arms. I yelp and wrap my legs around his waist as he lifts me in the air like a small kid when I'm anything but.

He steps into the tub and sits us both down in the warm water. I suck in a breath and wince a little as my tender flesh meets the liquid. Brick slides his hands down my back and cups my ass. He kisses my nose and looks into my eyes.

"My childhood was fucked up," he begins. "Your daddy saved my life. If it weren't for Cage, I probably wouldn't be alive and I damn sure wouldn't be where I am.

"My family just ain't shit, darlin'. My father beat the fuck out of me and in the trailer next door his sister allowed her boyfriends to do whatever they wanted to my cousin, Jemma."

"Oh my God," I breathe.

He nods tightly and continues. "When your daddy took me with him, I didn't look back. Jemma was a bitch to me. I hadn't known what was going on with her to know she had a reason for it.

"I found out when she showed up on my doorstep one summer after having the shit beat out of her. I handled shit for her and gave her a place to stay until she turned eighteen and took off on her own." His eyes are distant as he speaks and massages his hands over my cheeks under the water.

"I sort of felt like it was my fault. I believed that shit for a long time. Jemma has used that against me again and again. The fact that I was right next door and did nothing, knew nothing. I was a kid too. Took me a long time to accept that as truth. There was nothing I could have done differently.

"We're only a year apart, but the things Jemma has been through have damaged her deep and added years. When she returned to my doorstep with a friend and a sob story, I fell for it."

"Mags?" I ask and furrow my brows.

He nods and his lips thin. "Jemma and Magdalena came to me with a tale that sucked me in. I was full of guilt, young, and dumb. Mags was a gorgeous girl in need, and they suckered me right into being her knight in shining armor.

"I had no idea Mags was already in a relationship with my crazy as fuck cousin. I didn't know until after I'd been married to Mags for over a year. I came home to find my cousin, Jemma, fucking my wife."

Brick frowns and shakes his head. "That shit fucked my head up. Jemma was eating the same pussy I'd been fucking for more than a year. I knew I wasn't in love with Mags, but that shit still crushed my ego.

"I wasn't even turned on by the shit because Jemma is my fucking cousin. The two came clean and told me they were always lovers. They just needed me to keep Magdalena out of Brazil for good.

"Sad part is, Jemma doesn't realize Mags uses everyone until they're of no use to her anymore. It's only a matter of time before Jemma finds out who Magdalena really is. She's manipulative…" He stops talking, realizing his voice has started to rise and his chest is heaving.

I dip my head and kiss his pec, then lift to kiss his lips gently. He glides his hands up my back, crushing my breasts to his chest. His mouth hovers within inches of mine, he flicks his tongue out to sample my bottom lip, disintegrating the tender kiss I just pressed to his.

He places his forehead to mine and starts talking again. "I did everything they asked of me back then, but Mags decided she wanted more. She fought me tooth and nail on the divorce even after I used my connections to give her a new identity and new life.

"Mags is a liar, a cheater, and a virus of the worse kind. Trouble follows her and Jemma is always there to get her out. I was never married for love. I was married to help her get a green card and to have a safe place to stay.

"I didn't value love and a relationship like I do now. You feel me?" He finishes as he looks right through my soul.

"I feel you," I whisper right before he seals his lips to mine.

We remain in a heated kiss before he breaks it and looks me in the eyes again. His expression is impassive. I can't get a read on him.

"One more thing, darlin'," he says firmly. "Just like when we're fucking, when it's just you and me, I'm Owen to you. Brick is who I am to my brothers, not my woman."

"Okay, Owen." I smirk.

"Now turn around, I want to know everything I don't know about you and you can ask me anything you like," he commands.

I turn and settle between his legs. "Well, where do you want me to start?" I look over my shoulder to say.

I reach for his legs and run my hands over his powerful thighs that are beside me. "I'll be needing to feed you soon, so how about you start with what you like to eat? You still make those pancakes?"

I freeze in his arms and blink up at him. I know I must be looking at him with a stunned expression on my face. I search his eyes, not comprehending how he remembers such a thing.

"You remember that?" I say in awe.

I can't believe he does. One summer, when Brick was home from college, he and King had stayed out late partying. The next morning—because I knew it was the only way I could hang out with them—I made them breakfast.

He snorts. "Best damn pancakes I've ever had in my life. How could I forget?"

I made pancakes, eggs, and bacon. I recall they both devoured every last crumb. I was so proud of myself that day. I never in a million years would have thought he would remember that.

"I was like fourteen." I wrinkle my nose at him.

"Yeah, so, do you still make 'em, cause it's been that long since I had good pancakes," he says with a sparkle in his eyes.

I nod and give him a small smile back. "Yeah, I do. We may need to go to the store."

"No problem." He nods and starts to massage my shoulders. "Now, tell me what your plans are after graduation."

CHAPTER NINE

Forgotten Kings

Mix

Somewhere in the Georgia mountains…

"King thinks you're in New York checking on things?" the old man in the wheelchair asks. His voice is raspy and strained, not at all what it used to be.

"Yeah, I have my boys in New York seeing to things until I get there," I reply.

"He's running a tight ship, I see," he says with a firm nod and pursed lips.

"Yeah, the kid is doing well. I'm proud of him," I say and nod my head. I am proud of King even if I have a suspicion he's keeping something from me. I guess we're about even there.

In the end, it will all be a matter of who's willing to forgive who. I'd say I've had more time to deal with what I have been suspecting. King is going to be blindsided with this completely.

"Does he know trouble is headed his way yet?"

"No." I shake my head with a grim frown on my face. "I've kept a lid on things. I think his iron fist has held things off for this long. No one can find a way in. Too many are scared to come after the Lost Souls. They know about the Squad and are scared shitless of them."

The old man grins as much as his scared face will allow. "I would fear them if I didn't know the face of death for myself," he says. His grin falls as quickly as it appears. I know the conversation is about to take another turn. The same turn it takes every time I'm here. "Any change?"

"No brother, not yet." I don't have the heart to say there never will be. I know hope of there someday being a change is the only thing holding this brother up.

He swallows hard as he looks off into the distance. "How does an old son of a bitch like me get so lucky…" He doesn't finish the rest of his thought, but I've heard it enough to know what comes next.

"I'm hoping we all have your luck. Squad or not, this is coming for us all. He plans to finish what he started, and he has leverage and timing on his side this time. I think our clock is running out," I reply gruffly.

The old man nods. "I've been readying myself for this day. I think I've been readying myself long before I knew this day was coming. The bones in my closet are ready to rattle. We're going to see if the boy lives up to his name."

I snort. "King won't go down without a fight."

"Good, cause neither will I."

CHAPTER TEN

Just a Man

Eva

With yesterday forgotten, I find myself laying on Owen's chest. Yes, I have mentally started to call him Owen after he has growled at me a few times for slipping and calling him Brick.

After our bath, he called his housekeeper to get the things I needed to make us pancakes, as well as a few other things I asked for. By the time Owen had me dressed and we returned to his place in the old warehouse, everything I asked for and then some was stocked in his kitchen.

I made us pancakes for lunch and since he couldn't keep his hands off me long enough to allow me to cook, we had takeout for dinner. The beginning of yesterday had started off rocky, but it ended on a sweet note. Today has started off the same.

We only moved out of bed to relieve ourselves and freshen up. Then we ended up right back in bed cuddled up and have been that way since. It's been about two hours now.

"What were you thinking?" Owen chuckles as he runs his fingers through my hair.

"I don't know, I wasn't thinking." I giggle. "He pissed me off. I reacted."

"King has mentioned that temper of yours," he says with laughter in his voice.

"I'm working on it." I shrug. This is the millionth story I've shared with him. We've been trading stories about ourselves since last night. I think at this point, he knows me better than Misty does.

"He was only trying to cheat from your paper." He laughs. "Did you have to kick him in the balls?"

"Yes, yes, I did. I asked him to stop," I say with a sage nod of my head.

"I'm never looking at shit over your shoulder."

"I have a question," I say and pop my head up to look at him. "The apartment at the office is amazing. Did you design it all?"

"Every last detail. I didn't think we'd get those plans approved. We tried for this place, but no matter how deep my pockets are, it was too much glass for this structure, and they weren't willing to take the risk.

"I would have had to compromise on too much of the structural design to get approved. The office is exactly what I envisioned," he says proudly.

"You have a brilliant mind. We have to go back. I didn't get to take it in fully," I say in awe of his work.

"Anytime you want, darlin'." He chuckles again as he glides his fingertips up and down the center of my back.

The sound of my stomach growling takes over the room. I blush and bury my face into his chest. His chest rumbles with laughter.

"Come on, baby, let's see if we can find some leftovers," he says through his laughter.

"Do you cook?" I ask as we walk to the kitchen stark naked.

"Not often. I suck at it," he says with a shrug.

I laugh and wipe my sweaty palms on my thighs. You would think I would be more comfortable by now, but Owen is... Owen. Huge, sexy, and imposing. I feel so small as I walk beside him.

His body is perfection. I'm still trying to get used to the fact he's my man and he likes to see me walking around his place naked as the day I was born.

In the back of my head, I keep asking myself if I'm dreaming. I can't believe I've slept with this man, that thought alone is enough to continue to make me nervous. He has told me he can't get enough of me, but I still don't know if I'm doing all I can to please him like he pleases me.

"Well, how do you eat?" I ask and wince at my lameness.

I swear, I have a little more confidence around other people. I'm not claiming to be one of the cool kids, but I'm not normally this bad. Well... at least that's what I try to tell myself. Maybe it's being around Misty that gives me any confidence at all. I know I'm way out of my league here.

"There's a great Tai place that's close to the house and they deliver. There is also an Italian place by the office I go to a lot with my clients," Owen says with a smirk as he looks down at me.

"You always eat takeout," I say in disbelief. That can't be possible with a body like his.

"It's that or suffer through my own cooking," he says and pulls a face.

I giggle and shake my head. "Well, as long as I'm with you, I'll make sure you're fed properly."

He stops in his tracks and backs me into the wall behind me. He gives me a smoldering look as his nostrils flare. Placing a hand on either side of my head on the wall, he looks down into my eyes.

I squeeze my thighs and place my palms on his bare chest. Licking my lips, I peer up at him. He follows my tongue with his eyes.

"Keep saying shit like that, darlin'," he says, his voice dropping a few levels. "I may forget I'm trying to give your tight pussy a break."

"Owen," I whimper.

"No." He shakes his head. "I took you way more than I should've in the first place. I'm keeping my hands off you for at least twenty-four hours. We're still getting to know each other. It's your turn."

He pushes off the wall and turns to walk off into the kitchen. I'm left to melt against the wall in a pool of my own desire. I watch his hard, perfect ass walk away from me and groan. I don't know if I can wait another hour before he touches me again. I have to figure out how to seduce him or something.

I shake my head at my own thoughts and follow him into the kitchen. "I can make us pancakes again," I offer as I think of the way he devoured them yesterday.

He turns around with a boyish smile on his face. *How can such a big man be so adorable and so rough at the same time?* He nods his head emphatically. I burst into laughter.

It's right in this moment, I realize Brick is just a man. I've made him into something so much larger than life in my mind, but he is a man. My man.

Owen

"Out of the way," she giggles with that sweet voice.

My heart swells as it dawns on me that I have Eva Kennedy naked in my kitchen, getting ready to cook for me. After lusting after this young girl, who was too young for me when I first started to notice her, she is finally mine. My girlfriend is making me breakfast.

Girlfriend, I sound like a pussy to my own ears. I'm thirty-one, I've never had a girlfriend in my life. Never wanted one. Even when I was married, I knew in the back of my mind my wife was somehow unfaithful.

Hell, three months in, Mags had offered me an open marriage. She said I could fuck whoever I wanted. In her words, 'You're doing me a favor, I won't hold you to anything.' Yet, every time

I came home late or smelling of another woman, Mags was in my face.

For the first year, I hadn't done anything. I would smell of other women because of some club bunny sitting on my lap or a stripper giving me a lap dance when I would hang with the brothers. I would look, but I wouldn't touch.

After finding Jemma and Magdalena in my bed, I fucked anything that walked. I didn't care who and I didn't care where. I spent a year and a half feeling bitter and used. I wanted to make someone else feel that same way.

When I saw it was never going to make anything better, I threw myself into work. Now, looking at Eva as she bends over to grab something from the bottom shelf and her ass and pussy peek out at me, I only want her.

I can't even imagine placing my dick anywhere other than inside her. Her ass jiggling in the air has his full attention. I want her, but I promised I'm not touching her again until she's had a chance to heal from my bastard ways.

Eva straightens to her full height and turns to look over her shoulder to ask me something. I'm caught in the act of staring at her ass. Eva looks down and then looks back up at me.

"You're a dirty old man," she teases.

I give a deep belly laugh. I love when she has these little moments when she lets her humor peek through. Moments when she isn't analyzing everything she says to me before she says it.

I wink at her. "You have no idea how right you are," I say through my laughter.

Eva shakes her head. "So, it's my turn for questions," Eva says almost to herself as she places items on the countertop. She looks at me shyly, once again analyzing her words before she speaks.

"Just spit it out," I encourage her.

"You stopped coming to the clubhouse as much as you used to. I mean, I know you live all the way over here and all, but you used to come to the clubhouse at least every other weekend, then you just stopped. You show up when obligated from what I know…" her voice trails off as she chews on her lip.

"Do you remember when I stopped coming?"

I watch her face and see she's embarrassed because she knows the answer right away. "Well, yeah. It was right after my graduation BBQ. I waited all summer for you to come by before I had to leave for college. I...." She stops talking and tries to make herself busy with making us something to eat.

"You what, darlin'? Don't be shy. Come on and tell me," I coax as I try to hold back a smile.

"I heard that you lived here in Georgia. I don't know what I was thinking, but I had thought I'd worked up the courage to ask you to hang out sometime," she admits in a shy quiet tone. "I know, you were like twenty-seven and all, but I had hoped..."

She lets her words trail off again. I run my hand through my hair and snort. "I stopped coming around because of you." I let my words hang in the air. "I've wanted you for a long time, Eva. Way before you should've had my attention. When I saw you at that BBQ, I knew I needed to keep my distance."

Eva stops mixing the ingredients she has in a large bowl and looks me in the eyes. "But why? I was eighteen," she says innocently.

"Eighteen and too damn good for me. You're still too good for me," I grumble. "I was twenty-seven, I wasn't right for you."

"Oh," she says into the bowl and returns to mixing.

I stand and round the corner to wrap my arms around her waist. "You should want better than me," I whisper in her ear.

She places the bowl with the spoon in it on the countertop and turns in my arms. She brings her soft hand up to cup the side of my face. I turn to kiss her palm and pull her body closer to mine.

"You do know I was never following King around. It was always you. I've had a crush on you from the first time you rode up on your dirty bike with no shirt on." The vulnerability in her statement pulls at my heart.

It's clear in her eyes it was a big step for her to admit this to me. When she reaches her hand between us to wrap around my shaft, I hiss out a breath. All efforts of trying to ignore my hard-on fade away.

I move my hands to her ass to grasp a healthy amount of flesh in my palms. Dipping my head, I aim to suck her full lips into my mouth. As she gasps and her pretty lips part, I plunge my tongue in and deepen the kiss.

I groan as she starts to pump me with her silky-smooth hands. It feels so fucking good. I start to play with the lips of her pussy from behind. I keep chanting in my head that I will not fuck her.

Eva crumbles all of that shit when she pushes me back and drops to her knees in my kitchen. I watch those full lips wrap around my cock, like I've imagined so many times. It's then that I realize that I've always known she was made for me.

As I hit the back of her throat, I growl. I'm not a small man, but my baby girl takes me like a pro, all while her eyes are locked on mine. When she moans around me, causing my balls to vibrate, I crack.

I pull from her mouth, reaching down to toss her over my shoulder. I slap her ass then lick the sting away. Eva yelps and wiggles in my grasp.

"I think it's been twenty-four hours," I say as I step into my bedroom and toss her on the bed.

I shake my head at the wicked smile on her face. I don't know what I've gotten myself into, but I know I wouldn't change it for the world. With each hour I spend with her... *Shit, I think I'm falling in love.*

CHAPTER ELEVEN

Teach Me

Eva

"No, that won't work. Remember, we're looking to get them the most room and function out of each suite. Where can you get creative with the layout? Come on, use your innovation," Owen says as he places a hand on my knee and taps his finger absently.

I stare harder at the blueprints he has rolled out on the coffee table in his home office. Pushing a hand into my hair, I furrow my brows in thought.

Instead of heading into the office, we've been working from home. It's been more intimate, but in a one-on-one student-teacher sort of way. I love the patience he has for me. I've been so surprised he's allowing me input on projects.

This one is a multimillion-dollar project he's working on. I don't want to disappoint. I'm determined to pull my weight and learn.

I glance at the budget once again, allowing the math to run through my head. When I look back to the blueprints, I see it with new eyes. I nod.

"Okay, I can make this work," I mutter and bite my lip. I snap my fingers when it clicks into place for me. "I got it. Here. The plumbing would be more efficient and cost effective if we move the baths here.

"The closets can move here, giving each master suite a spacious master walk-in. That still leaves a huge footprint for the bedroom," I say, nodding at my own words.

Owen kisses the side of my head. "Perfect, baby girl, that's what I was thinking. Why don't you draw up the changes for me? I'll check them when you're done. I need to run some numbers and look at something else," he replies.

I take the pencil from his hand, staring at him in awe. He's really going to allow me to draw out these changes. It's only been a week and he doesn't do things totally by CAD. I've been sort of hyped to use paper and pencil. However, one mistake and I could ruin the entire thing, I could cost him thousands, if not hundreds of thousands of dollars.

He stands and gives my shoulder a squeeze. "You can do this. I'll look them over," he repeats.

He turns and moves to the drafting table with more blueprints spread out on it. I stare after him for a few beats, still in shock. Owen, however, gets back to work. I note how sexy he looks with his slacks on and his sleeves rolled above his elbows.

I smile to myself. We may work from his place every day, but we dress as if going into the office. I wish I would have packed more.

I shrug off the thought and turn my attention back to the table. As I wipe my hands on my circle skirt, I give myself a pep talk before I scoot to the floor and get to work. I can do this.

Apparently, I get so focused on the blueprints I lose track of time. I've just finished addressing the rooms in the west wing when Owen grabs my attention.

"It's quitting time, darlin'. It's time you eat something," he says as he stands with a tray in his hands.

I furrow my brows, but quickly roll up the blueprints and move everything aside. When he puts the tray down, I see he's made us sandwiches and has a pitcher of sweet tea and two glasses. I can't help but smile.

"You made this for us?" I tease.

His cheeks turn red under his beard. "Don't get too excited. Pastrami and cheese are the extent of my culinary skills."

"And here I thought you were hopeless in the kitchen."

"Bite the sandwich first. I might be," he says with humor in his voice.

I pick up the sandwich and take a bite. It's amazing. I don't even mind the onions on it. I nod my head and look over my shoulder at him sitting on the couch.

"Not bad at all."

He smiles and grunts before grabbing the plate with his sandwich and tucking in. We eat in a comfortable silence. I'm too busy musing at the fact that he made us sandwiches instead of letting me know he was hungry.

I've cooked for us every day since I've been here. As I clean my hands on one of the napkins, I can't help but wonder if he doesn't like my cooking. Maybe my pancakes are the extent of what he thinks tastes any good.

He leans to place his plate on the tray and fills a glass before he picks it up, drains it, then replaces it on the tray. I look away when his gaze lands on me. He shifts over on the couch and wraps his arms around me from behind, bringing me into his warmth.

He buries his face into my neck. It's like a reflex the way I take a breath and close my eyes. I could get lost in this feeling so easily.

"No work tomorrow. I want to take you for a ride," he murmurs.

"Sounds good. I had planned to sleep in and read a book, but I like your idea better," I reply.

"You can bring your book." He kisses my skin. "I like having you here with me. My days end peacefully."

I can't help myself. I have to ask. "Is my cooking bad?"

"What?" he says.

"Well, you made those sandwiches. I thought maybe you didn't like my cooking and didn't want to hurt my feelings."

He roars with laughter. "Darlin', you were so into those blueprints and I was hungry. You've cooked every night this week. The least I could do was make a couple of sandwiches, so my woman doesn't starve or have to fuss over me."

"Oh, I would have stopped sooner. I lost track of time."

He tilts my head back and pecks my lips. "You're fine. I'm going to have a few beers on the roof for a bit. You want to come with me?"

"Sure, but I want to hit the shower first. I've been sitting here in these clothes all day," I reply.

The thought of pulling on one of his T-shirts brings a smile to my face. I love wearing his things. His clothes smell like him.

"On second thought, those beers can wait," he says before clasping a hand over my throat and devouring my lips as he holds me in place.

He nibbles at my lips, coaxing my mouth open. I breathe him in as he pushes his tongue into my mouth. I reach for his hair and hold him to me.

This is my favorite part of the day, drowning in his intensity. It's something I look forward to. When he growls and lifts me, I smile.

It might be a while before we get to those beers. I don't mind. Being consumed by this man is nothing short of amazing.

Brick

"Eva, baby," I say as she rests across my chest.

She mutters something and nestles deeper into my body. We were just talking before she drifted off. We never did make it for those beers. Watching her writhe beneath me is a much better pastime.

I stroke her soft skin with a smile on my lips. This week has been what I've been missing in my life. After a hard day of work, I get to watch her in my home and ravage her body in my bed.

Right as my mind turns to King and how I'll handle things with him, my phone rings. I inhale, ready to face my brother. However, when I pick up the device, it's Jemma's number that appears.

"Shit," I grunt.

I don't realize my body has stiffened with irritation until Eva stirs and looks up at me. I'm even more pissed now that she's been awakened by my cousin and her bullshit. I ignore the call and cut my ringer off.

"Everything okay?" Eva asks sleepily.

"Yeah, it's fine," I reply.

She gives me a quizzical look. I'm not going to get into what's annoying me. When my phone lights up again, I flex my jaw and tighten the fist not pressed to Eva's back.

She keeps those brown eyes on me. Her thoughts running across her face as they often do. A tiny, wicked smile graces her lips.

"Maybe I can help you relax," she says, reaching beneath the covers for my soft cock.

It hardens the moment she touches me. As she looks at me through her lashes and moves to settle between my legs I tense with anticipation. Blood rushes through my veins and all is forgotten other than my woman.

Yes, she will make a great old lady.

"Yes, baby, just like that," I coach as she gets a rhythm going.

"Mm," she hums before sucking up the saliva she covers me in.

The sound of her slurping and the feel of her head bobbing take me to another place. What have I done to earn this woman? I don't know, but I'd pay the king's ransom to keep her.

CHAPTER TWELVE

Let's Ride

Eva

I press my face to Brick's back. I don't know why I can only think of him as Brick while on the back of his bike. This is heaven and my dreams come true. It's a gorgeous day for a ride.

Disappointment fills me as he pulls to a stop. I wanted the ride to last forever. However, the magnificent view of waterfalls and green grass draw my attention.

I hop off the bike and nearly bounce in place. This is a dream come true. I close my eyes and let the peaceful sound take over.

"This is tranquility. If there was a picture for the word in the dictionary, this place would be it," I say and sigh.

I open my eyes when he wraps his arms around me, pulling me into him. The smile on his face is so enchanting, I'm entranced immediately. He's so gorgeous. The picture of perfection and I'm me.

How did this happen? Once again, I berate myself for my poor choice of clothing and awful packing skills. Although Owen has made me feel special all morning, I can't help feeling self-conscious in the oversized sweatshirt and leggings I dressed in for today's trip.

I keep thinking of his ex-wife and her expensive looking clothes and thin body. On a good diet and a lifetime at the gym, I'd never look like her.

Owen guides one hand under the back of my shirt and into the waistband of my leggings to squeeze my ass cheek. His voice brings me deeper into him and all things Owen. "I thought you would like it here. You can get lost in one of your books. I always find myself deep in thought while out here," he says.

"And you made us sandwiches," I squeal teasingly as I think of the things I watched him pack.

He shakes his head at me and places a soft kiss against my forehead. His beard tickles my skin. Releasing me, he goes to get the blanket and food basket he brought along for our ride. My heart melts. This man is sweeter than I ever thought possible.

I never want this to end.

"Me either," he says and pecks my lips.

I give him a surprised look. I hadn't realized I said the words out loud. My cheeks heat. I'm such a dork.

"Come here," he commands as he begins to lay out the blanket.

He steps into the center and holds out a hand for me. First removing my backpack, I then take his hand and follow him down to sit. Without hesitation, I curl into his lap and snuggle into him.

What did I do for comfort before him? It's as if these days when I want to center myself, I seek him out. It's a welcome but scary feeling.

Like free-falling and knowing someone's waiting to catch you. I try not to read too much into it. Sometimes I'm still not sure this is all really happening.

"Are you hungry?"

"Not yet," I answer, turning my face up to the sky and closing my eyes.

I smile as he traces my face with his thumb. His callused hand is gentler than a soft blanket brushing across the skin. I feel precious in this moment.

"You're beautiful. I've watched you grow into a gorgeous woman. You've always been an old soul, but you still amaze me," he says.

I flutter my lashes open, locking eyes with his intense green gaze. There's something in Owen's expression that appears and disappears so fast. Before I can inquire, he leans in and captures my lips.

I'm breathless within seconds. I turn into him to wrap my arms around him and get closer. The kiss goes from heated to scorching so quickly I whimper as it's all I can do.

He groans loudly when his phone goes off. "This is club business, I have to take it," he says.

I move out of his lap and he stands. He walks away and I shrug my shoulders and dig into my little backpack, pulling out one of the books I've been reading for my final independent study class. I get lost in highlighting and making notes.

When Owen returns, he startles me a bit. He hadn't walked off that far. I had just become so absorbed by the pages in front of me. Something Misty and King chide me about all the time.

You need to be more aware of your surroundings, Eva.

As their words play in my head, I become aware of Owen and his change in demeanor. I put my book away as he sits facing me, a distant look in his eyes. Placing a hand on his knee beside me, waiting for him to meet my gaze.

When he does I give him a bright smile and the tension between his brows release. He returns the smile, and those beautiful green eyes light up with it.

Brick

I forget all about the call I was on as soon as her smile sucks me in. It's like the sun above, bright and coaxing, making you want to bask in it. Her face is so adorable and innocent.

Eva has no idea what kind of man she sleeps with every night. If I were a better man, I'd tell her. However, King has always said Eva is oblivious to the club life around her and he intends to keep it that way for as long as he can.

I can't say I blame him as her eyes tell me how truly sheltered she is. And I'm fulfilling my duties with little remorse. That call will result in someone being put in harm's way. I did what I had to do.

"You want to eat now?" We say at the same time.

We laugh. I've found we've been doing that more often. Speaking each other's thoughts and finishing one another's sentences. I narrow my eyes for a second as I think on this.

Eva is taking up a place in my heart. Each day, more and more, I see her in my life in a permanent way. When I wake, she's the first thing I seek out.

Eva's cheeks glow and she ducks her head. "Let me feed you," I say. "We can take a dip after."

"A dip?" she says with wide eyes as she snaps her head back up.

"You're not afraid of a little water, are you?"

The defiance that sparks in her eyes reminds me my Eva may be all kinds of innocent, but she's a Lost Soul deep down at heart. She's Cage Kennedy's girl. Blood or not, Cage taught her to be tough and fearless.

"I don't have anything to swim in," she says thoughtfully, but with that confidence I love to see.

"Yes, you do. You were born with it."

"You want to skinny dip?" she says, the doe-eyed look returning.

I lean in and kiss her lips. "I plan to do more than skinny dip. I want to hear your voice echo off the walls of the cave behind that fall." I nibble her soft lips for good measure.

The look of lust in her eyes when I pull away gives my naughty girl away. My jeans tighten. If her stomach didn't pick this very moment to growl, I'd forget about lunch and take her straight to the cave.

"Later," I say and wink.

***

I brush my finger over Eva's hair as she rests her head in my lap. We're digesting our meal and enjoying the quiet. I've been running what I'll say to King over in my head.

"Hey, Owen," Eva says softly, causing me to look down at her and come out of my thoughts.

She's watching me closely. I move from her hair to trace her full lips. As if I'm prying the words out, she slowly opens her lips.

"You're older than me. Do you remember my mom or Cage?"

I smile at the fond memories that surface immediately. "Yeah, I remember them. Rose was like the mother I never really got to know and Cage, he was the only real father figure I had. I owe everything to him," I reply.

I think back to when Rose sat me down and talked to me about the birds and the bees. She had started to notice the club bunnies taking interest in me. Cage's old lady told it straight.

"Don't stick your dick in anything you can't pull yourself out of. Handsome young boys like you and King, headed for great things, these women will eat you alive," she had said that day.

I chuckle at the memory. I should've listened more closely. I never got mixed up with the club bunnies, but Mags was ten times worse.

"What?" Eva asks.

"Just remembering something your mom said to me. She was full of wisdom. I see why Cage was crazy about her. She never minced words. It was what I loved most. She called me on my shit," I say fondly.

"Yeah, she had a way with words. She made everyone feel special. I guess you can say that about them both."

She's right. It was a gift they both had, just in different ways. Cage guided you to where you needed to be. Rose had a way of telling you the truth about where you were going.

I think back to Eva's graduation from high school. The way she didn't look like a girl celebrating a great accomplishment at her BBQ. I felt then she might be missing her parents.

My heart aches for her. "You do know they would be proud of you. All you've done and how far you've come?" I say thoughtfully.

She doesn't answer right away. When she does, the longing is clear. "Yeah, but that doesn't keep me from wanting them here so I can hear it for myself."

Damn, what do I say to that? If I could trade my lost and broken soul for her to have them back, I would. Not being able to do anything tears me up as much as hearing the pain in her voice.

Eva breaks into my musing again. "Sometimes, I wonder if Cage would have seen something different in me and pushed me in a different direction," she says.

"You know, darlin'. I don't think he ever pushed any of us into anything. He only pointed us in the right direction. You have natural talent. I'm sure Cage would have placed you on my doorstep sooner or later."

"I remember when he first started coming by the house to see Mom. He would bring me Legos. I was obsessed with the things. New books and Legos," she says thoughtfully with a wistful smile.

The air turns thick with melancholy. I hadn't noticed I allowed both of our thoughts to become heavy. Looking at my watch, I see it's been almost an hour since we finished our lunch.

A lot of time to let the shadows try to creep in. That darkness will sneak up on your ass in a heartbeat if you're not careful. I've had less of those moments with Eva around. I make it my business to pull her back to the light she is. This conversation will only weigh on a day that's been going great so far.

"Eva," I say to get her to turn toward me. When she looks at me there's so much emotion on her face. "Cage lived life to the fullest. I remember he laugh hard and often with the brothers he kept close. He was a hard man with a soft center, but he also told me I had to make the most of everything in my life.

"We can get lost in our past and what ifs. Or we can live in the present and create moments out of pleasure with those we are with," I say.

Eva seems to catch what I'm throwing. She lifts to her knees and pulls her sweatshirt over her head. Her gorgeous full breasts jiggle within the confines of her pink bra.

I tug off my cut and rip my T-shirt over my head. Eva reaches for my belt buckle and releases it. I grunt as she reaches inside for me.

"Slow down, baby girl. No need to rush," I say despite fighting for my own restraint.

She nods and bites her lip. I cup her face and kiss her sexy mouth. Sliding my palms down her throat and over her smooth skin, I savor the moans coming from her.

Wanting to elicit more of that sweet sound, I cup her breasts and knead them as she combs her fingers through my beard. In an instant, I'm the one in a rush. I lean in until she falls back, then go straight for her leggings, breaking the kiss to pull them down her thick thighs.

"You're so fucking sexy," I say as I pluck her sneakers from her feet so I can pull her pants and panties all the way off.

Pausing, I take her in—fully naked and waiting on me. Like a rare pearl that's been awaiting my discovery. Her curves are on display just for me.

I lower and start a trail of kisses, the first sampling those full lips. I make my way past her chin, down her throat. I love the way her neck moves as she swallows down a moan.

"Don't deny me your pleasure, Eva. I want to hear that shit, baby."

"Please," she says breathlessly.

I continue my descent, taking a moment to give her breasts my full attention. I roll one hardened nipple in one hand and hold the other mound up for my mouth. Sucking her peak into my mouth, I can't help wondering how I got so lucky to have this gorgeous woman give herself to me so easily.

She arches her back, trying to feed me more of her breast. I don't disappoint. I draw the bud deeper into my hot mouth and flick it with my tongue before nipping it and releasing it from my warmth.

"Are you wet for me?" I groan.

"I want you so much."

"Good, spread your legs. I want them as wide as you can hold them, baby."

She spreads her legs and brings them into her chest. I wrap my arms around her thighs as I pass her belly with a few more kisses and lower to settle in.

"Owen," she cries out as I start to savor her core.

She tastes so sweet. I groan and push in deeper, adding my fingers to the mix. I open her folds wide and lavish her pretty pussy.

It doesn't take long for my face to become saturated in her juices and my saliva, making a sticky mess. I twirl my tongue around the string of her honey and my fluid that clings to her folds and connects to my lip as I back away. Turning my head to the side, I then move in to suck on her inner thigh.

"O-o-wen," she drags out on a moan.

I grin and turn back for her hot center, diving in to pull her first orgasm from her. It doesn't take long for me to devour her, sending her body into a quivering, shaking, convulsing mess beneath me.

Damn. I need more. This isn't enough.

I'm rock hard and want to thrust into her here and now, but I made a promise and I'm a man of my word. Every true Lost Soul is. I kick my boots off and shove my jeans down with one hand.

With one final suck of her clit for good measure, I lift and scoop her up in my arms as I stand. She gasps as she always does when I lift her.

This woman was made for a real man. I don't think twice about having her in my embrace with her full figure and lush curves. I move for the waterfall to make my way into the hidden cave.

The water is cool, but our heated bodies allow us to go unfazed. Once I make it to the nearest wall in the cave, I press a hand against it and hold Eva's back inches away, not wanting to press her skin to the rough rock.

"Please," she pleas.

I grin. "You need something, darlin'?"

"Yes, you," she whimpers.

I reach between her legs from behind and guide my cock into her tight walls. She feels so good as she sucks me in. She locks her arms around my neck tight as I bounce her on my length.

Soon she begins to take over, grinding her hips and using her upper body to ride me. I press my forehead to hers while still looking into her eyes. She gushes and throws her head back.

"Oh God, Owen," she starts to scream.

I smile and growl as her voice echoes and the rushing of the waterfall roars in my ears.

"That's my baby. Keep coming," I say tightly.

I bend at the knees and take control for the both of us. She's building toward her next orgasm before the second one can die down. I shiver at the feel of her pebbled nipples rubbing against my chest.

"Yes, yes, yes."

I growl at her cries and burrow my face in her neck. My sweet baby girl. If only she knew the demons she holds at bay.

Not for the first time, I acknowledge that a man like me should never get his hands on a woman like Eva, but now that I have, I'll die before I let her go. My chest tightens as the clock in the back of my mind ticks loudly. I'm going to have to answer for all of my sins. Making Eva mine seems to be the one I'll have to pay the piper for first.

Come get me. I'm ready motherfucker.

CHAPTER THIRTEEN

Time to Shop

Eva

I can't wipe the smile off my face as Owen and I walk hand in hand heading for the next store. I officially need some things to wear. I've gone through all of the stuff I packed, and we'll be returning to the office in another week as per Owen.

I've enjoyed having him to myself for a few weeks, but I know he has a company to run and we can't stay in our little bubble. I've spent two weeks in this amazing man's arms. I could truly pinch myself as reality keeps tiptoeing back in.

He squeezes my hand, causing me to look up. "What are you smiling about?" he says as he opens the store's door and holds it for me to walk in.

"Nothing." My face heats and I duck my head while walking through the door before him.

He keeps close, placing the hand he had used to hold mine on the small of my back. Goose bumps run over my skin. There's something about the protective way he always hovers around me.

I always feel safe and cared for. It's almost like the way King makes me feel, except with Owen, it's more possessive and in an intimate sort of way. Sometimes, I catch him glaring at others around us, but I never catch why. Only the way he moves closer to me, drawing my attention to him and the secure way he makes me feel.

"Make sure you get things for home and the office," he reminds. "It's on me, so don't worry about the cost or how much you get. You can get more than you did in the last store."

My heart skips a beat. The way he says home is as if it's my home as well, not as if I'm a guest. Not to mention, his offer to pay for my things.

"You don't have to pay for anything. I can take care of it," I repeat for the millionth time today.

I start for the T-shirts. He follows me, crowding my space. "But you won't," he says next to my ear.

The warmth in my belly threatens to spill over when he leans in and kisses my forehead absentmindedly. It's so natural and effortless. I shake off the feeling and start to pick up a few pairs of jeans.

Owen grunts, grabbing my attention. I look up to catch him rolling his eyes at me. He plucks the jeans and T-shirts from my hands.

I stare at him in confusion as he waves the clerk over. When she eagerly comes over to attend to his needs, he wraps his arm around my waist and pulls me into his side.

"How can I help you?" the clerk chirps.

"This is my girlfriend, and she doesn't always realize how sexy this body is. I need you to help her pick out everything you have that will cater to all her beauty. I'll wait," he commands as if he's the king of the world.

I look up at him with my mouth open. When he turns his green eyes on me, I have to gulp from the sight of the heat within them. He gives my side a squeeze and his lips lift in the corner.

"I can do that," the woman says adoringly. I blink to clear my thoughts and look at her. She turns to me and leans in to whisper.

"I wish my boyfriend loved me like that. Just this morning, he told me I need to lose weight."

I frown. That's pretty awesome coming from a boyfriend. Like February 30 is the best day of the year.

Owen snorts. "Sweetheart, you need a cheeseburger and a new boyfriend," he says gruffly before walking off.

"Oh, my God, Brick," I call after him.

He turns and gives me a look. I can only shake my head at him and mouth, *Owen.* He smirks at me and shrugs his shoulders.

"You're an attractive woman. Your boyfriend's an asshole," he says to the clerk, a little nicer this time.

"Thanks," she says with a goofy laugh. She turns to me to whisper. "You two are such a beautiful couple. I can tell he loves you."

My heart stops. For but a small moment, I let my mind hope she's right. I know I'm in love with him, but I'm not ready to bet the farm on the feeling being mutual.

At night, when he makes love to me, I often fight not to confuse it with the feeling of love. I get sex is sex and what I'm feeling is something more. Owen looks up from his phone he has been tapping on.

A smile comes to his face and I wonder if—just maybe—she could be right. I mentally kick myself. I'm thinking too much.

"Thanks," I whisper in reply to the clerk and allow her to lead me to a rack.

"I have some things I think would look great on you." She lowers her voice again. "I'd kill for curves like yours. Especially your hiney. Five days a week in the gym and mine is still flat as a board."

I bite my lip to keep from laughing. She keeps talking the entire next two hours I spend in the dressing room trying on clothes. Eventually, I tune her out.

I spend most of the time in my thoughts, wondering what she saw that I didn't. By the time she piles everything on the counter to ring me up, I realized she has half the store ready for me to purchase. I spin to face Owen.

"You can't get all of this," I say, startled.

He pins me with a glare before reaching for me with one hand as he holds his card out to the clerk with the other. Before I can protest any further, he dips his head and takes my lips. I completely lose track of what I had planned to say.

"Thank you," I breathe when he lets me up for air.

He nods. "You'll need shoes for all of this."

I go to decline the offer, but he shoots me that glare once again. He kisses my nose. "You'll need work boots for the construction site too."

I can only smile. I don't know if it's love, but I know he cares. At least I think he does. What do I know? I'm still in shock over all the things he's just purchased for me.

It's enough to keep me wordless as we head to the next store.

Brick

"You got my message?" King asks, his voice full of stress.

"Yeah, I got it. I can have that all handled within the next few hours. I've got you, brother," I reply.

"How's Eva? Is she giving you any trouble?"

My gut twists with guilt. I should tell him now, but from the sound in his voice, I bite back the words and swallow them. Whatever is going on with King it's weighing heavily on him.

This is my best friend. I don't what to add to his plate. Not now.

So, I go the safe route, knowing I won't lie to him. "Just finished picking her up some work boots for the sites," I reply.

"Thanks again. I know this is asking a lot."

"It's nothing. Hey, she's actually in the truck waiting on me. I'm starving so she probably is too."

"Yeah, all right. Call me if anything goes wrong with that thing we were talking about."

"Got it."

I hang up and climb into the truck. Eva has her nose in her phone. When I close my door, she looks up as if surprised to find me. Her eyes light up.

"Everything okay?"

"Yeah, King was checking in," I say.

Her smile falls a bit. "Did you tell him?" I lean in to kiss her lips.

"Nope. Not the time."

Without another word, I start the truck and pull out of the parking space. I have a million things on my mind, but I'll get to all of that when we get home. I have a few calls to make.

"I'm hungry, what do you want to eat?" I turn to Eva and say.

I catch the light in her eyes before facing the road again and know exactly what she's gonna say. At the same time, we call out, "Chinese."

"That place is so good. If you want something else, we can get what you want," she says sheepishly.

"If you want Chinese, Chinese it is. I wouldn't mind some of their garlic chicken."

"I promise to cook tomorrow," she says as I pull to a stop at a light.

I turn to look at her. Reaching over, I grasp the back of her neck and begin to knead it. She looks into my eyes.

"Darlin', you don't have to promise me anything. It's late, I wasn't looking for you to cook anything. I'm good with takeout and a few beers. I'd much rather have you in my bed than at the stove. The sooner I feed you, the sooner I can feast on you," I say and wink at her before turning and stepping on the gas.

I smile to myself, catching her heaving breasts out the corner of my eyes. Two weeks and I'm still affecting her as much as she affects me. I already dread having to share her with others.

My chest fills with satisfaction as I think of all the bags in the back of my truck. Eva truly doesn't know how sexy she is. I'm still semihard from watching her try on clothes.

I've never taken such pleasure in purchasing things for a woman. However, with Eva, I would have cleaned out the store to see the awe in her eyes and smile on her face. I want to spoil this woman with everything her heart desires.

"Will you watch that documentary I was telling you about with me?"

I glance over and smile. "Yeah, sounds good. We can do that."

"What was it about again?"

"The history and Evolution of American Architecture. I'm so excited to watch it. I heard it's awesome."

"Speaking of which. I found those books you were asking about. I brought them out of storage," I say, referencing some old textbooks and other books I've accumulated over the years.

Eva is more than an avid reader. She devours books and information. I think at times she forgets I'm even around as she gets lost in the pages she reads.

Her voice shows her excitement. "Oh, maybe we should wait on the documentary. I'm so glad you were able to find them," she says.

"Told you I would. We can do either."

I should've known she'd opt out of the movie for the books. I shake my head. I'll never fault her for her brilliance. It's sexy as fuck to me.

As I think on it a little more, I come up with an idea. "How about this? When we get back, I'll order our food, you can start reading and once the food arrives, we'll eat. Then we can watch the documentary and then relax in a bath," we say the last part at the same time, bringing a broad smile to my face.

"You've got it, darlin'," I say.

"Sounds good to me," she sings.

I smile at the road ahead of me. Not for the first time, I muse over how good Eva is for me. I've spent the day with her shopping and I've never been more content.

When I think of my future, I see her in it. Her bright smile and those gorgeous eyes. I reach over to place my hand on her thigh.

I think I'm trying to hold her in place, so I don't lose her. My chest tightens at the thought of being without this woman and I know I need to move things along where King is concerned. The more time that passes, the bigger problem this will be.

I'm falling in love with her.

CHAPTER FOURTEEN

Our World

Eva

"Come on, baby. You were the one that wanted to play," Owen teases.

I stick my tongue out at him. "Whatever," I mumble to myself.

This was my idea, but I'm having a hard time getting into it. We have been in his game room, playing pool for the last two hours. It's not that I don't like pool. I have other things on my mind.

If I wasn't totally in love with Owen, I've fallen ten times over in the last three weeks. We have worked together from home during this whole time. He has run out to a site once or twice a week to put out a couple of fires and check on things, but I stay behind to work on whatever design tasks he trusts me with.

I have to say I've learned so much. During working hours, Owen is all business. Not like that day in his office on his desk. He may rest a hand on my hip, thigh, or the small of my back, but those are all possessive gestures that are becoming natural to him.

He's always aware of where I am and what I'm doing. I feel like we finish each other's sentences now. I haven't been this happy in… yeah, not ever. I love me some Owen, and I love the bubble we have built around us.

That's why I'm pouting now. Meetings and clients need his attention. Our time here is up. I knew it was coming, but it still stings to know the time is here.

I understand, but I don't want to share him with the world. This weekend seems like it has gone way too fast. I continue to pout as I chalk my pool stick to take my next shot.

He's kicking my ass because I'm distracted by the feeling of dread I have for tomorrow. Tomorrow, I will have to remember Owen is my boss, not my boyfriend. I won't be able to lean over and kiss his cheek or reach over to run my hand through his hair. All things I haven't had to think about in the last three weeks. Things I've started to do daily.

"Okay, baby girl, what's going on in that pretty head? I've watched you hold the record for kicking ass in pool at the clubhouse since you were thirteen. I know I'm not that good." He crosses his arms over his chest as I miss yet another easy shot.

I sigh and place the stick across the table. "Things are going to be different tomorrow. We still haven't told King about us, so we have to be careful of how we are together," I murmur.

He moves into my space, crowding me against the pool table. "Let me worry about King. As far as work goes, we'll have too much work to do to worry about anything else." He reaches for my face and turns it up so I look him in the eyes. "I've loved having you all to myself, but I have an empire out there to run and club shit I've been putting off. King will start asking questions if I don't handle that shit."

"Why don't we just tell him?" I ask, feeling insecure.

I haven't said it outright, but I've wondered if he is keeping this secret because he doesn't want to take this any further. I know he said in the beginning he's my man, but who's to say he isn't tiring of me.

"I plan to, baby." His voice rumbles through me as he presses his lips to my forehead as he speaks. "King has his own shit going on, and I think it's best to wait for the right timing. He's not going to like this. We'll give it a little more time."

I sigh and nod my head. "Okay," I say.

He glides his hands down my sides and around to cup my ass. With a tight hold on me, he kisses my forehead and moves to the side of my face with another, then places a trail of kisses down my neck. "You know. I can't wait to tell the world you're mine. And I'm really looking forward to seeing you in those tight jeans and your cute little construction boots tomorrow," he breathes against my neck.

I moan when he flicks his tongue out against my skin. I giggle and snuggle into his chest. "You really didn't have to take me shopping," I say breathlessly as he sucks my skin into his mouth.

It's been almost a week, but I still can't believe all the money he's spent on me. My belly drops and twists every time I think about it.

"That's where you're wrong, baby girl. You needed something, so I'm here to give it to you," he says against my skin, sending goose bumps over my flesh and shivers through my body.

I moan again as he kneads my ass cheeks with his big hands. I try to focus because I have a point to make here. While I really appreciate him buying me new things since I packed so poorly, I want him to know how much it really meant to me.

It's not like I don't have my own to take care of myself. Cage left money for us all to be good if anything ever happened to him. King wouldn't let me touch that money for school, so I haven't put a dent in it.

I push gently at his chest, so I can focus and get my point across. "No, Owen, I want you to know how much it meant to me." I cup his face in my hand and scratch at his beard. He turns his face and kisses my palm. "Thank you."

"I know how you can really thank me, darlin'. I think it's time for bed." He wraps his arms around my back, drawing me into him.

He lifts me, causing me to wrap my legs around his waist. I cup his upturned face in both hands and take his lips in a kiss. He takes over the kiss, devouring me.

However, before we can get too lost, his phone starts to ring. A growl rumbles from his chest as he places me back on my feet. He pecks my lips as he pulls the phone from his pocket. I watch as he pulls a face while he lifts the phone to his ear.

"Prez," he answers. I suck in a breath.

I don't even move a muscle as if King can hear me. As it does every time King calls, my stomach churns. He trusted Owen with me all those nights ago. We have both broken that trust in a big way.

King is going to kill us.

Owen

"Hey, brother," King grunts into the phone. I can hear already he's in a mood. "How's my sister?"

"She's good, she'll be going to her first worksite tomorrow. I have a few clients who love some of her ideas and want to pull her in on their project teams already," I reply with a proud smile on my lips.

Eva stands before me frozen. I chuckle inwardly and move to pull her into my arms. I know she's concerned about how King will react to our relationship.

I don't blame her. I know it's going to be a hurdle to get over. I'm only trying to time it right.

Every time I've spoken to King in the last three weeks he has sounded so stressed out. I know he's about to blow any minute. I'm giving him the time I know he needs to sort shit out in his head, before he brings whatever it is to me.

I know my best friend, that's why I know it's not time to tell him I'm fucking his little sister. I bury my face in her hair and inhale. *Shit, it's not the time to tell him I'm in love with his little sister.*

My chest feels blown through as the realization hits me. I love this woman. I'm no longer falling.

I've watched her stress out all day, but I've been thinking of the same things. It's going to be hell keeping my hands off of her at work. It was risky for me to fuck her in my office the day of her interview.

There are Lost Souls members all throughout my organization. Sure, most work the construction side and are out in the field, but all it would have taken was one to go back and mention something to King.

It's another reason I made it so Eva and I could work remotely for three weeks. I needed to be able to ensure I could hold it together throughout the workday. I still haven't managed to keep my hands off of her, but I haven't tried to fuck her brains out during the workday.

That's something, given how much I crave this woman. I can't wait to lay her body down now. I want to show her what I know. I love her.

"Good, I need a favor, brother. I'll be by the worksite tomorrow to talk in person. Give me the location," King says, bringing me from my thoughts.

My gut tightens. King being in South Carolina is one thing. Him being here in Georgia is another.

Fuck!

My workers, I may be able to fool them into not knowing anything is going on between me and Eva. King will see right through that shit. He knows me too well.

I press my face closer to my shoulder that has the phone balanced on it. I tighten my arms around Eva. I'm so lost in thoughts of how much of a clusterfuck this is, I haven't responded to King.

"Brick, you hear me?" he grumbles, snapping me back to the present.

"Yeah, yeah, I hear you. I'll text you the address in the morning," I finally reply.

"Good." King sighs. "I need one more favor. I need to borrow one of your trucks. You can bring my bike to the club on the weekend. Need you in church."

"Got it, see you tomorrow," I reply, knowing this conversation is done.

I hang up the phone and look down at Eva. She has her bottom lip trapped between her teeth and her eyes are filled with worry. I kiss her cute little nose.

"Stop worrying about shit I plan to handle. I know King. I'll tell him when the time is right," I reassure her.

"He's here, in Georgia?" she asks with her brows wrinkled.

"Yeah, but I'll handle it."

Eva looks at me skeptically. Instead of trying to reassure her with words, I go back to my original plan. I take her lips and kiss her with everything I have.

This is my woman, and nothing is going to change that.

That's what I confirm in my head. I mean it. Let anyone test that fact and they will learn the truth.

CHAPTER FIFTEEN

My Woman

Eva

I am nervous as shit as we pull up to the site. I can already see King waiting by his bike. I narrow my eyes as his face comes into view.

I groan. This doesn't bode well. I know my brother and I know that look on his face. He's going through something big.

Maybe Brick is right about waiting to say something. The realization only makes my heart sink and my belly tighten.

"You ready for this?" Owen says.

However, I don't get a chance to answer as King pulls my door open to let me out of the truck. He wraps me in his embrace and gives me a bear hug. When he places me on my feet to look me over, he purses his lips and shakes his head at my outfit.

"You didn't have anything else to wear?" he grumbles. "This is a construction site."

"I—"

He holds his hand up before pulling it down his face. "Ignore me. You need anything?"

Owen rounds the truck at that very moment and hands me a hard hat. I take it and smile, catching myself before I say *thank you, Owen*. It's right on the tip of my tongue. I quickly turn and reply to King for a distraction from Owen's intense eyes.

"No, I'm fine."

King nods, still frowning at my outfit. I have on a pair of well-fitting blue jeans, with a black Soul Deep Construction Polo and the tan construction boots Owen bought me. I'll admit as simple as the outfit is, it's not something I would normally wear because it places my body on display.

However, when Owen looked at me this morning and licked his lips, I took a look of my own in the mirror. I mean, a real look. What I saw for myself was an attractive, curvy woman who shouldn't try so hard to hide herself or from herself.

Although observing King's reaction makes me believe all he sees is the trouble I'll get into dressed like this. He sucks in a deep breath and shakes his head before waving for Owen to follow him.

"Let's talk," he says.

"Give me a sec." Brick nods but takes a moment to wave over one of the guys working.

When the worker comes over, Owen leans into whisper something to him. They both turn their attention to me. "Eva this is Anthony, the foreman here. You'll stick with him until I get back."

"Okay," I say quietly.

I can totally read Owen doesn't like this introduction one bit. He's not doing well at hiding it either. I glance at King, but he seems distracted.

"Good to meet you, Eva," Anthony says with a lingering look at my breasts before he reaches out a hand to shake mine.

I reach out my hand but clumsily drop the hard hat on the ground as I look to Owen out of the corner of my eye. I bend to reach for the hat and when I straighten, I find Anthony smirking at my ass.

I shoot my gaze to Owen. His ears are so red, I know he's ready to blow. The only thing holding him back is King standing right next to him. King is looking at his phone and misses the entire exchange.

Quickly, I shake my head at Brick. Reminding myself again not to call him by his real name. I keep my hands busy with the hat instead of trying to shake Anthony's hand. Something tells me that's not such a great idea.

"Mr. Mason spoke highly of your crew. Nice to meet you too," I say.

"We are the best," the foreman replies with pride.

"Anthony," Brick bites out. He gives Anthony a dirty glare as a warning.

"Got it, boss."

I can tell Brick wants to say something more, but he doesn't.

Anthony gives a smile and waves for me to follow him. I start after him but look back to see King watching me for a moment with that same frown on his face before his phone grabs his attention again. I rub my hands on my jeans self-consciously.

Yeah, I might be dressed for trouble if King looks so disturbed. If I go by Anthony's appreciative looks and Owen's death glares directed at Anthony, I'm pretty sure King is right. It doesn't take long for me to find out for a fact.

***

King and Owen disappeared to talk club business hours ago. I knew King had something on his mind, because he totally missed the entire thing that passed between Brick and Anthony. Usually, he would've been the one to threaten to cut the guy's balls off, if he didn't keep his eyes to himself.

A part of me wishes Brick had said more earlier. I would love to have my baggy clothes back right about now. At the moment, I'm sitting through an awkward lunch with a bunch of guys drooling over me. Anthony is on my right, sitting way too close. I've been asked out on a date twice by two different guys.

"So, you're the big boss's new personal assistant?" one of the guys asks, I think he said his name was Rock.

I nod and nibble at the sandwich Anthony insisted he pay for at the truck. I wipe at my mouth and sip my soda. With a swallow, I give a real reply, since everyone seems to be looking for me to elaborate.

"Yes, I'm an intern for the summer."

"I'd love to have an intern following me that looks like you," one of the other guys says. I can't remember his name.

"I'd watch that," Texas, a guy I recognize as a Lost Soul, cautions. "That's Prez's little sister."

The guy who made the comment and the two who asked me out look like they're about to lose their lunch. I almost laugh at the look of horror in their expressions. I guess they heard enough about my brother.

"Damn, I still wouldn't mind climbing that family tree," Anthony murmurs next to me.

The growl that rumbles through my back nearly has me jumping in the air. I turn to look over my shoulder to find Owen is standing at my back, looking down on Anthony with rage in his eyes. I go to touch his chest to calm him but think better of it.

"Brick, the guys were only joking," I squawk.

"It's sounds like sexual harassment and it won't be happening on my worksites. If I hear it again, the mouth it comes from will be out of a job," Owen seethes.

"I… I meant no harm, boss," Anthony stutters.

"The fuck you didn't," Owen growls out. "Eva, let's go."

"I didn't finish my lunch. I don't want to waste Anthony's money," I say stupidly, wincing as soon as the words are out of my mouth.

"He paid for your lunch," Owen says tightly.

Owen's face burns red and his ears turn purple. *Oh, shit,* I know that look and it isn't good. He's about to go DEFCON. I chide myself for my stupid mouth and get up from the plank I'd been sitting on with the rest of the guys.

"I'm ready," I say as I move toward where the cars are parked.

I chance a look over my shoulder, hoping Owen is right behind me. He's not, instead he has a hand on Anthony's shoulder as he whispers something in his ear. Anthony's face has gone white as a sheet.

My mouth falls open and I stop right in my tracks. I turn, wringing my hands and look around for King. I'm not sure if he has left. When my gaze lands back on Owen, he's stalking toward me with fire in his eyes.

When he reaches me, he clasps my wrist and pulls me along to King's bike. I wrinkle my brows as Owen hands me a helmet. My brother is so picky about anyone touching his bike.

Honestly, Sal and Brick are the only people I've ever seen ride it other than King. Reap is the only one he lets work on it other than himself. So, to see Owen straddle it has my mind racing.

"Let's go, Eva," he barks.

I know he's extremely pissed, so I bite my tongue, place the helmet on my head, and climb on the bike behind him. I squeeze my thighs against him and tighten my arms around his taut waist.

Some of the tension seems to leave his body as he places a hand over mine and takes off. I'm not sure what's in store for us when we get to wherever we're going, but I can tell it's going to be intense.

Owen

"Son of a bitch," I say under my helmet as I push King's bike and try not to acknowledge Eva's hold on me.

I can't do this shit. Eva is my woman, but I had to watch as my workers drooled over her for hours. I had my eyes on Eva the entire time King laid his shit on me. I should be optimistic after my talk with King, but this shit has only gotten worse.

King's ass isn't going to handle this well. He'll get over it, but he isn't going to like it at all when he finds out. His current situation and the turmoil over it is going to set this whole thing on fire.

However, each time I watched one of my guys glance at Eva's ass, I almost pulled the Band-Aid off and told him. If for no other reason than to be able to stake my claim publicly. Just to let them all know to keep their fucking eyes off my woman.

Shit, this is my fault. I wanted to bring her out of her shell and allow her to see she doesn't have to hide in those baggy clothes. Now, all I want is to rip my own shirt off and cover her in it.

I'm burning up with rage. Anthony is lucky to still have his life, fuck his job. He'll be in Vegas by the end of the week. We just started a new division out there. Tiny has been asking me for a few good foremen. Well, now she has one.

All I want is to take Eva home and show her who she belongs to, but I can't. I have a meeting with a new client at the office in thirty minutes. I rev the engine on King's bike and floor it to the office. The sooner I get this over with, the better.

I may not be able to get my hands on her now, as bad as I want to, but I'm going to make it through this meeting with one goal in mind. Oh, I plan to fuck her brains out as soon as this meeting is over, and nothing is going to stop me.

Did she do anything wrong? No, that's my fucking problem. She's so sweet and innocent; people prey on that. I want that fire I know she has to be on display to let people know she belongs to me, but I can't pull that shit out yet. Why? Because we haven't done shit right.

No, this shit is on me. I fucked up and now I'm paying for it, big time. When King narrowed his eyes at me and said he had to go, I was able to take a breath of relief. King had come and gone without things coming to blows, and I was finally able to go get my woman.

I have to make this shit right, because it's about to make me crazy. I know what I'm about to do is on the border of insane, but I don't give a flying fuck. In my own head, I need to prove she's mine.

"Fuck."

CHAPTER SIXTEEN

Mine

Eva

We get to the Soul Deep Enterprise Building and park in the garage. Owen helps me off the bike but doesn't say a word. I wring my hands together after he takes the helmet from me and puts it away. His face is an expressionless mask.

"You'll sit in on this meeting with me," he says.

With a nod, I follow him wordlessly, but I can't help noticing how detached he sounds. We walk to the elevator and climb in. I know this is during work hours. However, when he moves to stand across from me in the car with his arms folded across his chest, my heart sinks a little.

I swallow as my mind starts to spin. I move on autopilot as we get to the floor Owen's office resides on.

"Mr. Mason, the clients are in the boardroom," Holden says, after lifting his head up and spotting Owen storming forward ahead of me.

I recognize him from back home. Holden is the little brother of Tracks, one of the Squad members of the Lost Souls. I shudder to think of the Squad. It only takes a second to figure out Holden must be taking over for Beth.

"Good," Owen replies, taking the clipboard that's handed to him.

Owen seems to be keeping his distance from me. You would think we were just two co-workers, like we should be. I'm not sure how to feel about that.

"This client wants us to bid for this project. I'm not completely convinced I want to take this one on yet. We'll head in after I get these docs signed," he says as he flips through the pages on the clipboard.

His tone is gruff but still professional as he explains the purchase orders and contract he scribbles his signature on. I note he doesn't fail to show me what he's working on. "Always make sure the spec sheets match the purchase order. I can't tell you how many times the wrong thing has been ordered because of one simple mistake," he mumbles as he shows me what he means.

"Got it."

"Holden, this all looks good. They have my signature. Get it all processed this afternoon," he says, handing the clipboard back to Holden who has been walking with us.

"On it. There are some messages for you on your desk," Holden says before turning and disappearing back to the reception desk.

Owen gives me a few more notes about the meeting we are going into before we get to the conference room. I listen to him while he gives me details on what I need to do and the tasks he's trusting me to handle in this meeting. Although, he has kept at least a foot of distance between us since we got on the elevator from the garage.

I'm not sure if he's pissed at me, or what happened back at the worksite. However, I get that now isn't the time to ask. I think to myself; his demeanor will change once the meeting starts.

It doesn't, other than the tight smile he gives the clients. Owen is just as gruff with them, rushing the meeting along. Everyone seems to be flustered but him.

This is where I realize he's the best at what he does. The clients seem to bend over to please him, not the other way around. They really want him to bite at this bid.

The meeting isn't fifteen minutes in when Owen interrupts the ramblings of the pretty, nerdy project manager. "Ladies, gentleman," he says.

She pushes her glasses up her nose and her mouth pops open as she stares at Owen.

I almost laugh. I've had that expression many times in his presence. Her mocha skin does nothing to hide her blush as concern covers her face. Her brown eyes go round as Owen lifts from his seat.

"Sorry, sir, did I say something wrong?"

"No, Andy, I'll send over my proposal. If you still want Soul Deep as the lead on this project after seeing the specs and designs, we can move forward," Owen says.

She looks relieved as she falls back in her seat. "Oh, thank you so much," Andy breathes and rubs her temple as her two co-workers start to look relieved as well.

Owen starts for the door to the conference room. "Eva," he barks.

I rush from my seat and follow him to his office. He calls over his shoulder to Holden to hold his calls. Owen holds the office door open for me and I walk in.

As soon as the door is closed, he clasps my wrist and drags me over to the bookshelf. He stands behind me and lifts the wrist he is holding to cover my fingers and hold my thumb.

He nuzzles my neck before breathing in my ear. "This is why I printed you the other day. The only way to open this panel is to have print recognition access. Everyone else that knows about and has access to the apartment has to go through the service entry." He flicks his tongue out against my ear. "Stick your thumb here."

He places my thumb in the groove and the panel pops open. Owen backs us out of the way for the door to swing open. This time as I move forward, I'm able to focus on the design of the stairs.

Not having to worry about my heels or breaking my neck, I admire the glass steps as they light up one by one with each step I take with my little booted feet. I start singing "Billie Jean" in my head as I reach the top of the landing and snicker to myself. My laughter is cut off as two large hands cup the sides of my ass. Owen rests his thumbs under my ass cheeks as he squeezes.

I nearly choke on a gasp as he buries his face in my crack, while he uses his thumbs to spread my cheeks. His hot mouth is on my sex over my jeans. He growls behind me, reaching to unfasten my jeans. He starts to pull them and my panties down my legs.

I bend to release my shoes strings to kick my boots off, causing him to growl. I barely get one boot off before his face is back between my legs. He sucks my left lower lip into his mouth before twirling his tongue into me. He moves to the right side and repeats.

I look over my shoulder to see him on his knees on the top step. The light from the step illuminates him as he laps at my pussy. His face is completely consumed by my ass. His beard brushes my skin and it only sends my tingling flesh into a fever.

"Oh, God, Owen," I cry out.

"Shit, Eva. I'm going to kill this pussy."

He reaches to tug my other boot from my foot and tears my jeans the rest of the way off. He stands and grabs my hips, moving me over to the nearest see-through glass wall. He places my palms to it and drops to his knees.

"Owen," I moan as my head drops down between my shoulders.

His response is to lift my leg and place my ankle onto his shoulder, while he attacks my core from behind. I beat my fist against the glass as he devours me. He's never been this intense and that's saying a lot.

"You're mine," he grunts into my folds. "I want everyone to know you belong to me. I can't take this shit, Eva. Fuck!"

I know he's thinking out loud, and even if he weren't, I couldn't reply. My legs turn to jelly and the one leg that's supporting me threatens to give out.

"I'm coming," I scream.

"Damn... fucking... right," he grunts as he lifts to his feet and pushes his jeans down his legs.

I cry out as he plunges into me. On penetration I come around him. "Fuck, fuck, fuck."

Owen does a combination of a chuckle, groan, and moan. He cups his hand under my chin, lifting my head up from between my shoulders. He thrusts his hips forward and pins me to the wall.

With a slow measured grind of his hips, he moves in me with a swivel type of motion. We both moan. "Fuck yeah, baby girl. I'm not giving you up, Eva. I can't breathe without you," he says hotly in my ear before biting down on it.

I was expecting him to take me hard and fast after making me come. I mean, he did say he was going to kill it. He doesn't though, I mean, he is killing me and my pussy, but not hard and fast.

Nope, he continues the slow roll and swivel of his hips. Each time that thick, hard meat between his legs stirs inside me, I gush and spasm around him. He has a bruising hold on my waist with his right hand that's keeping me pinned to the wall.

I pound the glass with my fist as I sob his name. When he starts to rock in and out of me, real tears start to fall. Owen dips his head and licks the tears soaking my cheek.

I reach my fingers into his hair and tug, causing him to groan and pant harder against my heated flesh as he moves to suck on my neck. *This shit ain't right.* He knows it.

He's punishing us both for what we've gotten ourselves into. He releases my face and reaches for my clit. I'm a shaking writhing mess against the wall.

I come so hard I see stars. Meanwhile, Owen grips my hips and releases me from being pinned to the glass we have steamed up. I'm breathing my way around multiples, when Owen's hand comes down on my ass.

"Mine," he grunts as he starts the pounding I'd been expecting. My butt stings from his slap, but it only turns me on more. "I'll take a bullet for this shit, baby. I'm never going through that shit again. I'm taking you home and clearing this shit up. You're my woman. This is my pussy. *Fuck, Eva.*"

Holy shit.

I swear I think this grown ass man just gave a husky whimper on that last part, as I clinched my walls around his cock. His strokes get choppy for a moment before he regains his control. He slaps my ass again.

"Baby," I gasp.

"Shit, you're going to bring me to my knees. I shouldn't want you this fucking much," he says through clenched teeth.

I reach for his hands and dig my nails into his skin. His hold on me tightens. His powerful thighs are the only thing supporting us as my feet start to lift up off the floor.

I'm so wet and full. Our grunts and groans are bouncing off the glass in front of us. The sound of his skin slapping mine is the only thing that's louder.

Owen reaches for the neck of my polo shirt and rips it right down the middle. My bra is the next casualty. My breasts bounce free and he places his hand in the center of my back. He presses forward, smashing my breasts to the glass wall. The coolness of the glass against my breasts is a soothing sensation to my skin.

The nerd in my brain babbles about Owen being a genius architect. I'm sure the walls have central air cooling them. As if knowing my inner geek has tried to break the moment, he proceeds to break my back.

He grips a handful of my hair and tugs my head back. Then he shoves his free hand between the glass and my breast to knead it. I blink back more tears of pleasure.

"We're coming," he announces loudly and increases the pace.

"Mother of... oh, my God, Owen," I scream.

Don't ask me what happens next. All I know is that I feel his hot seed flood me as I ripple around him. My heart pounds as I collapse in his arms.

Owen

"Eva?"

I look down at baby girl in my arms. She has blacked out on me. I chuckle and lean to kiss her sweet lips. God, I love this woman.

Yeah, I'll be following King back to Georgia. He needs to know the truth. This woman is mine. Maybe we can have something in common soon.

I can only wish.

I want Eva Kennedy as Eva Mason. The real Mrs. Mason.

CHAPTER SEVENTEEN

Unwanted Courtesy

Eva

I close the file I'm working on and reach for the next one. I'm in Owen's office working while he's out at a worksite. After Monday, I haven't been to a site since.

"Knock, knock." I look up at the sound of Troy's voice.

I have to hold myself back from groaning and rolling my eyes. He finds his way to this office whenever I'm here and Owen isn't. I'm so tired of his corny jokes and prying.

"Hi, Troy," I say, trying to hold back on my annoyance.

"You look busy. Hope we aren't working you too hard."

If I look busy you would think he would leave me alone. Not a chance. He saunters into the office and takes a seat in the chair across from me.

"Nothing wrong with a little hard work. How can I help you?" I reply.

"Oh, I thought I'd come and check on you. You know, see if everything is working out for you. If there may be some questions you have about the internship and your role here," he says and gives me a cheese smile.

I try so hard not to roll my eyes. Glancing at the clock, I wonder how much longer Owen will be. I'm never comfortable around this guy.

"I'm fine. Working my way through the list Mr. Mason left for me," I say.

"Maybe you should take a break. Have you eaten? I'd love to take you to lunch. You fascinate me. I want to get to know more about you," he says.

"I have a lot to do here. I'll get lunch when Mr. Mason returns. Thank you."

"Oh, come on. You have to be hungry by now." He looks down at his watch. "It's the perfect time for this little spot I know. They serve great drinks as well."

"I'm not much of a drinker. Besides, these are working hours for me. I'll be fine here. I have some blueprints I need to get to after sorting these files. Thanks, though."

"Shame. I would have enjoyed your company," he says.

He stands and moves closer to my chair. I draw back in my seat. This guy really doesn't get I'm not at all interested in him.

Please go away.

Too bad he doesn't get the message. Instead, he reaches over me and picks up the file I just finished working on. He flips through it as if he's overlooking my work.

I frown. Ugh, his cologne is giving me a headache. I pluck the folder from his hand.

"I have this one completed. Don't want anything to fall out of order," I say.

"I can see why the boss wanted you as his intern. You're pretty thorough. What do you say I take a rain check on that lunch date?"

Oh my God, is he slow?

"I like to eat here. I'm not sure that rain check will happen," I say pointedly.

"Keep it in mind. Totally my treat. We can go anywhere you want, doesn't have to be my suggestion."

"Yeah, sure," I reply to get him out of here so I can finish my work.

"You know where to find me. It was good to see you, Eva. Always a pleasure to see you," he says with that smile I'm sure he thinks is charming.

Like your ass hasn't been in here every day so far this week. Ugh! Dick.

I only stare at him in confusion. I've never shown him any interest, and yet, here he is, again. I shake my head as he moves for the door to leave.

I pick up my phone to see if Owen has sent me a text. Troy has only served to remind me of how much I miss Owen. I bite my lip when I see nothing.

Pushing down my disappointment, I remind myself he's a busy man. There were a few hiccups he had to deal with today. I'm more than aware it could take him longer than usual to return.

Doesn't mean I can't miss him a little bit. Okay, a whole lot. I flip open the next file.

Keep busy, Eva. He'll return soon enough.

Brick

As I type a message out on my phone and send it, my attention is pulled by movement from my office door. I look up and stop in my fucking tracks. The smile I had on my face—thinking Eva would be the one stepping out—disappears and I nearly snarl as I see Troy.

"Why the fuck are you coming out of my office?" I snap.

He has no business on this side of the building. His office is on the other side of the building down the corridor with all the other finance officers. I have no need for him today, anything he has to communicate with me could have been said in a fucking email.

I look past him to the door. Eva. He's been sniffing around her from what Holden has told me.

I'm going to cut this motherfucker's balls off. I have to count to ten to remind myself not to lose it here in my place of business. Troy looks back at me with wide eyes.

I lift my chin and hold my phone at my side in a death grip, waiting for an answer. Troy has gone completely pale. I begin to storm in his direction, the only thing that saves him is the reply text from King I'd been waiting on.

I shove past Troy and head into my office. I'll deal with him later. The moment I step inside, my anger wanes.

The sight of Eva in deep concentration brings my smile back. She looks up as I close the distance between us. I read the text from King and send a quick reply to let him know I have him covered. The distance between me and the club allows for more reach.

I get shit done. I send one more text to carry out my task for the club before placing my phone away with one hand and shoving the other into Eva's bun. I tilt her head back and take her lips in a lingering, searing kiss.

I try not to do this here in the office, but it's been a long day and I miss her more than I'm willing to admit out loud. When she clings to my bare forearms and whimpers, I know this is going to get more serious than a kiss. I groan, knowing I'm willing to stay overtime to help her finish whatever she doesn't get done because of me.

"Let's go," I grunt as I break the kiss.

I tug her up from her seat and guide her to the bookshelf. I can't get her upstairs fast enough. When her heels seem to make her too cautious on the stairs to move as fast as I want, I pause and toss her over my shoulder.

"Owen," she yelps.

"I've got you," I say and slap her full ass.

She smells so good. My mouth waters. Somewhere in the back of my mind, I know I've needed this all day. Tension has been high. My gut keeps telling me something is coming.

King's requests have been somewhat light. However, they are all building to something. For once, I want to forget all of that.

I want to get lost in the feeling of being just a man with his woman. A man who goes home at night and doesn't have to feel lost and at times alone. I'm the one who distanced myself from my brothers and it's all because of this woman over my shoulder.

I kick the bedroom door open and march inside. The place still smells of Eva from the last time we were here. A smile comes to my face as I think of how much she's made her place in my world.

"What about work?" she says and laughs as I drop her down to the bed with a bounce.

I kick my shoes off and place a knee on the mattress. With a shake of my head, I pluck her shoes from her feet and toss them over my shoulder. "We're taking a break. I'll help you finish up later."

The smile she gives me makes my heart skip a beat. Simply gorgeous. I can't wait a second longer.

I hover over her body and take her lips. I don't know where I want my hands more, so I used them to roam her sexy body. Eva returns the kiss with as much heat and desperation as I place into it.

Pushing her skirt up with my palms on her thighs, I revel in the smooth skin of her legs. When I get to her warm center, it's like my entire body turns into flames. I find her wet with need for me.

"I see you missed me, darlin'," I say against her lips.

"Yes, I need you."

With a grin, I take my hands from her body and back off the bed. She widens her eyes in surprise, before pinching her brows in confusion. When I fold my arms across my chest and widen my stance, her mouth pops open.

I let my lips turn up slowly. "Strip for me. Take your time, I'm going to enjoy this," I command.

Anticipation lights her eyes. However, I can see her shy hesitation. I wait her out, knowing she'll come out of that shell for me. Like a flower ready to bloom she does just that.

She sheds her clothes like the temptress she is. A clear sign she doesn't know this is what turns me on most. She's a natural beauty who hasn't a clue how much power she has.

When she gets down to her panties and bra. I hold up a hand to stop her. "Leave those for me," I say.

I have to reach to squeeze my cock in order to think straight. I'm ready to burst from my slacks. The fabric of her panties has been soaked through by her essence. The stain is begging me to suck it.

I unroll the sleeves of my dress shirt from my elbows before I start on the buttons to take it off. The desire in her eyes as she watches me almost causes me to rush through this. I'm already holding on to my restraint by a single thread.

"On your knees," I command and move closer to the foot of the bed.

She comes without question. Always so obedient to my requests. I wonder if she's figured out that I'm just as willing to do her bidding. All she has to do is ask.

With my shirt gone, I stand before her, tracing my thumb over her full lips. I bite down on my own bottom lip from the thought of having these plush pillows wrapped around me. She parts her lips and I do the same to mirror the action.

"Take me out," I say as my cock beats at the fabric of my pants, demanding its way out.

She licks her lips and reaches to unzip my slacks. I release the bun from her hair and watch as it springs out in my palm. I grasp a handful of her coils and slowly bring her head down to my length that she's holding so lovingly.

"Yes, you know how I like it," I say as she draws me into her mouth. "Take your time, Eva. We're in no rush."

I drop my head back and rock my hips slowly, all while guiding her head at the pace I'm looking for. The tension that had built from the frustration of the silly mistakes made at not one but two of the worksites and King's latest request begin to float away. Eva's warm mouth is the only thing I focus on.

"Fuck," I grind out when she backs off with a gasp and a slurping sound. "Turn around and lie flat. Keep your legs closed."

She nods and does as I say. I shove my pants down the rest of the way and kick off my shoes. In a flash, I have my socks off. The bed dips when I climb on and straddle her legs.

I dip my head and nibble on her ass. "You like that, baby girl?" I ask as she moans.

"Yes, Owen, please."

"I've got you, baby."

I lick circles on one of her cheeks, biting the fleshiest part. Take a globe in each hand and spread them, moving to feast on my favorite snack. The sweet sounds coming from her bring me to a painful full mast.

I consume her until she's boneless beneath me. The moment I know she's right where I want her, I move until my length lines up to her entrance and I slide into her wet heat. Releasing a loud groan, I roll my eyes to the back of my head. I ride her ass while straddling her thighs and its heaven.

"You're so tight, extra tight like this," I say.

I fist the sheets and growl as it gets too good to see straight. Eva starts to lift her ass and roll her hips and I'm nearly done for, but I'm not letting go that easily.

I pull out and reach for one of her legs. "Come here," I say and flip her over, onto her side.

"Owen, yes," she cries out as I thrust back inside her.

She's been screaming all this time, but that's the first thing that's made sense in a while. I hold her leg over my forearm as I pump into her from behind.

I can't get enough of watching her ass bounce against my pelvis. From this angle I can watch her breasts jiggle too. I release her leg and reach for her clit to take this up a notch. Wrapping my other hand around her throat, I cover her lips and swallow her cries.

"Yeah, that's what I want," I breathe into her mouth.

I fuck my way through two of her orgasms, keeping my own at bay. Our bodies are slick with our combined sweat. Our scents mix in the air making my new favorite fragrance.

"Owen, please, please, please," she sobs.

I drop my gaze to her bouncing breasts. Goose bumps pebble her skin. She soaks me as a silent scream catches in her throat and her face contorts with pleasure.

When her body quakes with the third, I roar my own release. The back of my head tingles with the force of it. I have to blink a few times to clear my vision.

I look down at Eva. She's watching me with a dreamy look on her sweaty face. I kiss her lips and tug her to my chest.

"I missed you too," she giggles.

Nuzzling her neck, I chuckle. "It was one of those days."

She runs her fingers through my hair. "Glad I could help."

You have no idea.

CHAPTER EIGHTEEN

Stay Like This

Brick

"This hotel is going to be amazing," Eva says as she scans over a set of blueprints I'm finalizing to be sent out.

"If we can get the design approved, it will be. We've redone the plans four times already," I murmur.

"What's the hold up. I mean, what won't they approve?"

It's a simple question. As an intern it's good she's asking. However, there's no simple answer for me to give her.

This is where the road meets muddy waters. Business versus club business. The shit she has no business next to.

"It's complicated. If you ask me it's all red tape. Someone's getting a hard-on from blocking the project from moving forward. Nothing was wrong with the original design, nor the second or third. Politics."

"Really," she says with rounded eyes. "They can block your plans just to block them?"

"You have a lot to learn, darlin'. I've had multiple projects blocked at once because someone had a problem with me."

"What did you do?" she asks.

"I have bigger friends in higher places. A few phone calls and things were as they should be," I reply and shrug.

"What's so different about this one?"

I look up and stare her in the eyes. I'm already up shit creek with King. This is getting too close to club business. Something I know he wants to keep Eva out of.

I'm not going to lie to her, but I can't go and tell her I normally throw around my Lost Souls weight either. However, this time we need to be more careful of the doors we kick in. I always go with my instincts and something tells me this project has had eyes on it from the word go.

I almost walked away without placing the bid, but the revenue was too great for me to let the opportunity pass by. Not to mention, the location is prime. I want to build in this district.

Instead of lying to her face. I crook my finger for her to come to me. She lifts to her knees from her place on the floor near the couch beside me and closes the gap.

I peck her lips and nuzzle my nose to hers. "You've been doing really well with the blueprints. That computer shit doesn't have the same feel as doing it the old fashion way. I'll make sure you master both, you never know when you need to fall back on the old-school skills," I say and peck her lips again as another distraction on top of redirecting the conversation.

Her cheeks glow. "I'm glad I took the internship with you. I'm learning a lot more than I would have if I went back home to intern with someone else," she says.

I furrow my brows. I never considered she would have gone back home to intern with someone else. When King asked me to look at her portfolio and consider her, I only thought of placing her somewhere within Soul Deep Construction.

For the life of me, I can't tell you why this makes me a bit insane for a moment. Eva places her hand on my cheek. She presses her lips to mine but pulls away before I can deepen the kiss.

"You have to remember I didn't put two and two together. I didn't know you were the brother King had put a word in with. I had planned to go back home before you walked into this office," she says as if reading my mind.

I grunt.

"You do know I'm happy you were the one to walk through that door, right?" she breathes.

I wrap an arm around her. "Why is that? Because I fuck you within an inch of your breath for lunch and help you get your work done after hours," I tease.

She slaps at my chest. I catch her hand and bring it to my lips for a kiss before capturing it against my heart. We stare into each other's eyes for I don't know how long.

"I wish things could stay this way," she says, breaking the trance.

I wish they could too, but change is inevitable. With the talk I need to have with King and all that's about to change around us, I know things won't always be this way. I haven't fooled myself into thinking they will be.

Hell, Misty and Eva are best friends. However, Eva hasn't spoken to her much. Eva has really only had communication with me. Once friendships and life start to press on this new bond, we don't know what will happen.

Yet, in this moment, as hope fills her eyes, I can't find it in me to say all that. Instead, I smile and hold her tighter. "We'll take it a day at a time, darlin'. That's the best we can ever do."

This time when I take her lips, I don't let her up for air until I've had my fill. Yeah, I'm probably going to be up all night finishing her work I didn't let her get through. I'm grateful for the apartment upstairs.

Eva

I watch Brick in his sleep. He looks so peaceful. Tonight, I felt like there was so much weighing on his mind.

If I'm honest, it was there before tonight. It reminded me of something my mother used to say. I can hear it clear as day.

"Be his peace. No man wants to take on the world and have to take you on too. Be his peace."

I think I understand that now. Mom was Cage's peace. I reach to trace the tattoo on Brick's chest, snuggling deeper into his side. His hand flexes on my hip, but he doesn't wake.

I place a kiss over his heart. "I want to be your peace," I whisper.

I climb out of bed and grab my phone off the nightstand before creeping into the bathroom. Tipping the phone against my lips, I debate whether or not to call King. Maybe I'm the one who should call him. He's my brother.

He might take all this better from me. I frown. That might not bring Owen the peace I want.

I blow out a breath and look at the time. Yeah, calling King is definitely a bad idea. However, my sister is always up late. I could call her.

I've been trying to text Misty, but lately she's been ignoring my calls and sending me vague text messages. I sigh, decision made. I need someone to talk to.

"Hey, Eva. Is something wrong?" Sal says into the phone.

"No, everything is okay. I mean, it's not but it is."

"O-kay."

I release a long sigh. "Do you ever miss mom really bad? Like, can't breathe, wish you could get some of her advice, but know you can't type of miss her?"

"More than you could ever know," she replies with a hint of something haunted in her voice.

I get a chill. Looking around the bathroom, I move to climb into the tub. Once inside, I slump down and look up at the ceiling. Tears start to fall.

"It's not fair. We didn't just lose one parent we lost them both. I miss Cage too," I choke out.

"He was the only father I ever knew. So much would be different…" She trails off and goes silent for a few beats. "What's going on, Eva?"

I wipe at my tears. "Nothing. I'm just thinking. Remembering some of those things mom used to say. I don't know. I think I just needed to hear your voice," I reply.

"Eva?"

"Yeah?"

She's quiet again. "Nothing, I'm glad you called. It's good to hear your voice."

"Yeah, yours too. I miss you. I have to come see you or something. Maybe when my internship is over."

"Oh, yeah, how's that going? King mentioned it. Do you like it?"

I smile, thinking of my talk with Owen earlier. I am learning a ton from him. I was a bit intimidated by working with actual paper blueprints and not a CAD program, but I've learned so much.

When I do get to work on a computer, I see the plans differently. It makes me feel like I'm getting things done more efficiently.

"I like it. It's better than I thought."

It's on the tip of my tongue to tell her about Brick, but I swallow the words. As I do, movement at the door catches my attention. I turn to find Owen with his eyes on me as he leans against the doorjamb.

"Hey, I have to go. I love you, Sal. Talk to you later."

"Love you too, Eva."

I stand as Owen walks over to me. "I thought I put you to sleep," he says, reaching to caress my face.

"You did. I woke up and my mind was wondering."

He lifts me out of the tub. "Come on, let's see if we can do something about that. I'm having trouble sleeping without you by my side."

I smile.

Be his peace.

CHAPTER NINETEEN

Trouble

Eva

I smirk at the blueprints in front of me. I can feel Owen's eyes on me. He's on the phone at his desk behind me, but his attention has been on me all day. I think it's the white sheath dress I took a chance on this morning. Or it might be the blue heels I bought at lunch yesterday with him in mind.

After having so much on my mind the other night, I had wanted to go shopping with Misty, but she's still ignoring my calls and she's answering me with these damn vague text messages. It wasn't until yesterday morning that I found out she actually went back home for the summer.

She was supposed to stick around with me for the summer break if I got the internship. I feel bad. I've wondered if she left because I've been staying with Owen. I was so depressed about it all, I went shopping.

It would be what Misty would want to do to try to cheer me up. It never does, but it makes her happy, which does cheer me up. Only yesterday, I found myself really happy. The idea of Owen seeing me in these blue four-inch platform heels had me all types of giddy.

We are supposed to leave for SC tonight. Owen has church and he needs to return King's bike. Work has kept us both busy this week. Owen is a workaholic and he wants things just so.

I still haven't been to another worksite since Monday. I guess Owen trusts me here with Holden. I get the feeling that's because rumor is that Holden is Tracks' little, gay brother.

I've never seen him with anyone, but I've never seen him look at a woman either. I've never gotten too close to Holden or Tracks. Again, Squad members are next level Lost Souls. I stay far away.

I used to think Owen was Squad. I guess that was a part of my bad boy fantasies I made up in my head. Now, I just can't see him as a part of the truly Lost Souls. *Nope, not at all,* I think as I feel him walk up behind me.

He places a hand on either side of me on the drafting desk. His cologne engulfs me, making me bite my lip. I turn my head up to him with my smirk still in place. He leans down and pecks my lips.

"I need to feed you soon," he says as he searches my face. "What do you want today?"

"I don't think you can order what I'm hungry for," I purr up at him.

He gives me a sexy wolfish grin. When he dips his head again, he captures my lips in a searing kiss. Dropping his hand to my belly, he groans into my mouth.

My main concern about this dress had been my soft fleshy belly. Owen killed that worry when he walked up behind me in the mirror this morning. He made me feel beautiful.

He deepens the kiss as he moves his hand up from my belly to my breast. I cup a hand behind his head and lift from my seat a little to get closer. He moans and bites at my lower lip.

"Boss," Troy's voice fills Owen's office.

Oh, shit, we didn't close the office door. Owen pulls away from the kiss, allowing me to see Troy standing frozen in the doorway. His mouth is hanging open and the papers in his hand are hanging limply from his fingertips.

Owen had contained what happened in this office a few weeks ago. That whole scene with Beth and Magdalena was as good as buried. I haven't heard so much as a whisper about it.

This, however, is not how Owen wanted our relationship to get out. We usually close the door for privacy if we know we just can't keep our hands off each other. Troy has been making more and more unnecessary trips to this office over the last week. Including the one when he tried to ask me out on a date.

Troy pulls a face, looking as if someone has stolen his new puppy. Owen grunts, then leans over me to kiss my lips once more. *I guess since the cat is out of the bag.*

"Go have Holden order our lunch. Get me whatever you like," he says as he pulls me from my chair. He pats my ass and kisses my temple.

Yeah, this is more than the cat being out of the bag. Owen has been waiting to stake his claim on me in front of Troy. He's been annoyed with him since my interview.

I shake my head at Owen and start out of the office. I put a little extra sway in my hips as I feel his eyes on me. I smile and wave at a flabbergasted Troy on the way out.

I am still giggling when I get down the hall to the reception desk. Holden hangs up the phone as I put my elbows on the desk and peer at him. I smile and reach to ruffle his hair.

Holden blinks at me like I'm crazy. I laugh. He always has such a serious look on his face. I know he's my age, I also know he and Tracks came around right before Mom and Dad's accident. They didn't get as much time with Cage as the rest of us.

Tracks is still loyal to King and the club, though. That much I know. You can't be on the Squad and not be loyal.

"You're trying to get my ass kicked," Holden whispers as he looks down the hallway toward Owen's office.

I stop laughing and tilt my head to the side. "What do you mean?"

Holden rolls his eyes and pokes out his twisted lips. "I'm not stupid. Shit, anyone paying attention can see it. You're fucking the shit out of the boss." He wiggles his brows at me. "I've seen the hickeys and claw marks on his neck."

My mouth falls open. I lean over the desk. "How do you know they're from me?"

"Oh, come on. Have you seen the way he looks at you? Girl please, he's probably in there handing Troy his ass. I've seen it coming for days now."

Holden props his chin on his hand as I gape at him. I lick my dry lips. "You haven't told anyone?" I whisper.

"Not my thing, I don't gossip. Besides, you're good for him. Squad members need something to keep them from going into the darkness." He shrugs.

My eyes go wide and I take a step back. "What?" I choke out.

Holden looks at me like I'm stupid and bursts into laughter. "Wow, everyone's right. You don't pay attention to shit around the club. How could you not know you're fucking the Squad captain? It don't get no darker or more fucked up than your man."

"But… how is that possible?" I say.

"Eva, what do you know about the Squad?"

I think about that. Well, damn, nothing really. I know Tracks, Gutter, Grim, Beau, and Diggs are all Squad and there are seven more I've never met or at least, I never thought I knew them. There are twelve in all. Like apostles. They cover King.

Essentially, they go to hell and back for the club. Forget enforcers, the Squad rolls in when shit is about to turn apocalyptic. The ones I know of are batshit crazy. I close my eyes and groan.

"*Fuck*," I whisper.

"Yup, you get it now. Have you seen his Lost Souls tat? All Squad members have a reaper with wings and a sword in his hands. It's not the standard reaper," Holden says as he watches my face for recognition.

I blink, he sure as hell just described the tat on Brick's back. The wings span his shoulder blades. The sword in the reapers' hands takes up the center of his back in the most realistic design I've ever seen.

When you watch his back flex, it's like the tat comes to life. "I never knew the difference. Daddy and King have the winged version with the crown on the hood." I shrug my shoulders as my mind races.

"Yeah, well, your dad was the prez and now King is. The prez always gets the crown." He shrugs back. "If you've paid attention you noticed Brick's sword has five stars etched in the blade."

I frown before scratching my head. Again, he's right. "Five-star general, Eva." He lifts a brow. "In the Lost Souls' world, when it comes to the Squad, Brick is second only to King. They say your daddy set things up that way. Prez never changed it. They've just grown since." Holden pauses and looks at me pointedly. "Your man *is* the Squad."

I move back to the desk and put my elbows on the counter. "How do you know so much about club life?" I question.

"I wanted to be a prospect. Tracks doesn't think it's a good idea. I get it. He's extra protective when it comes to me. We're all we have. Tracks thinks the brothers will be extra hard on me. You know, cause they think I'm gay," he says the words with such a straight face, I can't help but ask.

"Are you?"

Holden frowns and shrugs. "I don't know. I've never been attracted to a guy, but I haven't been attracted to a girl either," he says sadly, and his eyes go distant. "Well, not in a really long time, I don't think."

"Really?" I wrinkle my brows.

"What? It's because of the way I dress, isn't it?" He chuckles. It looks good on him. Holden is actually very attractive with his dark blue eyes and mop of light brown hair. "Just because I wash my ass and iron my clothes, doesn't make me gay. I mean, I think you're extremely pretty. I just don't get... I don't know. I'm supposed to feel something, right? Shit, I think Brick is a good-looking guy, but I don't want to fuck him, either."

"What happened?" I blurt out.

Holden looks at me long and hard. "I… I can't remember. Tracks knows everything. He remembers everything. I don't. I have this one memory of a friend I once had. It's not a big one, just this sliver of a memory. It's the only time I think I might have once felt something."

"Wow."

Holden waves his hand at me. "Your dad saved us. At least, that's what Tracks says. Whatever happened fucked my brother up pretty bad to get him on the Squad." Holden pauses as if he has said too much.

"Don't worry, I won't say anything to anyone." I tilt my head to the other side. "I get that you don't care what everyone thinks." I stare at him as I read his face.

Holden snorts. "They think anyone not chasing ass around the clubhouse is gay," Holden frowns and grumbles.

I laugh because he's right. Rumors fly around about Gutter, but everyone's too scared to death to say that shit to his face. Like Holden, I don't think Gutter gives a damn and prefers it that way.

"So, the big guy wants lunch. Let's feed my baby before he gets grumpy on us." I laugh.

"Sure, what's your man got a taste for today?"

"Well, he said I could pick. I think he'll growl at both of us if I order wraps like I want." I giggle.

Holden lifts a brow at me. "Steakhouse it is. I want to stretch my legs. I'll go get it."

I laugh and shake my head. "I'll man the desk for you while you're gone. No need to bother Adriana."

Holden looks up the hall toward the office and wrinkles his nose. We hear Owen's voice raise and we both jump. Holden lifts a brow at me.

"Sure, you don't want to take a walk with me." He smirks.

"Yeah, that sounds good." I laugh.

Holden nods and picks up the phone to place the lunch order. He then calls Adriana to come sit at the desk for him. I don't even bother going back for my purse. Holden gets some cash from the petty cash box.

"Come on, it's about to get real in here." Holden chuckles as Owen gets louder.

He's right. It's best to get going while the getting is good. Owen sounds beyond pissed. I bet Troy wishes he stayed his silly ass out of Owen's office today.

Owen

I shake my head at Eva's swaying ass as I adjust my cock. I have something for her later. I want to get my hands on her one good time before we have to go to South Carolina and pretend we're nothing to each other until I talk to King.

I know Troy has had his ass in my office every time I step out of the building. He's supposed to be working in HR and finance. How the fuck his ass always knows my comings and goings already has me gritting my teeth.

I sent Eva out because it's time I make something clear to this kiss ass. Troy is the best at half of his job. It's the reason I've kept him around. As long as I keep him up here on the executive floor, I usually don't have a problem out of him.

"You know she's young. She could sue the company for sexual harassment," Troy has the balls to say to me after he watches Eva leave my office.

I should have closed and locked that fucking door. Troy is the least of my worries, but someone that could make this weekend hell could have walked in. I need this relationship to come from my lips to King's ears.

When I looked up to see Troy, I was honestly happy he did walk in on us. He's been sniffing around Eva all week. His ass doesn't know I have eyes everywhere. Especially when it comes to Eva.

None of them would find it strange that I want to keep an eye on King's little sister. The club princess is always priority. So, it's been easy to keep the brothers in the office on the lookout.

I slowly turn my head in Troy's direction and narrow my eyes, cocking my head to the side. "You want to repeat that shit?"

I'm already on edge because I have to be in church tonight and that means taking Eva back to South Carolina with me. I don't know why that's not sitting right with me. I had planned to before. Then King and I both agreed for me not to leave her behind.

I know King hasn't told me something. I only get called to church for one of two things. Either King needs me to get in some bigwig's ear or shit is about to get real.

I mean, usually my presence is optional depending on the nature of business. When King needs my squad, it becomes mandatory. It's another reason he called me to go rescue Eva.

I stay out of shit unless needed. My mind has been turning over the fact that King requested me in church for almost a full week now. When I saw him Monday, his mind was preoccupied with something totally different. I can't say it's not club related, but his shit wouldn't require my whispers or the Squad.

"I'm only saying, she's a summer intern. We don't need the complications. We're doing so well in the industry these days," Troy says, straightening his tie.

I think Troy is about to find out who the fuck I am. The real Brick Mason. I bare my teeth and close the space between us.

You see, the Lost Souls have your ordinary enforcers like any other MC. Grim and Wolf are our official club enforcers for the South Carolina, Georgia chapter. You might as well throw Reap into that equation. She's not an official club member, more like the property of Grim, but you tell her that and see what happens.

Cage always treated Reap like one of the guys. She's never seen herself as anything but. Reap is smaller than Eva, but you would think she was my height.

However, she's half the height of every brother in the squad, but just as insane. It's the reason she's the only female Squad member. I tried to stop that shit, but she wasn't having it.

Where you find Grim, Reap is sure to follow. They're both crazy as fuck, but I will always want them in my corner and on my squad. I was proud the day I watched Reap get her reaper on her right thigh, wings, sword, and all. She grumbled the whole-time *Property of Grim* was etched into a ribbon wrapping the sword and knuckles of her winged reaper.

"Let me get this straight," I say low. "You've been eye fucking my woman since her first day here. You bring your ass to my office for bullshit all day to ogle her and now you're talking to *me*." I touch my chest incredulously, trying to have a moment to reel my shit in. "About sexually harassing *my* woman? Are you stupid or slow?"

It's been one of those mornings. I've had so much bullshit floating through my mind as I sat through call after call, watching Eva in those heels and that white dress. I couldn't wait to get off the phone so I could get close to her. I wasn't even thinking when I walked over to the drafting table she sat at.

"I... I... I," he stammers.

"*I... I... I*," I mock. "Shut the fuck up! What do you want? Why are you in my office this time?"

"I needed you to sign off on the Sheldon account." Troy blinks stupidly.

I swear, I lose my half-sane mind. "Are you fucking shitting me?" My voice rises with my ire. "I told your ass to email those to Holden and he would print them off. Where is the shit I actually pay you to do? The Cooper file was a fucking shit show. The figures are a mess and I have that pitch on Monday."

"Owen, I thought you wanted to see the numbers for the revisions they asked for," he tries.

"Are you fucking with me? Please tell me you're fucking with me." My voice gets louder by the moment. "Those are the same bullshit numbers you beefed up two weeks ago. I told your ass then I wanted clean numbers and details on the shit you were piling onto those spec sheets."

"I... I can do that," Troy murmurs.

"It's not a matter of you being able to do it. Why the fuck has it not been done? There's one reason I've been keeping you around here in the first place and you're fucking that up," I growl.

"I'm sorry," Troy says.

I open my mouth to go completely off, but my cell vibrates. I pull it from my pocket and frown. It's a text from Gutter.

King has activated him. I clench my jaw. If King went direct, some shit is going on.

I text Gutter back to let him know I got his message and I turn my attention back to Troy. Once again, my words are cut short by my phone. This time it's a call from King.

"Get the fuck out," I growl at Troy, dismissing his dumb ass.

I pick up the phone and bring it to my ear. "Prez," I grumble.

"Get my sister home, now," King roars into the phone.

My heart sinks into my stomach. For a moment, I think he knows. I can't breathe for a few seconds. The thought of losing Eva steals what little bit of soul I have left.

"Is there a problem? I got a text from Gutter," I manage to ask.

"He's on the way to get Sal and bring her in. Her apartment was broken into and trashed. They took her bike," King says tightly.

I think I start to see red. Nobody fucks with our girls, but I know what really sets me off is that King doesn't feel this is isolated to Sal. If he wants Eva home, she could be in danger.

"I need all twelve ready. Get her here. I'm locking shit down until I have answers," King snaps and hangs up.

I close my eyes as a growl vibrates through me. This shit is just not happening right now. I was hoping this trip home would be a simple one. Not the giant one my instincts have been warning me about.

My mind turns to my cousin and my ex-wife. They've been too quiet. I should've been paying them more attention over the last few weeks. My name isn't Brick Mason if those two don't appear soon to make this shit worse. I feel it in my bones.

"Shit."

CHAPTER TWENTY

New Friends

Eva

Holden and I stroll slowly up the street. One, because of my heels and two, because we're not in any rush to get back to the building. Not from the sound of the bellows coming from that office.

"Those heels are going to take you out," Holden taunts.

"Ugh, they were not meant for me to walk in them. I hadn't planned to do more than go into the office and back to the truck to go home," I groan.

He throws his head back and laughs. Fine, we can both laugh at my pain. It feels good to do that after all my worrying lately.

Taking a glance at his outfit, I grin. Holden is a tall lanky sort of guy. Not lanky in an awkward way. He carries himself well enough.

His burgundy slacks are a slim fit and his loafers give him a polished look. He actually looks like he could be on a magazine cover. Edgy, but not rough like King and Brick can pass off.

"Look, you modernized James Dean. Just because we all can't pull off the loafers and caviar look doesn't mean we've all failed at life," I toss out.

"Oh," he bursts into laughter. "Loafers and caviar? James Dean? Good one."

"Thank you."

"You know, I like you this way," he says.

I look up at him, drawing my brows in. "What do you mean?"

"You smile more here and… I don't know. You seem happy. Back home, you were always… off to yourself. Sort of guarded, I guess. I can't blame you. Things are always intense back there. I can't imagine it's easy being the prez's sister," he replies.

I shrug. "I think I blocked it all out years ago. The bunnies have never been too nice to me and the brothers kept their distance for the most part. My books were better company, with the exception of Misty and Reap."

"Reap, now that's one I keep my distance from."

"Really? Why?"

He looks at me like I've lost my mind. "You're kidding?"

"No, why?"

"Can I ask you something? How much do you know about the club?"

I take a moment to think that through. "Honestly?"

"Yeah, honestly," he replies.

"My dad was the prez and then my brother took over. We're one of about ten chapters, I think. I get the whole business thing with some of the brothers. Oh, and Uncle Mix is the VP.

"There's a subdivision in our chapter. That's the Squad, they can be a bit scary. At least, the ones I know of, but after what you told me back at the office, I'm questioning that knowledge a bit," I say truthfully.

"Yeah, you should. Maybe you should ask Brick to fill you in a bit more. I'm feeling a little out of place now that I know how little you know."

I look up and catch the nervous look in his eyes. I make a note to ask Brick a few questions. I chew on my lip, if he considers it club business he may not answer.

That could be a problem. I'm starting to want to know more. Although, I'm still processing this Squad captain thing.

"Hey, do you remember that orgy you walked in on at the clubhouse?" Holden says.

My mouth pops open and I palm my face. With a groan, I shake my head. "You were there?"

"Nearly blew my cover laughing so hard at you," he says. "You should have seen your face."

"Well, I walked in by mistake. What were you doing in there?"

He snorts. "Technically, I was there first. I was trying to get high in peace. Not my fault they picked my hiding spot."

I laugh as I remember that night. I'd been reading and walked into the room not paying much attention. Otherwise, I would have noticed the room was occupied.

"Wait, do you remember that time that one brother got so drunk he couldn't find the bathroom so he pissed right in the middle of the clubhouse?" Holden asks next.

"Oh, yeah, I do. I was in the corner reading and looked up right as he whipped it out."

"See, you're always around. Just not paying attention."

"Fine, I get your point," I say and bump my arm into his.

"Do you remember Molly dancing on the pool table until her wig fell off?"

I squint my eyes as if that will help me remember better. This one doesn't come back to me. I try to think harder, but still nothing.

"No, I don't recall that one," I say.

"Come on, you were sitting right there. You have to remember," he says.

"What? Really?"

"Well, damn. That's pretty amazing. No wonder you didn't react. You weren't paying attention."

"Can I ask you something?"

"Go on."

"What brought you here to Georgia? How did you end up Brick's assistant?"

I peer up at him in time to catch him rolling his eyes. "I needed a break from my brother. He means well. I know he's just looking out for me, but it gets to be a bit much. I talked to King and here I am," he says.

"I can totally relate to that. King can be intense sometimes. He definitely means well. I guess college gave me a reprieve," I muse aloud.

"But he doesn't know about this thing with Brick," he says with a bit of caution in his voice. "I mean, Brick told me to mind my fucking business in but so many words, but I'm not going to run home and tell either way. Like I said, I like you like this."

"No, he doesn't know. It sort of just happened. We're going to tell him. Brick is waiting for the right timing," I say.

"No need to explain to me. If King ever asks if I knew, I'm blaming the memory." He taps his temple.

"Ah, but then you would be breaking a Lost Souls rule, we don't lie."

"Wait, so you do know more about the life," he says teasingly and bumps my shoulder this time. "Besides, I'm not a Lost Soul, remember? My brother has blocked that one."

This time when he says the words, I hear something in his voice. It's a longing or disappointment. I peek up at him once more.

"Why do I get the feeling there's a lot more to you, Holden?"

"Because there is. I'm this great mystery hidden in the Lost Souls' world," he teases.

"Aren't we all?"

CHAPTER TWENTY-ONE

Family

Eva

I had such a good time with Holden as we walked to get lunch. He got in a few more teases about my deer walk in my heels. I managed to throw a few more of my own jabs. We're laughing to the point of tears when the elevator opens to a raging Owen, pacing in front of the car bay.

He doesn't give me or Holden a chance to get off. "Let's go," Owen demands as he storms right on and jabs the button for the lower level.

I look to Holden with wide eyes. He looks forward, but I can feel the anticipation rolling off of him. I'm not sure what's going on, but Owen looks too angry for me to even ask.

"Both of you, get in the car," Owen barks when we reach the parking garage.

Holden doesn't ask questions as he holds open the BMW's front passenger door for me, before climbing into the back. Owen pulls out of the parking garage like a madman. My stomach tightens.

I get the feeling something big is going on. My thoughts go back to what I've learned. Brick is the Squad captain.

I swallow the implications of that thought. The silence of the ride is deafening. The only sound that registers is the pounding of my heart.

"Holden, take the keys to my Harley," Owen orders when we arrived at the house.

Holden does as he's told as he jumps out of the back seat. I get out of the car right before Owen reaches my door. He tugs me to the elevator by my wrist.

Still, he hasn't done more than bark a few orders. Once on the apartment level, I have to kick off my shoes to keep up with his long strides. He drags me to the bedroom where he sets me on the bed.

He pulls out a duffel bag and starts to throw things in for me. Once the bag is packed, he tosses me a pair of my old jeans and a baggy T-shirt. I dress in confusion. I don't understand what is going on.

Has King found out about us? Should I be worried? I have so many questions, but my tongue is tied.

Within ten minutes, he has two bags packed and has changed into jeans and his cut. We return to the garage where Holden is waiting for us. I see the lunch we bought resting in the trash can, all but forgotten.

Owen tosses Holden one of the bags. "Let's ride," he says, climbing onto King's bike.

We are on the road before I can clear my head. Holden is on Owen's bike and Owen and I are on King's, heading to South Carolina. I'd never seen Holden handle a bike, but he keeps up with Owen the entire way.

I'm frustrated and exhausted by the time we pull into the compound's gates. The three-hour ride has taken its toll. I stumble off the bike on jelly legs.

"You all right?" Owen asks as he reaches out to steady me with a hand on my hip.

I watch the frown that mars his face as he quickly pulls his hand away. I know my sadness shows in my eyes because his frown deepens. I tuck my helmet under my arm and nod my head to indicate that I'm all right.

"Listen, baby," Owen starts, but he cuts his words off as King comes marching out of the clubhouse. Owen draws his lips into a thin line. "We'll talk as soon as I get shit straight," he says low enough for only me to hear.

King stops in front of me just then and pulls me into a bear hug and kisses the top of my head. "Thanks, brother," King says over my head, not letting me out of his embrace. "I mean it. Thanks for keeping her with you for so long while I got shit in order."

I pull out of King's arms and turn to look at Owen. If my eyes read hurt a few moments ago, they're telling him I'm crushed now. I thought I was staying with Owen because he wanted me to. Not because King asked him to babysit me.

I wish the hurt ended there, but it doesn't. King's next words kill me. I feel the knife as it runs through me.

"This problem is growing, brother. Jemma and Mags showed up asking to be inside the gates for lockdown. I need you inside to handle that crazy-ass wife of yours," King grunts.

"Ex-wife," Owen growls as he locks eyes with me.

"She ain't seeing it that way. Just go handle that shit," King retorts.

King wraps an arm around my shoulders, totally oblivious to the fact I'm falling apart inside. I can't even look at Brick. I follow King into the clubhouse lifelessly.

When we step inside, the last voice I want to hear reaches my ears. Magdalena is demanding something of Jacks, one of the oldest members of the club. He sits staring at her like she has lost her mind.

Magdalena turns in our direction and a grimace reaches her lips. "What the fuck is she doing here? If she's staying, I sure as shit am," she shrieks.

"Shut your damn mouth, before I shut it for you," Brick snaps as he rushes pass me.

"Handle that shit, Brick. She disrespects my sister again, she's out on her fucking ass. I don't give two fucks," King says hotly.

"Your sister?" Magdalena says with wide eyes. A smug grin comes to her lips as she looks between me and Brick.

"Brick," King warns. He turns to me. "You look exhausted. Why don't you go to your room?"

"Yeah," I say and turn to leave.

I should have known there was nothing truly going on with me and Brick. He had to watch over me and made the time useful to himself. He's a Lost Soul. It's what they do.

Owen

"I said shut the hell up," I growl and grab Mags by the top of her arm.

I glare at Jemma, warning her to follow me. Thank God Mags zips her fucking lips. I can feel King watching us as I pull Mags simple ass outside with me.

I march to the edge of the property, way out of ear shot. I am hanging by a thread. I need to talk to Eva. I saw her face. I know she's thinking all types of shit I need to expel from her brain.

I'd take ten Eva's over Mags any day. In any category—looks, personality, and hell, brains. Baby girl has me so wrapped around her finger I can't see straight. I'm dying inside right now and feeling like the pussy I sound like.

I stop and spin Magdalena to face me. Before I can lay into her ass the smug grin on her face makes my blood run cold. I've never wanted to hit a woman. Fuck, Mags has made me want to choke the life out of her more times than I can count, but here and now I want to slap that smile off her face.

"She's King's sister?" She cackles out loud. "Holy shit, Brick. He has no idea you're fucking her, does he? You dirty son of a bitch. Oh, my God, she's the little fat one who used to watch you every time we came here. This is priceless."

"You're fucking Eva?" Jemma gasps. "Are you crazy?"

I pinch my eyes closed. "I'm not fucking her," I growl.

"Are we forgetting I walked in on you pounding her ass into your desk," Mags snorts.

I open my eyes and give her a death glare. I then look at my cousin. "I'm not fucking her, she's mine," I finish this time.

"Oh, God, Brick. You have to fix this shit. King is going to lose his fucking mind. We can't afford for you to be stripped of your patch now," Jemma says frantically.

"Enough," I bark. "Stay out of my business. What you two need to be telling me is why you are here. What the fuck have you gotten into this time? And how the hell did you know to come here for lockdown in the first fucking place?"

"Rodney has been keeping me updated," Jemma says in frustration. "I told you we needed your help."

I run a hand through my hair. The Squad is going to have to teach Rodney the meaning of loyalty and keeping his fucking mouth shut, *again*. I swear, if he wasn't Mix's nephew... Give him pussy or alcohol and he's an open fucking book. That shit is going to get him killed.

I narrow my eyes at Mags. First, she bribes Beth, my receptionist, for a full fucking year, now this shit. I couldn't believe that shit when Diggs reported it back to me.

I'm at the end of my fucking rope with these two. I've given them more than enough slack to hang themselves, especially Mags. I have no doubt she's going to choke soon.

"What have you done?" I look at Mags.

"It was me," Jemma whispers.

I whip my head in Jemma's direction and narrow my eyes. "Oh, come on, Jemma. What now?" I groan.

"She didn't do it alone." Magdalena sighs.

"Look, spare me the lovers' quarrel. What did you two do?"

I watch as fear registers in Magdalena's eyes. For the second time, it dawns on me, I'm not the only one she has feared lately. Mags likes to push my limits, but she has always feared taking things too far. I've seen it in her eyes.

In this moment, she has something else in her brown depths. These two have definitely gotten their selves into some deep shit. I shouldn't care, but my instincts force me to focus.

King says shit is brewing and these too show up here. Mags' visit to my office is nagging at the back of my mind now. I was more worried about Eva then. I know I should have kept my eye on these two, but I've been wrapped up in my woman instead.

However, my common sense kicks back in. This is Mags and Jemma. These two live to stir shit up. I'm not getting dragged into their manipulation. Not this time.

Whatever they want, I plan to squash that shit and get them far away from here. I don't need their brand of trouble. Messy, I can do without.

The longer I'm out here with these two, the longer Eva has to spend in her head, thinking all types of shit that ain't right. I feel in my very bones she's questioning everything about us in her pretty little head.

Straightening that shit out is more important to me, but I hold back to get to the bottom of this little evil duo. I resolve in my mind I need Eva to know she's the only one who matters. I don't give a shit what Magdalena or Jemma have to say, because with each second that passes, I can feel I'm losing my woman.

Bitterly, I shove my selfish needs down. These two showing up here isn't good for the club. I don't like the way Mags looks at Jemma as we stand here, I need answers.

I don't want the song and dance Mags is going to give me. I don't need it. I know the way these two work.

Jemma is known for skirting as close to the truth as she can when she's trying to manipulate me for Magdalena. I can count on ninety percent of what she says to be true. Tonight, that ninety percent is better than being blindsided.

So, I hold my hand up when Mags opens her mouth, and I point to Jemma. "You, start talking, now," I command.

Mags opens her fucking mouth anyway. "What are you going to do for me to keep my mouth shut?" she asks.

"You don't want to go there with me," I say. "You assume I'm too much of a gentleman to really harm you. You play that game, but let me remind you of this, Reap is itching to put you to ground. All I have to do is say the word."

"Calm down, Brick," Jemma says, pinching the bridge of her nose. "You two drive me crazy."

"I want to know what she means to him."

"Why do you care?" Jemma glares at Mags.

"I want to know." Mags shrugs.

"None of your fucking business. The only thing I want to hear coming from your lips is what the hell you've gotten yourself into and how you dragged my ass into it this time," I seethe.

Magdalena changes her expression. I guess my willingness to listen trumps her curiosity about Eva. I start to pace and shrug out of my cut. I'm becoming pissed and overheated.

I feel my muscles become taut with tension as I wait for this shit show to start. My biceps flex and my jaw tics as I tighten my grip on my cut. Jemma starts to pace. I swear, I can touch the tension between these two. I can read the trouble in paradise.

I look at Mags to study her and watch her gaze run over me. I snort at the lust-filled look in Magdalena's eyes. I once relished in that look.

My ex-wife is a conniving bitch, but she's an attractive one. Mags has the type of beauty that grants her whatever she asks for from fools. I was once her fool.

However, that will never happen again. Magdalena has received all the attention she will ever get from me. I wouldn't touch her with a ten-foot pole now. She's a costly mistake for any man willing to entertain her. That won't ever be me.

"Spit. It. Out," I roar.

Mags shakes her head and licks her lips. "You never used to be so mean to me," she pouts.

I tighten my fist in frustration. "I don't have time for your games. You tell me what the hell is going on or I'll find out on my own. You and I both know you don't want me prying into your life," I rumble.

Mag's shoulders sag. "They're coming for me," she whispers. "Miguel has found me."

I narrow my eyes as I feel my whole body tense. "She's kidding, right?" I look at Jemma, waiting for the joke.

Jemma shakes her head with tears in her eyes.

"How did that happen, Magdalena?" I bellow. "I spent a fortune and called in a million favors to reinvent your life. I gave you a new world to hide in.

"I married you so this shit wouldn't happen. For three years, you made my life fucking hell, all so that I could make you disappear. So, please tell me... how the fuck is this possible? How the hell did you two fuck that up?"

I am livid.

Jemma and Magdalena came to me with a sob story that sucked me in. Mags was a gorgeous girl in need, and they pulled me right into being her savior. I had no idea Mags was already in a relationship with my crazy-as-fuck cousin.

I did everything they asked of me back then, but Mags decided she wanted more. She fought me tooth and nail on the divorce, even after I used my connections to give her a new identity and life.

I narrow my eyes at Mags. They're leaving something out. That ten percent that never comes to the surface because it doesn't benefit them. I'm going to lose my shit. I know I am.

"What are you not saying?" I grunt.

"We need your help, Brick. Please," Mags says with less confidence. It's an act. I know it is.

"How... tell me, how?" I snap.

Jemma stops pacing, but she won't lift her head. These two will be the cause of my heart exploding. I grind my teeth to keep from shaking them both.

"Mags and I found a new mark." Jemma winces with her words. There's no need. I know I was their mark. I had money and power, and my own cousin and her girlfriend played me for a fool. "He fell for me hard. Mags was just a bonus for his ego."

"They started to do things without me," Mags interjects, cutting Jemma off with heat and anger I notice. "He wanted to surprise her with a trip. Jemma didn't know he was taking her to Brazil until the plane landed. Jemma freaked and demanded he bring her back home, but one of Miguel's men noticed her on the tarmac." Mags closes her eyes and licks her lips.

"We didn't know he was related to Miguel. David is Miguel's cousin, but we didn't know. I was made and Miguel figured out the rest. They're coming for her," Jemma whispers with panic on her face. "For us. I'm tired of this shit, Brick. I didn't mean for this to happen, this time. I really didn't mean for this to happen."

"Unbelievable," I roar and run a hand through my hair. "You two are unbelievable. Why do you let her drag you into this shit?"

"I don't twist her arm." Mags rolls her eyes.

"The fuck you don't."

"Brick," Mags says softly, causing me to cringe. I know she's going to drop a bigger bomb on me.

"What?"

"He knows about you. He knows you're a Lost Soul. He's invested in you and your brothers. Finding me is only the icing. You and your brothers are the cake," Mags breathes.

I swear, I want to snap her neck. I was stupid to ever help her. Knowing it's possible Mags has now dragged my brothers into this shit has me fuming.

Most of all, I'm pissed because I know I'll most likely help her again. Not because of her, but because of who I am. I won't let Jemma be thrown under the bus like I should.

I'm all she has. The rest of our family ain't shit. It's the reason Jemma is so fucked up now.

I need them both where I have eyes, until I can sort this all out. I don't trust them out of my reach. For that reason, they're staying.

"Get your shit." I point in Mags face. "Stay the fuck away from my woman. If you two start any shit, you're on your own. Eva's my priority, I need to keep her safe."

"Why the—" Mags starts.

"Finish that sentence and you're on your own. For all I know, you could have led trouble right to our door. You're lucky I don't leave you to the wolves."

I turn and leave Mags standing with her mouth hanging open. I don't have time for this shit. I need to get to the bottom of this before it blows back in my face.

I storm into the clubhouse ready to track Eva's ass down. I feel Jemma following behind me, but I don't want to talk to her right now. I'm pissed as fuck.

"Brick," she says nervously behind me.

I whip around, ready to lay into her, but I stop as I see the tears run down her cheeks. Jemma isn't a big crier. She has to really be going through something to break down.

I heave a heavy sigh and pull her into my arms. "I'm going to need you to stop getting into this shit," I say into the top of her hair.

"My baby is going to need me to stop getting into this shit." She sniffles. I pull away and look at her with disbelief.

"You're shitting me, Jemma," I groan.

She shakes her head. "I fucked up. David didn't just fall for me. I fell for him. Mags is lying. She knew David was taking me to Brazil. I was supposed to tell him about the baby. She was pissed…"

"Wait, what?" I fume.

"She told David to take me to Brazil. I think she was trying to set me up, but it blew up in her face. She didn't factor in David's relation to Miguel. It was the one thing she didn't know about," Jemma whispers and looks around. "I don't trust her or a word she says.

"Listen Brick, I haven't talked to David. I don't know if Miguel is really after the Lost Souls or if Mags is trying to drag y'all into this to save her own ass. Something's not right, but if I don't help her, I'm going to get me and my baby killed. She has lost her mind."

"Really, you're just figuring that out?" I snort.

"I know I fucked up. I was wrong for what I did. Please help me and my baby. David's gone. I don't know what Mags did, but he up and left. I told her not to go to him for help, that I would get you to fix this, but she must have dragged him further in. I'm sorry to bring this to the club's door," she's sobbing now.

I bite my fist as I pull her into my arm. I have a whole lot of shit that needs fixing. I don't make idle threats. It's about to get real fucking uncomfortable for some.

CHAPTER TWENTY-TWO

Club Business

Owen

"Brick," King bellows my name as I come from the room I set Jemma up in. Far away from where I plan to have Magdalene staying.

I curse under my breath. I am finally making my way to Eva. My lips pinch when I see Mags over at one of the pool tables trying to gain some attention. No one with two ounces of sense is going to entertain her.

I push her out of my mind for now. I'll be making a phone call later. I still need more facts to make sure Jemma and my little cousin on the way are okay.

I follow King's retreating back into his office. I close the door behind me and lean against it. King takes a seat behind his desk and props his feet up on it.

"I know anytime I see those two in the same place, it's trouble," he says pointedly.

"Jemma's pregnant. Mags is a dead bitch, and we may or may not have trouble headed our way. But it's all on me," I say as I push off the door and stumble my tired body over to the chair in front of his desk.

I might as well get this shit over with. That way I can go curl up in bed with my woman. I need her in the worst way.

He chuckles humorlessly. "We know how to get into some shit." He drops his feet to the floor and reaches for his drawer where he keeps *our* bottle of brandy.

"Yeah, well, I really didn't see this one when I was wet behind the ears just trying to get my dick sucked. You tried to warn me. Your dad would've kicked my ass." I chuckle.

"Yeah, he'd be up my ass by now too," King grunts.

"How is she?" I ask, seeing an opening for what I need to talk to King about.

"Sick as fuck," he groans.

I smirk. "They say that shit passes. Listen, King, we need to talk," I start.

He slides a glass in front of me. He lifts his glass in salute and knocks it back. I swallow mine, letting the liquid warm my belly.

"Yeah, we do." He nods. "I need to know if what's going on in New York has something to do with your ex-wife. I need to know why someone is after Sal. What do you think is coming to our door, Brick?"

I guess this isn't the time to talk about Eva. "Miguel Silva," is all I have to say.

"Fuck." King sighs. "How, why?"

"When Jemma brought Mags to me, I was willing to help because she was in need and hot as fuck, but when I found out she belonged to him, I knew I was going to do whatever I had to do to help her." I shrug.

"You're one crazy son of a bitch." He smiles and shakes his head. "Fine. He finally wants to end this. Let's rock."

"No, this is my mess."

King pins me with a hard glare. "No, brother, that motherfucker is our problem. He has been lying in wait for years.

We embarrassed the shit out of him. Trust me, this shit ain't about some pussy he's chasing."

"Maybe." I rub my beard.

King looks down at his phone and frowns. "Gutter hasn't checked in since he met up with Sal," he mutters.

"They could be riding." I shrug. I watch him purse his lips in thought. "Actually, they may have stopped to rest. The three hours from Georgia are riding my ass right about now. Give them 'til the morning. If you still feel like something is off, we can send reinforcements to meet them."

"Brick, we've been brothers for a long time. Tell me this… why do I feel like we haven't seen the tip of the iceberg? This shit isn't the beginning. Whispers have been coming in from New York and Alabama. That's why I wanted you in for church, but now I'm thinking I need to keep this one close to the chest. I need you to do what you do."

"Talk to the Mayor?" I lift a brow.

"The Mayor, Governor, all our greedy friends who have their hands in our pockets. Someone isn't happy with their cut. I want to know if they're involved with Miguel or if we have more than one problem."

I rub the back of my neck, but what I really want to do is throw this chair across the fucking room. This isn't a request for tomorrow. What King actually just said is, *"Get your ass back on your bike and find out what the fuck is going on, now. There will be no more talk."*

I get it. Sal is involved, in his mind nothing else matters. This is priority. I nod.

"When does Mix get back?" I ask, knowing the club VP is up north.

King sighs and purses his lips. "He's checking into some things, but he's heading in after."

"You ready for that?" I ask, knowing Mix's return holds a heavy weight over King's shoulders for reasons I'm still trying to wrap my head around.

"I love that old man like a father." King pauses. He shakes his head. "I just don't know where all this is headed. I can see it all coming from miles away, but I can't tell you what it is. Not just the shit I started. Something bigger is brewing. I'll work shit out with the old man, but I think that's the least of my worries."

I sit forward with my brow furrowed. "The old man practically stepped out of the way to make you prez. He has a lot of respect for you. I don't think this is going to be as big a problem as you think. As for the rest, we'll shut that shit down. We've been running a tight ship for years. If it's time for clocks to be cleaned, you know I've got your back."

"Well, saddle up, brother. I think we're in for a bumpy ride," he grunts. He looks me in my eyes with his next words. "We're dealing with Mags this time."

I know his words are not a request, but a command. She needs to be handled one way or another. Mags is reckless.

King knows it and I know it. He doesn't need to know why she's here to know she's here to cause some type of trouble. This isn't the first time she has caused trouble around here for a little attention.

King has left dealing with her up to me. Mags should count herself lucky. Not anymore.

"Already done," I say through my teeth.

King lifts to his feet. "Call me when you have information," he says, dismissing me.

I don't want to delay this anymore than I have to. I need to be on the road and back as soon as I can, so I can handle things with Eva. I get up with a heavy heart and leave. I won't be holding Eva tonight and this shit is going to get a chance to fester.

"Motherfucker," I mutter under my breath as I make my way out to my bike.

I'm getting too old for this shit. I'll be glad when things pan out the way King has been planning. A big transformation has been in the works for the club.

I smile, that change is coming. I have no doubts about that. Everything is changing.

CHAPTER TWENTY-THREE

Darkness

Eva

"What do I do now?" I say into my empty bedroom.

I've spent the day locked in my room at the clubhouse. I hate lockdowns. Honestly, I only come to the club because of Misty. It's not that I hate the life or the club.

It all has its ups and downs. For me, I've just never fit in. Or should I say I've never tried. The fact of the matter is, Cage wouldn't have it really. When we were younger, he tried to keep me away from the club as much as possible.

It was Sal that shadowed him when she was home from school. Cage would let her tinker around with his bike, same as he did with Reap. Me, Cage kept a book and drawing supplies in my hands.

Cage was good like that. He knew who belonged where and placed them there. I wish he were here now to tell me where I belong.

I feel so lost. I don't want to go out there and get strange looks from the guys and dirty glares from the women. Most of all, I don't want to run into Brick and his ex-wife.

"You're such a fool," I mutter, berating myself.

I guess I now know why Brick didn't come clean right away with King. He never had any intention of doing so. I feel so silly. I've been crying since I got in here last night.

I hate that I hurt like this and I'm letting the stupid tears get the best of me. I don't know if I can go out there and face them yet. A part of me thought Brick would at least respect me enough to come say he was sorry.

I was wrong again.

My stomach growls for the hundredth time and I don't think I can ignore it anymore. I push the covers off and scoot out of the bed. It's late.

Most brothers are probably shacked up for the night or in bed with their old ladies who have been forced into lockdown as well. There are probably only a few hanging around in the main den and around the bar.

I can make it to the kitchen and back if I move quickly. I toss on a pair of sweats and an old T-shirt. When I crack the door to my room open, I peek down the hall. All is quiet from what I can see.

I rush out and down to the kitchen. When I enter the kitchen, I sag in relief as the small figure in front of me comes into view. Misty is sitting on a stool with a pint of ice cream in front of her.

As soon as she sees me the spoon pops from her mouth. "Thank God, Eva," she sings my name and hops off her stool. She rushes over to hug me.

She is wrapped tightly around me before I can even process her flying across the room. For someone who hasn't been answering my calls or texts, she sure is clinging to me now. Honestly, I cling back because I need my best friend. I need to tell someone how stupid I've been.

"I'm so sorry I've been such a bad friend," I blurt out as I hold on to her.

She pulls away and frowns at me. "What are you talking about?" She wrinkles her nose. "I feel like shit for ignoring your calls and not talking to you and here you are apologizing. You're going to wring my neck—"

"No, I'm not," I cut her off. "You should be trying to wring mine. I fucked up so bad. I slept with him," I whisper the last part quickly when I see her about to protest.

I look around to make sure no one else has entered the kitchen. When I look back at Misty her eyes are as large as golf balls. They look like they're about to pop out of her head.

"You slept with Blain?" she says. "Oh, my God, Eva."

I purse my lips in annoyance and roll my eyes. "Who the hell is Blain? What are you talking about?" I huff.

She wrinkles her brows. "Blain, Jeff's friend. The guy you went on that date with."

I wave my hand at her. "He was a jerk. I would never sleep with that asshole."

"Oh, thank God. I'm sorry about that. I should've never sent you out with him in the first place. My head was messed up—" Misty starts and stops midsentence. "Wait, heifer, you lost your virginity? To who? You don't know any guys. You little slut."

A huge grin spreads across her face, softening her words. I look around again because she's talking way too loud. I grab her by the arm and pull her with me to the pantry.

I release her as we step inside. I pace a little and rub my forehead. When I collect my thoughts, I turn to her.

"I slept with Owen," I whisper.

She frowns. "Who the fuck is Owen?" she asks as she pulls a face.

I shake my head and huff. "Owen Mason," I say with wide eyes. "Brick," we say in unison. Misty's voice comes out in a gasp.

I nod as she stands with her mouth hanging open. She closes her eyes and her next words put weight on my shoulders. "This is not good. King is going to lose his shit. Shit," she says with a distant look in her eyes when she opens them.

"I don't think it will be that bad," I mutter and look down at my feet. "I mean, we're not even together. It was a mistake. His wife is here."

"Who, Mags?" Misty snorts. "I never liked that hot mess. You don't have to worry about her. She's a problem for Reap to handle. She just doesn't know she's a sitting duck."

"What do you know about her?" I ask, then wince. What does it matter? I shake my head and hold up a hand to stop Misty from answering. "Never mind, forget I asked. It doesn't matter," I say sadly.

"Was the sex bad?" she asks as she looks me over. "Was he too rough."

I shake my head as I try to hold back my tears. "No, it was amazing. I… I think I thought it was more than it was. I just want to forget him."

"Eva." She reaches for my arm.

"No, Mist, for once, let me let this go," I plead.

Misty sighs. "For now, and only because I *need* to finish that ice cream."

I laugh, she's so freaking silly. I pull my best friend into a hug. I missed her something awful and I feel terrible now for ditching her for some guy.

My stomach growls right as we break apart. She lifts a brow and bursts into laughter. "Sounds like you need some ice cream of your own," she teases.

"Yeah, something like that." I snort.

I wiggle my brows and grin. I scurry over to the corner of the pantry everyone knows to steer clear of. It's King's shit. There's even a lock on the cabinet. I pull the key from the pocket of my sweats and open the cabinet to get to what I'm looking for.

Misty lets out a long slow whistle when she sees what I pull out. "You're trying to make him kill you. Not the Cookie Crisp." She giggles.

"He'll get over it. I mean, he wouldn't have given me and Sal a key if he didn't really want us to eat his shit." I laugh.

"Yeah, but he grumbles about it every time. Hey, are there any candy bars in there?" she asks and moves closer to look over my shoulder.

I laugh and reach in to grab one. She shoves me out of the way and takes three. I frown at her and place my hand on my hip. "Look who's talking about trying to make him kill you. What's up with all the junk food. Weren't you just talking about going on a diet?"

Misty snorts. "As if he…" She trails off and gets a funny look on her face. "Spider is going on a food run in the morning. I'll have him replace them."

"Whatever." I laugh and close the cabinet back and lock it. "I don't know who has a worse sweet tooth, you or King. I swear you two shouldn't even have teeth left in your heads."

"Remember that time he was so sick he was flat on his ass in bed for like a week?" Misty asks with a twinkle in her eyes. "I brought him a bag full of candy bars and ended up as sick as he was 'cause I tried to keep up with him eating the stupid things."

We both burst into laughter as we exit the pantry and sit on the stools at the metal prep table in the kitchen. Misty tears into a candy bar and goes back to devouring the ice cream she was eating when I arrived.

I lift a brow and shake my head. It must be that time of the month. I smile as she closes her eyes and moans while she eats a mouthful of ice cream and candy bar.

"So, Brick," Misty says as she reopens her eyes.

I huff and narrow my gaze on her. "Misty," I warn.

"No, Eva, wait. I know you, and you always miss what's going on around you if it's not in a book or a drawing." She puckers her lips in thought. "I hope you're not letting something slip by that—"

"That what, Misty?" I cut her off. "That can never be? You're right, King would lose his ever-loving mind and then what? Besides, I told you. I misread things. I mean, look at his ex-wife. I'm clearly not his type."

She drops her candy bar into her ice cream. "I will never understand how you don't see how gorgeous you are. You're hot, young, and smart as shit. Why wouldn't he want you? Mags is as dumb as a bag of rocks and she's trifling."

"How do you know so much about her?" I mumble.

Misty frowns and twists her lips in disdain. She turns back to her ice cream. "I pay attention." She shrugs.

"Well, if you pay attention, then you already know he has moved on. I haven't seen him since we arrived," I mutter.

"That's because he's been gone since you guys arrived. King had him head right back out," she says and points her spoon at me.

I'm a little thrown and hopeful with this new information. Maybe Brick would have apologized, at least if he were around. I'd like to think our time meant enough for him to at least say he's sorry for using me.

"How do you know King sent him out?" I ask to distract my thoughts.

"I told you, I pay attention," she says and shifts on her stool.

I start to pay attention. My best friend is hiding something from me. I watch her right as her phone buzzes on the tabletop. Her whole face lights up as she looks down at it.

"Is that your latest boy toy?" I ask as I watch her.

Misty tries to reel in her smile. "I guess you can say that." She smiles.

I reach for one of the bowls stacked in the center of the table and fill it up with cereal. I groan inwardly as I realize I've forgotten the milk. I slide off my stool and head to the refrigerator.

I hear someone else enter the kitchen as I rummage through the shelves. I stop and smile as I recognize the voice. I grab the milk and spin to close the door.

"That's not food, Misty," King growls as he towers over my best friend.

King is a gorgeous man. Those blue eyes and his blond dreadlocks have most of the women around here drooling and lusting after him. On the rare occasion that you get a smile from

King, it's breathtaking. I've just never seen him as more than my big brother.

"Um, Eva and I wanted something quick," Misty says nervously.

I wrinkle my brows as King's head shoots up in my direction. Misty is usually anything but nervous around King or anyone else. She's known for her sassy and feisty personality.

King looks back at the table as he takes a step away from Misty. "You little shits were in my cabinet." The smile on his lips tells me he could care less. He reaches for one of the candy bars Misty stole and opens it.

"Hey, that was mine," Misty pouts.

"No, it was mine and you stole it," he grunts around a mouthful of candy.

"I was going to have Spider replace it," she grumbles.

King laughs, but he's distracted by his ringing phone. He frowns down at it and his face darkens. "I gotta handle this. Eat some real food, Misty," he commands before he turns to leave.

I sit and pour milk over my cereal. "What's that about?" I ask.

King is just as protective of Misty as he is of Sal and me. However, there was something different in that last command he gave. Something a little possessive, I guess you could say.

"What?" she asks around a spoonful of ice cream.

"Why is he up your butt?" I ask with a lift of my shoulders.

"I haven't been feeling good since I arrived. I guess he's checking up on me." She shrugs back.

"Yeah, by the way. I'm so sorry I bailed on you," I say, feeling like crap again for totally failing as a friend.

Misty gets that weird look on her face again. For the second time, I know she's keeping something from me. I decide to pry this time.

"Hey, did like something happen? You know with you and that guy? His friend was a jerk, by the way," I say as I watch her.

She started acting strange around the time I went out on that date. Honestly, now that I'm thinking about it, it may have been way before then. Misty had been acting out of character for a couple of months. First, she was all dreamy eyed. Then, she was sort of nervous all the time.

"Who, Jeff?" She waves a hand at me. "I blocked his calls and deleted him weeks ago. I think I'm going to head to bed. I probably ate too much junk. I'll see you in the morning."

With that, she slides off her stool and gives me a hug and kiss on the cheek. She's gone before I can ask any more questions or think about what's really going on with her. I'm left with my bowl of cereal and my own thoughts.

CHAPTER TWENTY-FOUR

Owen

"Good evening, Mr. Mason," the bouncer says as I move to the entrance of the club.

I nod and grunt.

Exhausted is beyond what I am right now. I'm annoyed, tired as fuck, and I miss my woman. I didn't know I could miss someone this much. It's been three days since I left Eva at the clubhouse pissed off.

So far, I have shit. No one knows anything. For the most part, I think that's true. Just one person has me believing otherwise. That's why I haven't returned home.

Something stinks in the Mayor's home. Not the Mayor in South Carolina, no, his ass was clueless, and I believe it. The Mayor of Georgia is the one I'm finding an issue with. The more I think about it the more I know his ass is up to something.

Mayor Finch has been in for quite a grip with the club for about a year now. He knows King is going to come knocking for that bread sooner than later. Helping someone bring down the club would be in his favor.

Finch has no morals and he's a sniveling piece of shit. I also know one important fact about that motherfucker. Finch has a nasty tell. When he lies, his right brow twitches.

That shit was a twitching mess last night, when I paid him a visit. That's why I'm on my way to see a friend. Clayton Hennessy may not be a brother of the Lost Souls, but he's like a brother to me. We met in college as roommates. Clayton helped me smooth out my rough edges to get through the doors Cage was counting on me to break through.

Clayton and his family have connections. If you so much as breathe in the South East, North East, or East Coast Clayton knows about it. Anywhere else, he'll have access to the information soon enough.

Clayton and I have an understanding. Ask what you need, act as if the rest doesn't exist. It works for us. Has for the last decade or more, no need to change it now.

"Welcome back, Mr. Mason," a pretty brunette with a tray of drinks in her hand says as I walk into the club. I'm positive I once knew this one biblically.

I look into her hazel eyes and confirm, I indeed once fucked her. She has a come-hither look as she lets her gaze roam over me. Not Eva, not interested.

Hell, I can't even remember this one's name or how long ago we fucked. Clearly, she didn't leave the impression I so obviously left with her. Ignoring her flirtatious looks I keep moving.

Dressed in a tailored black suit and black dress shirt with the top three buttons open, I move through the club Clayton and I silently own together. I've learned it's always a good idea to have my eggs in more than one basket. Not that I don't trust King and the Lost Souls. I just wanted something to call my own.

King is the same way. He and I both actually have businesses outside of the club together.

After Cage died, we always wondered what truly happened that night. We knew who we could trust and who we needed to keep an eye on. We also knew we needed a nest egg in case we needed to regroup.

I spot Clayton up in VIP and head straight there. Although, this isn't a Lost Souls business, I have hired Diggs' Security firm to handle the place. I don't trust anyone else.

Clayton stands with a smile on his face as I reach him. He pulls me into a big bear hug. Not many men can dwarf me. Clayton comes pretty close.

The ginger is a jolly red giant without the perpetual jolliness. He's the guy who everyone is drawn to, it doesn't matter that he's brooding most the time. He has a way of talking and moving that makes people gravitate to him.

When Clayton smiles your way, you move because it seems like a gift he's bestowing. I have seen it work on women and men alike. I've been amused more often than not to watch him in action.

"It's good to see you," Clayton says as he releases me and nods for me to take a seat. He goes to wave over one of my usual girls, but I hold up my hand for her to stay put.

Again, I'm not interested. If it's not Eva, I want nothing to do with her. The busty blonde pouts and turns back to her seat, looking deflated. I've already forgotten her. When I look at Clayton, he has his brow lifted at me.

I shrug my shoulders. "Things have changed," is all I say.

Clayton looks me over and smiles. "Is the wife back in the saddle?" he asks, but I know he's about to answer his own question and a few I've come to get answers to. "I hear she has ruffled some feathers. I can't believe she has unraveled all you've done for her.

"Mayor Finch has been looking for a way out of his debt to your circle." Clayton pulls a face. He never likes referring to the club in public. "He had nothing, not until your crazy wife went barking up some of the wrong trees. This is less about your brothers than it is about her. Miguel is coming for her ass. However, he does seem to have a bit of a problem with you and King as well."

"Tell me something I don't know." I snort. Although, his words confirm Jemma's suspicions and my own.

"I think you have two problems on your hands here. There's a hidden player in this all. Someone not involved with Miguel, but who's watching what's going on to make a move. I'm hearing talk, but I'm still digging on that one."

"What kind of talk?" I ask, leaning in with my forearms on my knees.

"Listen, this unknown, they're after anything with the name Kennedy or attached to it. Friends, family, associates. The LS included. Someone wants that whole club to burn." He frowns, his eyes turning hard.

A growl rips through my chest at the thought of a price being on my woman's head. I'll take care of me. If someone wants to come knocking at death's door, I'll open that motherfucker up nice and wide, but don't come for my woman.

That will get your ass a straight visit from me. You don't have to come to my door, I'm going to blow your shit in. This has gone to a new level.

Everything has changed. I stand, unable to sit knowing someone is after everything I put my life on. My woman, my family, my brothers. Not to mention, Mags silly ass is playing with an open can of worms. I could ring Magdalena's neck. Yet, there's another can out there that's waiting to burst.

My nostrils flare and I crack my neck. My fists are balled so tightly I know I'll break skin. The rage going through me is hot and coiling to a boil.

Clayton gets my attention with his next words. "Whoa, Brick, I'm not done. What is she worth to you? I know that look in your eyes, does Mags still have value to you? She's going to need to because you may not like what you learn next." He tilts his head to the side as if studying me more closely. "This third party. They don't give a fuck about her, but Miguel still does. He wants something.

"Have you ever wondered what she's really running from? Good pussy will drive you to do some crazy shit, but I get the feeling there's more here. I did some asking. I couldn't get much. Everyone's scared to mention her, but Magdalena was never his woman," Clayton says as he looks me in my eyes. "No, brother, she has some other value to him. Some value he's been waiting a long time to collect."

I nod as I take his words in. "Thanks," I grumble. Clayton has answered most of my questions.

"And Brick," he calls as I turn to leave.

"Yeah." I look back over my shoulder.

"Tell him before he finds out from someone else. The streets are whispering," Clayton gives me a knowing smile.

I close my eyes and nod. *Fuck.* I already knew I wasn't as careful with my relationship with Eva as I should have been, but I thought I would have gotten a chance to talk to King by now. I had no idea I would be out handling club business.

Now that I have what I need, I need to head home. I have some things to iron out and a woman to protect. Someone has written a check on their own life.

I decided to ride my bike here despite the suit. This area can be packed, even on a Monday night. Parking my bike would just be easier. The moment I leave out of the club I feel them.

I act as if everything is fine as I walk to my parking spot. A smile creases my lips as anticipation floods my veins. I have a taste for blood after what I've learned from Clayton. I welcome my beast to the forefront.

Cage had a knack for picking everyone for a role that would fit them best. He didn't just send me to school to become an architect. Cage had me trained to be a soldier. Not just any soldier, a Lost Souls soldier. The Squad general.

You don't become Squad because you're willing to fight and kill for the club. No, Squad members are broken. Most of us came to the club that way. Cage found us all before we were completely lost and made us something in between the darkness.

It's why we're so damn loyal. We were saved from the broken hell that was meant to be our fate. We've known loss, that deep rooted scar your soul shit. So, we have no fear of it.

No, I don't fear shit. Like I said before. The Lost Souls don't allow me next to the trouble, *I am the fucking trouble.*

Don't let the suit and tie fool you. As a Squad member, you know and understand the importance of getting in and out. We move like ghosts.

We handle business and disappear like a soul lost in the wind. I reach my bike right as the unlucky souls advancing on me close in. I turn and toss a blade into the neck of the one on my right.

His gurgles fill the night air and send a delicious tingle down my spine. I move swiftly to retrieve my blade and sheath it in its hiding place once again. Another rushes me, getting a good right across my left cheek.

I feel my flesh split and smile wider. My left, right combination hits him faster and harder than his hit me. I body check him and he crumbles to the ground. The next asshole goes to pull the trigger on his gun, but I was in motion to stop him all along.

I have a small double edge glaive blade sailing through the air faster than this prick can think. His hand and gun are on the way to the ground as I catch my returning blade and toss my leg over my bike.

"Tell whoever sent you, I'm coming for them," I bark as the motherfucker screams over his severed hand.

Before anyone can make me out in the shadows, I'm ghost. Just like the winged reaper I am. Some unlucky bastards are going to learn how I earned my patch and my tat.

CHAPTER TWENTY-FIVE

Report

Brick

I pulled over halfway back home. I need to fill King in on what I've found out. I pull my phone out and dial while still straddling my bike.

All exhaustion is forgotten as rage and adrenaline pump through my body. I've been turning this information over and over. Clayton's voice ringing in my head.

"What have you got for me?" King says as he answers the phone.

I don't waste time in my answer. "We're looking at a few problems. Finch doesn't want or can't clear his debt so he's selling us out so he doesn't have to pay."

"Son of a bitch. I'd been showing him a courtesy because of my old man. He's done," he grates out.

"I feel you. I'm on that one as soon as you give the word," I reply. "Someone's lurking in the shadows. Trying to take you and the club down. They want everything dear to you to burn."

"What the fuck?"

I blow out a heavy breath. "I couldn't get names. No one has one for me yet, but trust me, I'll get it or them. Whoever's behind this has my full attention now."

"What else have you got? I hear it in your voice," King says tightly.

"First, Mags has shaken some shit loose with her games. She's a bigger player in this. Her problem, it's ours, but ours is aware of her problem and wants it to be ours. You feel me?"

"Yeah, I got you. It's time to handle her ass. We remove her and that clears a path," he replies.

"Yeah, but something's incomplete. I'm not ready to move her off the board. Soon brother," I say thoughtfully. "I think it's better to keep her close for now."

"I'm trusting your judgment, but you know how I feel. Reel that shit in."

I grunt and move onto the other part of the night that has my attention. "Second, I was attacked outside the club. I sent a warning, but it's clear these motherfuckers are bold."

King starts to curse, and I believe he throws something across the room as the mushing sound rings out over the phone. I can hear the rage building inside him over the line. I know the feeling all too well. I've been trying to ride it off on my way back to South Carolina.

That hasn't happened yet.

"Get your ass back here. We need to strategize." The line goes dead.

CHAPTER TWENTY-SIX

Mine

Owen

The rest of the ride back still doesn't help to release the tightness in my chest or the rage coursing through my veins. The more I think about it the more pissed I get. The open road has done nothing to clear my mind this time around either.

What I need is in the form of a little brown, five foot four package. I need to get my hands on Eva. In this moment, seeing her sweet face would be enough to soothe my soul.

My mama died when I was five and that's what caused my daddy to move close to his sister in South Carolina. Before she died, my mama was my place of comfort. She was always gentle with me. Always had a smile for me.

I guess that's what draws me to Eva. I can't remember a time when she hasn't had a smile for me, well, with the exception of the night I left her here at the clubhouse.

I climb off my bike, the exhaustion returning, but the first thing on my mind is to find my way to Eva. My room here at the club is nowhere near hers. Cage made sure that the girls' rooms here were off on their own end of the club. Nowhere near the brothers' bedrooms.

Any brother awake who gives two shits will see me making my way to her, but at this point, I don't care. As has become the norm, I have no value for my life over hers. I need to make things right. I'd been too tied up while I was gone to give her a call.

As I drag my tired body toward the clubhouse, I pull out my phone with the intention to send Eva a text to let her know we need to talk. I curse under my breath. It's nearly five in the morning. I rode hard to get here as soon as I could, but it's still the middle of the night.

"I should probably mind my own business," I hear someone say, causing me to look up.

I grin when I find Misty looking back at me. Misty is one gorgeous girl. She and Eva have always been able to find trouble with their looks. Only difference is, Misty knows what she's working with and will intentionally bring a man to his knees without batting a lash.

"Is that right?" I murmur.

"You and I both know it is. I'm just making things worse for myself. He hasn't told Mix, yet. I know he's still struggling with the age thing. This thing with you and Eva is going to set us all back." She frowns.

"I take it she told you." I lift a brow at her.

Misty nods. "We're best friends. We tell each other everything."

"Really?" I ask and watch for her reaction.

I know this not to be a fact. Misty's face falls as she looks down at the ground. She begins playing with the hem of the oversized T-shirt she has on. I make a mental note of who the T-shirt most likely belongs to.

"I want to tell her. I will soon. With everything going on, it's not like I'll be able to hide things for much longer," Misty says quietly.

I nod in understanding. "What are you doing out here anyway?" I ask.

"Waiting on you." She shrugs her little shoulders. "Besides, I needed the fresh air."

"What can I do for you?" I say tiredly as I prop a shoulder against the side of the clubhouse.

"Actually, it's what I can do for you." She perks up again. She reaches under her oversized shirt into her shorts pocket and holds out her hand. Dangling from her fingers is a key, on a heart shaped keychain.

I tilt my head and eye the key. "It's the key to her room. She always keeps it locked. I have a feeling she's in her feelings about something that can be explained. Eva doesn't know how gorgeous she is. She doesn't get that someone like you could want her." Her voice sounds sad as she speaks of her friend.

"She let you in. That's big. I know she's had a crush on you for forever. She tried to hide it, but I know her too well. Don't make me regret this, Brick. You two are going to make my life hell, but I think it'll be worth it in the end."

I reach for the key and push off the wall. "Thanks, and for what it's worth. She means the world to me. Your shit will work out too. He's stubborn, but he cares about you. He's not going to let anything get in the way of that," I offer.

"Yeah, I know. Things are intense around here. I can feel it all coming to a head. Something big is brewing and it's going to take us all for a ride." She sighs.

"We'll handle it just fine. We live for the ride." I chuckle and wrap an arm around her shoulder to lead her into the clubhouse.

She shouldn't have been sitting out here alone in the first place. I note the prospects patrolling the perimeters, but Misty is best safe inside. I welcome the warmth of the clubhouse as we step in.

One thing is on my mind as I see the clear path to the hall leading to Eva's room. *My woman, Eva.* I'm finally going to get to make this right.

Eva

I can feel him all over me. His heat, his hands, his mouth, there isn't a place left unconsumed by him. It feels so real. My heartache is forgotten as I get lost in his touch.

Right here, right now, all is forgotten and forgiven. The last three days of mourning are a thing of the past. All I want, all I need is him. I moan as my skin burns beneath his hot, wet kisses.

I can trust him here. It's not real. It's a dream my heart yearns for so much I can feel it all throughout my body. Even in my sleep.

When his tongue runs through my folds I feel my body quake like only Owen can make it. I whimper out in desperate hope this never ends. He's devouring my honey with such hunger. My thighs are quivering on his shoulders.

I clench the sheets in my fingertips and arch off the bed. My hips rock to a rhythm of their own as he clamps a hand over one thigh and the other over my belly. His huge warm hand pressing down on my flesh warms my whole body and wraps me in a heat that makes me feel safe and free.

His groans fill the room and create a sonic quake that booms through me. Yes, I can trust him here. I can allow this feeling here. It's what I need most. To feel, not to think, not to worry, not to cry. My only cries are cries of pleasure.

When my body explodes and I gush in his mouth, it is all too real. The feel of him latching on to claim my juices, the wetness between my cheeks, and my toes curling—it all sends me spiraling.

I bolt upright and blink the sleep away, my body is humming a song for the one man it knows. Only as I blink yet again, I'm startled by what comes into view. How the hell did he even get in here?

Owen's green eyes are glowing hungrily back at me. I compress my brows as I try to process whether or not I'm awake. I watch his bare broad chest and shoulders as he stalks up my body like a panther. He glides his hands up from my ankles, over my calves, to my thighs, up my sides, to stop right under my heaving breasts.

I'm stuck, my brain is still scrambled from the orgasm that's still rocking my body with aftershocks. I look down at his pale hands on my brown skin. My chest pangs because they look like they belong there.

I usually keep my door locked because I sleep in the nude or in my underwear. I know I locked that door. I flicker my eyes back up to his with questions in them.

He ignores the look and dips his head to wrap his warm mouth around my nipple. He draws it deep into his mouth as he rubs his rough thumb over the other tight peak.

I drop my head back as I gasp and whimper. I shake away the cobwebs and gain the strength to press a hand to his chest to push him away.

"Brick," I call out.

My nipple pops free from his mouth and he looks up at me with a loud growl. I eye him warily and get ready to tell him to get out of my room, but he has other plans.

He slides his large hand to span my back. I part my lips on a stolen breath as his thick tip pushes through my entrance. I sob. He covers my mouth with his heated one to absorb my cries. He moves his hips slowly as he thrusts in and out of me.

He kisses me for what must be a full five minutes, while keeping the same pace, before he breaks the kiss and locks his green eyes with my brown. I have to close my eyes to block out the intensity I see there. He places his forehead to mine.

I'm so confused. I don't understand how he can make love to me like this if I mean so little to him. I turn my head to break the connection.

I should know better. He's not having it. Brick grasps my face with his fingertips and turns me back to him.

He nips my bottom lip, then kisses the sting away. A single tear slips free and I'm so angry at myself. I push harder at his chest.

"Brick, stop," I say weakly.

"You're mine, Eva," he growls. "You know damn fucking well how I feel about you. And stop calling me Brick before I spank your ass."

I go from feeling sorry for myself to being pissed off. I reach to shove my hands in his hair. I wrap my legs around his waist and lock my ankles at the small of his back.

He growls as I start to rock my hips on him. He slides his hand lower to cup my ass. He squeezes my cheek and lifts me from the mattress. Just what I needed to take over.

I stare him in the eyes as I start to grind my hips and fuck him like I own him. His nostrils begin to flare like they always do when it's getting really good for him. He grits his teeth as I drip all over him.

He's never given me control like this and I've never tried to take it. I'm pissed but turned on by the power I have over him after feeling so helpless the last few days. I don't take my eyes off his as I let all my emotions show. All my hurt, disappointment, and betrayal.

"Fuck," he groans. "Damn, yes."

"You like that?" I grunt. "Is this what you want? This is what I know O-wen." I drag his name out. "I know you like fucking me. I know you can't get enough of this pussy. That's all I know."

Brick growls loudly again. I'm shocked and more pissed off when he slaps the shit out of my ass. He grabs my waist and takes control, bringing me down on his shaft hard.

He arrests my lips in a searing kiss. "The fuck you say to me?" His breathing is harsh as it fans my lips. "I love you. I'm in… fucking… love with you. I've never loved anyone the way I love you. Not just your pussy, baby girl."

He points to the center of my chest. "I love your heart." He brushes my hair from my temple. "I love your mind." He caresses my lip with his thumb. "I love your smile. I just love you, baby."

I freeze, searching his eyes. It's as if they are pleading with me to understand. I move my hands from his hair and cup his face. I noticed the small cut on his left cheek earlier. I run my finger right below it, allowing myself to care. He closes the distance to peck my lips.

"So, why are we hiding?" I whisper.

Owen sighs. "Eva, I want you wearing my brand as soon as I can get it on you. Things are fucked up. You know we did this wrong. I haven't had a chance to tell King, but I have every intention to. I'm not giving you up. I told you that."

"But you were only keeping me at your place as a favor. That hurt," I say and watch his face for a reaction.

He frowns and reaches a hand into my hair. "King asked me to keep you with me, but not before I had already made up my mind to do so. You. Are. Mine," he says huskily in between punctuating each word with kisses.

"You need to fix this, Owen."

"Don't tell me things I already know, baby girl."

"Okay." I nod and kiss him back. "Okay."

"Okay, what, baby?" He groans as he starts to move me up and down on his length again.

"Okay, I love you, too. I'm yours."

"Damn straight." He gives me the sexiest grin. "You're the one I need, Eva. You know you're my woman. Don't ever question that."

A smile spreads across my face. I slide my fingers back into his hair. "Shut up and finish what you started," I breathe against his lips.

"You sure that's what you want?" he grunts teasingly.

"Yes," I keen as he begins to thrust up into me.

"Damn, I've missed you. I'll handle this shit. I don't think I can handle not touching you," he says through clenched teeth.

"Oh God, baby, I'm coming," I gasp.

"Yes, baby girl, give me what I own."

The rasp in his voice sends a shiver through me, sending me over. I give Owen all I have before I slump against his chest. I'll have to ask about that scar later. Not that he'll tell me. Something tells me it's club business.

Owen

I cradle Eva to my chest as she slumps into me.

"I love you, baby girl," I murmur and kiss the top of her head.

My heart swells at the thought of her saying it back only moments ago. From the moment I entered the room and saw her naked chocolate body stretched out on the bed, I needed to get my hands on her. I couldn't think straight until I did.

I stripped right out of my suit and crawled between her thick thighs. I wanted to worship every part of her body. I must have licked and sucked on every inch of her before those pretty brown eyes opened to me. By then, I'd marked the sides of her breasts, inner thighs and ass with my mouth.

It was the only way I could mark and claim her the way I wanted to. It finally hit me hard. I love Eva.

Yeah, I said it. I love her. Finally, it's no longer a thought. Saying it has made it as real as it gets. I don't know how that shit snuck up on me, but I've fallen like a ton of bricks. She's what I want, what I need, what I crave.

I turn onto my back and lie down, pulling her body over mine. I miss falling asleep with her in my arms. First thing in the morning, I plan to fix this.

I'm shoving shit on the pile, but it is what it is. We'll all just have to deal. I know I should get my ass up and go to my own room. I've been playing with fire as it is.

However, my lids are too heavy, and my body starts to bleed into the mattress. Eva's warmth around me only pulls my exhausted body further under. Before I know it, I'm fast asleep with my woman in my arms.

CHAPTER TWENTY-SEVEN

Something is Up

Owen

I woke to my phone buzzing on the nightstand, where I placed it last night before climbing between Eva's thighs. I'm annoyed to be awakened from some of the best sleep I've had in days. For a split-second the feel of Eva's heavy breasts on my bare chest has me considering ignoring the text chirping for my attention.

Once I crack my eyes open and reach for the phone, I wish I had. With a grunt, I smoothly pull from under Eva's body. I find my clothes and tug them back on. As I button up my dress shirt, I bend and kiss Eva's forehead, and because I simply can't resist, I place a quick kiss on her lips.

I grumble under my breath, not wanting to wake her. Spotting her phone next to mine, I grab it and place it on the pillow beside her. When she wakes it's sure to be the first thing she sees, and she'll see my messages waiting.

Quietly, I slip out of her room and go to send her a text to let her know I have to handle some club business. I barely get to hit send when I stiffen as I hear, "Well, well, well, why am I not surprised to find you here?"

My lip curls back over my teeth as I look into Mags' eyes. Of all people to catch me coming out of Eva's room, it would be her. I want to wipe that devious smile right off her face.

"Let's get some shit straight," I seethe. "I told you to keep her and anything about her out of your fucking mouth."

"I told you I want to know why she's so important," she snaps back.

"You've never been this fucking dumb. Why are you testing me? Better yet, why the fuck are you here? Let's get to the bottom of that," I demand lethally.

"Oh, come off it. I can walk wherever I want. I just happened to be passing at the right moment," she says smugly.

I wipe that smug smile right off her lips as I crowd her space and get in her face. She recovers quickly and tries to give me a flirtatious look. However, my words crack into that look as well.

"I'm not talking about in this hallway, Mags," I grind out. "I'm talking about here, in my brothers' club. What's your endgame? What has Miguel really been searching for you for?"

Her mouth falls open and fear flashes in her eyes. She has no smart comeback this time. The truth hangs in her depths. She's been hiding something from the time she entered my life and it's time to unwrap that shit.

"Oh yeah, time to fess up. The reaper has come for you to pay. What the fuck did you bring to my door?"

"I don't know what Jemma told you—"

"Jemma didn't tell me shit." See, I knew these two have been hiding shit together.

My head is ready to explode. I get ready to light into her. I've had enough of this shit. I'm ready to hit the roof when King turns the corner to find Mags and I glaring at each other.

Being the conniving bitch she is, Mags slides her ass up under my arm and plays the situation. She knows this will cause me to have some explaining to do.

My clothes are rumpled, and my hair is sex messed. It's not the way I want to come clean to King. Mags being Mags knows this.

If I shove her ass off of me. King will have a million questions. I can see the questions in his eyes already as he looks at Eva's bedroom door at my back.

King only confirms my suspicion of his thoughts with his words. "Is my sister up?"

"I wouldn't know, right now I'm dealing with this." I nod at Mags.

It isn't a lie. I'd been out of Eva's room for at least five minutes. She could have woken without my knowledge. It's the closest I can skirt to the truth.

King narrows his eyes and nods. "I'm glad I found you. I need you on that situation," King says with fire in his eyes.

"Yeah, I was heading out," I grunt.

I know the situation he's talking about. It was in the text that woke me. Some of my squad has run into some action. I'm on my way to ride them in. At least that was before running into Mags.

Honestly, I do want to know what the fuck she was doing outside Eva's room in the first place. I don't believe that just walking around bullshit. I'll get to the bottom of all this shit with her.

"We'll finish this later," Mags purrs before sashaying her ass off down the hall.

"She's a problem, brother." King shakes his head. "Fucking snake."

"Yeah, I plan to fix that problem sooner than later." I look King in the eyes. "We need to talk when I get back."

He narrows his gaze at me for the second time. "Get my sister back here safe. That's what I need from you right now," King says gruffly and turns his back on me.

I sigh and head to my room for a quick shower and change of clothes. The sooner I get to Sal and my squad the better.

Eva

I was extremely disappointed to wake up to find Owen gone this morning. I started to second-guess our relationship all over again, until I found my phone beside my head. I had a few text messages from him.

The first one was to tell me he loved me and had some club business he had to take care of. The next text was to warn me that something had come up and he wasn't able to talk to King yet. The third and last one I received, was to tell me again that he loves and misses me. He also informed me he would be back tonight.

I'll admit. I'm still a little uncertain in all of this. King still has no idea.

A part of me wants to trust Owen and understand that's for a reason. The other part of me keeps wondering if this is all a part of Owen wanting to have his cake and eat it too. I keep trying to remind myself of Lost Souls' code.

They don't lie to family, but I don't know if Brick sees me as family. Then there's the fact that he's technically lying to King. This probably wouldn't be so hard if I hadn't had to see his ex-wife smiling in my face for the last three days.

"So, what happened?" Misty huffs at me as she climbs onto my bed, looking exhausted herself.

I showered and dressed in sweats and a tank top, but I haven't bothered to leave my room yet today. I actually haven't been feeling well this morning. I should have known Misty would be in here soon.

After all, I did figure out she somehow was the one who gave Owen the key to my room. She and King are the only ones who have a copy.

"Nothing happened," I murmur.

"So why do you look like someone kicked your puppy?"

"I just don't know. I'm second-guessing everything. I mean, what if he's telling me what he thinks I need to hear for sex," I murmur. "Let's face it Mist, look at me and then look at Mags."

She rolls her eyes at me, hard. "Are you shitting me?"

She scoots back off the bed and stomps around to my side. She grabs my arm and tugs me up. My stomach rolls a little, but I swallow back the nausea and allow her to march me over to the full-length mirror on my closet door.

"I want you to really look at you," she snaps. I go to turn away, but she holds her ground. "No Eva, look. You're gorgeous. Look at your eyes. I know women who would kill for your lips. Your hair is so perfect for your face.

"Girl, your body has been amazing since we were like fourteen. The difference between you and Mags is she knows that she's a beautiful woman on the outside, but she's ugly inside."

I shake my head. "I don't see any of that," I mutter.

"Oh. MY. God. Guys are always after you. How do you not see this?" she huffs.

"Maybe they're after sex, but that doesn't mean I'm pretty," I say and turn to look her in the eyes.

Misty's mouth falls open. "What would make you say that?"

"I've grown up my whole life watching men fuck anything on legs. Sure, the bunnies here aren't the worst. The Lost Souls have better taste than most, but I've been around MCs where it didn't much matter. A warm body was a warm body.

"Everyone thinks I'm clueless to things outside of my bubble, but I built my bubble for a reason. Before Mom met Cage, I was teased all the time. Then we came here. I've heard the bunnies whisper about how fat and ugly I am," I confess.

"Fuck them," she growls. "Eva, those bitches are just jealous. They always have been. Your mom was so gorgeous, and Cage loved her so much. He treated you all like gold.

"When we lost them, those whores all thought they had a shot at being something around here. That shit ain't never happened and King has treated you just like his daddy did.

"It's time for you to stop hiding under those clothes and lurking in the shadows like you don't belong." Misty pauses and smiles. I promise I see the light bulb go off in her head. I groan and palm my forehead. "I know exactly how to get Brick to come clean."

"What?" I wrinkle my brows at her.

"I know you. You think he's hiding things because he doesn't want you. I know how I'm going to prove you wrong and force Brick to come clean at the same time. I'm going to regret this shit, but I'm not letting you fuck this up. I saw his mug when he talked about you," she says with a big grin on her face.

"Misty, I'm not feeling up to any of your brilliant ideas today," I groan.

"Suck it up, sister. You're doing just what I say. The universe is working in our favor. Brick rolls back in tonight. I can't wait to see that bitch eat crow when that sexy beast stakes his claim on your ass," she chimes.

I roll my eyes. I open my mouth to respond, but Misty turns almost green. "Hold that thought." She rushes to say, taking off into my bathroom.

I run behind her, but she shuts and locks the bathroom door. I'm a little grateful she does once I hear her start to retch. My own stomach flips, causing me to back away.

I go to sit on the bed and think about Misty's words. I did feel beautiful while I stayed with Owen. I felt confident and sure of myself. Coming here has done more than make me feel disconnected from him. It's brought up old feelings.

Misty has always been my anchor here. Otherwise, I don't think I would have stayed around as long as I have. Misty has always said we have every right to be here. If it weren't for King, I don't know if I would believe that.

The guys have always treated me with respect, but sometimes I've wondered if that is only out of fear. I don't know, there are a small few who I wouldn't intentionally find myself alone with, especially after Mom and Cage died. They're the same ones I've noticed King keeps at arm's length.

However, if I'm honest, since being with Owen I've felt like I finally belong. Being unsure about him has made me unsure about everything, because he has become my new anchor. I sigh at my confusing thoughts and wait for Misty to finish in my bathroom.

She needs to get out here so I can first find out what the hell is going on with her, and second, find out what she has planned. It takes about ten minutes before the door unlocks and cracks open. I watch my best friend as she fidgets in the doorway.

I should have seen all this sooner. Misty's face is fuller. She's in a baggy Lost Souls T-shirt, that doesn't look like it was ever hers. She even has on a pair of sweats. These are all red flags. Misty wouldn't be caught dead at the clubhouse looking like this.

"So, you going to tell me what's going on?" I say when she creeps out of the bathroom.

She bites her lip. "I'm pregnant," she whispers.

My mouth literally drops open. There's no way I heard her right. I have millions of things floating in my head, but I settle on one. "Who's the father? Please, not that Jeff guy."

"No, it was never like that with him. He's a douche. I wouldn't drop my drawers for him if he paid me to." She pulls a face and waves her hand. When she absentmindedly places a hand on her belly, I see it. Her little baby bump.

"Holy shit," I gasp.

Now that I think about it, Misty has been in baggy clothes since I arrived here. I hadn't paid attention the first time I saw her in the kitchen. I narrow my eyes at her.

"Is that why King was concerned about you eating? Did you run back here for him to help you? Why would you come to him before me? Are you in some type of trouble, Mist? What's going on?" I rattle off.

"I'm not in trouble. You sort of have the rest right. I needed King and he came for me. I fucked up." She shrugs. "I switched birth control and got reckless."

I close my eyes and my world crumbles. I feel like the dumbest twenty-two-year-old in the world. I'm an A student, I can construct blueprints in my sleep. I'm a math genius, but here I sit, and it has *just* dawned on me I'm not on birth control. Owen and I have been fucking like bunnies.

Brick has never worn a single condom, not once. How could I be so stupid? For nearly a month I've been having unprotected sex. I never once thought about the possibility of getting pregnant.

Like really, Eva, really?

"Eva," Misty whispers. "You just went pale as a sheet. What the hell? I'm pregnant not dying."

I shake my head. "You actually just reminded me that I'm an idiot," I answer.

CHAPTER TWENTY-EIGHT

Trading Glances

Owen

My day has been shit since I pulled my body from under Eva's. Finding Mags outside of Eva's door and running into King has put me on edge from go. I thought that was my biggest worry.

Nope, I should have known this day was only going to keep turning to shit. I've never seen Gutter give two fucks about a woman since I've known him. Leave it to his big ass to start looking at the wrong fucking one.

King is going to go on a damn killing spree. I've been keeping him away from Gutter since we arrived back at the compound. Sal is safe, but she has been stapled to Gutter's side, only adding fuel to the flame.

"The one motherfucker I send because he'll keep his hands off my baby sister. Who the fuck can I trust around here?" King growls as he paces his office.

"They're not going to remain babies forever," I mutter, referring to both Eva and Sal.

I should come clean now, but this is my best friend. I know he isn't in the right headspace to lose both his baby sisters in one night. King totally lost his shit when Gutter climbed off his bike and wrapped his arm around Sal. The moment Gutter tipped Sal's face up to kiss her, I knew shit was going down.

I told the kid to let me handle this shit, but he had his own way he wanted to deal with it. I guess that makes me the pussy. Life or death, Gutter owned that shit up front.

However, Gutter doesn't know King like I do, and Gutter isn't nine years older than Sal. King will get over this shit with Gutter. With me, I don't know.

I represent his guilt. That shit is going to eat at him. We're two sides of the same coin. I pull myself from my own thoughts to put out this fire.

"King, we both know Gutter is a stand-up guy. It's not like you watched him whore around the club. We all considered the fact he might be gay a time or two. Seeing him with Sal, I don't think that's the case." I sigh.

"Stand up, stand up? That motherfucker is one step from being the most fucked-up brother here."

I have to chuckle. "You'd be right because you and I have that on lock. Don't we, brother," I tease.

He tugs at his dreads and locks his eyes on me. "Shit ain't right around here. That's on me," he huffs and looks up. "I... shit, I'm tired of talking about it. Let's get out there and get some beers."

I lift a brow. Last time we were out there he tried to get at Gutter's throat. "I promise, I won't kick his ass tonight. Tomorrow is a new day though," he grumbles. "He's lucky you're the only motherfucker I'll let hold me back."

I sigh and murmur under my breath. "Yeah, cause I'm really going to have to fight your ass."

He doesn't hear me because he's halfway out the door as I reach it. I spot Gutter standing tensely by a pool table with Sal tucked under his arm. Sal has a scowl on her face as she eyes King.

King shakes his head at the two, but then his body goes rigid and he stops in his tracks. I get ready to throw myself between him and Gutter, but it dawns on me that's not where his attention is.

I pivot my head to catch what has his eye. I nearly growl as I find what has King frozen. I told you this day has been shit.

My woman stands on the other side of the pool table dressed to kill or get someone killed. Eva has on a short black leather skirt that's showing off all of *my* thick brown thighs. The skirt flares out telling all my secrets about those shapely hips.

I grit my teeth when I see the red fuck-me heels on her feet. I run my eyes back up her legs and snarl. That skirt is so fucking short it's just barely covering her ass. I feel my chest explode when I look up further and her belly button comes into view. The T-shirt she has on is tight and cutoff a few inches under her breasts.

Eva thinks she's fat. I don't know where that came from, but she's anything but. Eva is a brick fucking house. Her curves are in all the right places. This outfit is not hiding an inch of the body I know for my own.

The outfit has my cock ready to burst out of my jeans, but when I see her face. Those lips, my lips, they're painted with a gloss that shows off their natural color and fullness. She has the face of a doll and has no clue how gorgeous she is.

Her looks have me weak, but she's completely oblivious to her power. Eva bends over the pool table to take the next shot and I see red. I get ready to go and toss her over my shoulder, but King's reaction brings me back to earth.

"The Fuck, Eva," King bellows.

I see Misty out of the corner of my eye. She looks like she wants to jump in, but she stays put. Sal, however, places her hands on her hips.

"King, if you haven't noticed, we've grown up. We became women at some point. Stop trying to embarrass us," she growls.

"Embarrass you?" King snaps. "Come on with that shit. I'm not trying to embarrass either of you. But that." King points to Eva. "That's not Eva."

And then shit goes to hell in a handbasket. I see my life slow down and play in slow motion before my eyes. This is the moment this bitch has been lurking around for.

CHAPTER TWENTY-NINE

Pound of Flesh

Eva

I try to swallow down my hurt and embarrassment. I knew King was going to have a problem with the outfit Misty coaxed me into wearing, but I didn't think he would go postal in front of everyone. King is usually gentler with me.

I flicker my eyes to Owen beside King. He looks just as pissed off as King does. I can see Owen is restraining himself as King loses his shit. I want to take off running.

Everyone who's been trying not to stare at me all night, is now taking the opportunity to ogle. I place the pool stick in front of me as if it can shield me. I bite my lip and teeter on my heels.

I love Sal for standing up for me. She looks so happy with Gutter. I've never seen him like this, but it looks good on him.

He gives my little sister a squeeze after her attempt to have my back after King's roared outburst. My heart sinks. The tears threaten to spill over and embarrass me further.

"Maybe she's trying to impress someone. Or get someone's attention," is cackled from across the room.

All heads snap in the direction of Magdalena as she saunters our way in a tight pair of jeans, a T-shirt, and heels. I just want to crawl into myself. She's making those jeans look good effortlessly. I told Misty this was a bad idea.

"Shut up, Mags, I swear to God you better shut your fucking mouth," Brick bites out.

"Why?" Mags flips a hand out to her side and points toward me. "She wants to be a big girl, let her. I can't blame her. I'd be threatened too."

I think that's the very moment I snap. It's all one jab, one dirty look, one low blow too much. This bitch has been getting on my nerves for days.

I forget about my insecurities and all the stares. Something rises up inside me and I let it loose. My temper that I normally hold on to jumps all the way out of the box.

"Why the fuck should I be threatened by you?" I growl as I storm right up to her, closing the distance. "I'm sick of your ass."

"You're not half the woman I am. You better watch out, little girl," Mags sneers back. "I think it's time you stuck that nose back in a book, bookworm."

I vaguely register King's, "What the Fuck?"

"I told you once, he already belongs to me, bitch. So, why the fuck do I have to worry about you?" I say.

Brick bellows my name from behind me in warning, but I'm too far gone. "Eva, damn it, *Eva.*"

"I also told your ass don't fuck with what's mine or I'd show you why it's a really bad idea to fuck with me."

I give no further warning before I haul back and punch the bitch right in the face. I'm Cage Kennedy's kid. You don't grow up one of his kids and not know how to fight, ride, and handle a piece.

Bookworm my ass, I know how to whip ass. I have Mags in a headlock while I repeatedly punch her in the head. I feel familiar strong arms wrap around my waist. My feet leave the floor and I start kicking.

"Damn it, baby girl, reel it the fuck in," Owen growls in my ear. "I said stop it, Eva."

I stop flailing, but my chest is heaving as Owen tightens his arms around me. He sets me on my feet and turns me to face him. I bite my lip when I look up at him and see how pissed off he is.

He shrugs off his cut and rips his shirt over his head. He wraps a hand around my waist, pulling me closer. Tossing his cut over his shoulder, he tugs the T-shirt over my head. His shirt swallows me and covers me up, which I'm sure is his intention.

"No," King roars. "No, you fucking didn't."

My eyes widen as I watch Owen heave out a heavy breath and close his eyes. I spin to find King staring at us. His head is tilted to the side as his blue eyes take in every detail of how Brick and I are standing.

I try to move away from Brick to place some distance between us. Owen places his arms back around my waist, pulling me into his chest. I feel his lips on the top of my head.

"I planned to tell you, brother. I just needed to do it at the right time," Brick starts.

"Are you fucking kidding me? How long?" King cuts him off.

Brick pushes my body behind his. I start to freak out. I know he's getting ready for King to come at him. I grab his arm and try to move back in front of him.

"Stay behind me, baby," Owen looks over his shoulder to say.

"Motherfucker," King growls and heads for Brick full force.

It all happens so fast. King is within inches of Brick right before both Misty and I jump in the way. I can feel her back pressed to mine as the two squish us between them.

"Move, Misty," King growls.

"No, calm down," she snaps.

"My sister, Brick? You're my fucking best friend, my brother. You know how I feel about my sisters, what the fuck?" King bites out. "Misty, move."

"King, come on," Sal pleads as she too tries to tug at King's arm. Gutter has enough sense to stay out of this. I'm sure this scene looks totally familiar to him.

"I know I did this shit wrong, but she's mine. I'll give my pound of flesh for her, brother," Brick says back.

"My sister, Brick? The fuck, I saw you with that crazy bitch ex of yours this morning," King says in anguish.

My body stiffens, then turns limp. I go to move out of the way, but Brick grasps my wrist. "No, brother, what you saw was me leaving Eva's room. I slept there last night. I ran into Mags lurking around her room. There's no one else for me. Just Eva, I swear that shit," Owen says the last part as he looks down into my eyes.

"I'm going to kick your fucking ass," King shouts. "How long?"

"Since the night I got her out of that bathroom situation." Brick sighs.

"You motherfucker," King growls and tries to push pass Misty.

"King, have you lost your fucking mind?" Misty shouts after she stumbles a little.

King's eyes widen and he reaches for Misty to steady her on her feet. "Baby, you all right?" King asks with concern.

My mouth pops open. "Oh shit… really, Mist? Oh, this is priceless, King," I scoff.

"Eva, don't talk about shit you know nothing about," King grumbles.

"Oh, please, King," I say and place my hands on my hips.

"What, what am I missing?" Sal asks.

King eases Misty behind him. I'm still in shock honestly. We were too busy dealing with my stupidity for me to get to the bottom of who Misty's baby's father truly is. She kept avoiding the topic and changing the subject back to me.

The bunnies keep a stash of pregnancy tests in their room. Something I didn't know. After I revealed what I'd so foolishly done, Misty went to retrieve a few.

In my defense, my mom was gone before we ever had the talk. I never had to think about birth control before. Sex was the furthest thing from my mind.

"It's not the same thing," King growls.

"Oh, yes it is." I smirk.

"No, it isn't." King moves closer as his eyes fix over my head on Brick.

"Oh. Yes. It. Is," I growl back. "It's the exact same thing," I say pointedly.

King's eyes snap down to mine and then my belly. He bares his teeth, but it's Brick who startles me. He spins me to face him. His eyes boring into mine.

"What are you trying to say, Eva?" Owen says as he searches my face.

"I swear on my father's grave. If you knocked my sister up, I'm carving you a new face," King says from behind me. He's right on my back now.

"I love her, King," Owen says as he runs his thumb over my lips. He holds his hands out at his sides. "I won't fight back, I owe for this, I'll take it. I love her, brother, and if she's saying what I think she's saying, we're getting married a lot sooner than I planned."

Owen smiles down at me. I give him a small nod and his whole face lights up. King is forgotten as he cups the back of my neck and pulls me to his lips. Owen devours my mouth in a toe curling kiss. I should know. My bare toes curl on the cool concrete floor. I lost my shoes somewhere along the way.

Owen brushes his nose up and down mine. "I'm going to spank your little ass. Don't put our baby in danger like that again, baby girl."

"I'm sorry, she's been fucking with me for days. I snapped." I pout.

"This motherfucker... hello," King says incredulously.

"Oh, get over it, King," Sal gripes.

"Exactly," Misty murmurs, looking pissed as hell at King.

"I'm not getting over shit until I beat the fuck out of him," King snaps.

"So, do I get to beat the fuck out of you before or after?" Mix booms through the room.

We all turn to see him propped against the bar watching, with his arms folded over his broad chest. The old man is still as fit as he was when he was as young as King and Owen. His skin may be a little windblown from riding, but he's still young in the face as well. Just a little gray has started to sparkle around his temples.

I watch as King's head falls back. He's vibrating with anger and frustration. He tugs at his blond dreads and blows out a breath.

"Mix," King starts.

"Son, I've known you two were sneaking around for months. You've been distracted every time we talked on the phone. I was saddling up to ride out the night Misty beat that girl's ass to get in your bed." Mix grins at Misty and lifts a brow. "What, baby girl? I was curious as to what you were up to."

Mix shrugs, popping some pretzels and nuts in his mouth. He chews as he watches King and Misty's stunned faces. King bites his fist as his whole body shakes.

"Why not say something?" King finally says.

"Why? *You* could have talked to me." Mix points to King and then himself. "You two have been dancing around each other for years. I knew it was only a matter of time before she got her hooks in you. My baby girl is determined."

Misty sinks into King. "Thank God." She sighs. "This shit has been stressing me out."

King wraps an arm around her, placing his hand on Misty's little bump. He kisses the top of her head. King then looks over his shoulder to narrow his eyes at Brick.

"You're too old for her," he grumbles.

Brick shrugs. "Are you talking to me or yourself, brother?"

"Both, you knew what I was dealing with." King frowns. "You were creating that same damn situation."

"Let me ask you something, brother," Brick replies.

"What?" King nods.

"Did any of that shit you were telling yourself in your own head stop you from claiming your woman as yours?"

King purses his lips. "Not for a fucking minute." He snorts.

"You were just waiting for Mix to get back to have a talk with him. Brother, I was waiting until your mind was here for me to tell you." Brick shrugs.

"I ain't got shit else to say to you tonight," King grumbles.

He walks off toward his room with Misty tucked up under his arm. I give my sister a weak smile and mouth, *"thank you."* Sal rolls her eyes at me but looks down at my belly and smiles.

Gutter walks up behind her and wraps his arms around her waist. I watch as Sal completely melts into him. They make a gorgeous couple, in a rough, gorgeous, biker way.

Gutter whispers something into Sal's ear that makes her smile and they turn to disappear into their own world. I look up at Owen and I can see the hurt in his face as he stares after King and Misty. I think he would have preferred to have King kick his ass.

Brick's face turns into a scowl as he looks over to Reap. "Get her ass out of here. Do what we talked about for now. She gives you any problems, put a bullet in her fucking head," he commands as he glares at Mags.

"What?" Magdalena squeaks.

Brick wraps his arm around me. "You're dead to me," he calls over his shoulder as he turns with me under his arm.

CHAPTER THIRTY

Precious Moments

Eva

Owen walks us to my room. I grin when he pulls out the key he hasn't returned to Misty. He pushes it into the lock to open the door and ushers me into the room.

I don't get too far inside before he wraps his arm around my waist, pulling me back to him. He reaches for the hem of his T-shirt he placed on me.

The cool air of the room hits my midriff and thighs as he tears it off. He continues to move me backward until we're against the closed door.

In one swift move, he has my back pinned to the door and he's on his knees before me. I inhale sharply as my eyes connect with his. They're not their usual green, but a deep dark hunter green. He nuzzles my belly button, before kissing a path around it.

He flicks his tongue out and laps at my skin then sucks it into his mouth. He hasn't taken his eyes off of me. With a look of awe on his face, he places his hands on my bare middle and glides them up my side to just underneath my bra strap.

When he releases the clasp and my bra slips down my arms, it's as if it comes undone by magic the action is so swift and smooth. He reaches to pull the right strap from my arm before he pulls down the left and removes the bra from my body without removing my shirt.

My nipples pebble against the soft fabric of my T-shirt. I lick my lips and bite the bottom one as he drops his hands to my ankles. I promise you, my skin melts under his touch as he slowly drags his warm hands up my calves, to my thighs, to the band of my panties. Tugging the fabric back down my legs, he caresses my flesh with his fingertips with the action.

I step out of my panties as he commands me to do so with only his eyes. It's honestly like I hear his gaze talking to me. My skirt is so short, allowing his breath to fan against my pussy before he leans in.

"This, you and this baby, are mine forever," he says against my mound. "You never have to worry about anything, baby girl. I'm here for whatever you need."

He kisses the top of my mound, then he delivers an open mouthed kiss to my pussy and weeping lips. I shudder as his tongue finds my nub. He grasps ahold of my pussy with his hands as he passes his tongue through my folds.

"Owen," I gasp and slip my hand into his hair. He groans into me, sending a buzz through my body. He pulls my hips forward for better access. I lift onto my toes and toss a leg over his shoulder.

He chuckles, but dives in deeper. I'd been so worried about how he would take the news. I fucked up royally. I grew up in this backward town.

Our school didn't believe in sex education. Everything I know about sex I learned from Misty. Honestly, sometimes I think she made up half of what she told me. Being that we both managed to get pregnant, I'm guessing I'm right there.

Owen has been my only real teacher, the true master of this body. That's proven as he laps at me with his tongue. I thrust my head back and forth against the door.

I try to pull my hips back, but he follows with his mouth. While he plants a hand on the door behind me and bobs his head into me, with his other hand he grips a tight hold of my waist.

The feel of his beard has my eyes rolling in my head. "Owen, I can't take it," I plead.

"Mm hmm," he moans in response. I tighten my grip and my toes curl.

I start to slide down the door as I come and seriously fall apart. He moves his arm from the door to wrap it beneath my ass and stands with me in his arms. He turns and I think he's going to walk us to the bed, but he doesn't.

I hear the clink of his belt as it releases. I'm in a dreamlike state, with my face buried in his neck. I inhale lightly and take in his scent. It's home. I smile and flick my tongue against his skin.

My smile turns into an open mouthed, silent scream as he adjusts me and thrusts into me right where we stand. His arms cradle me in the air as he bounces me on his thick erection, while thrusting up into me at the same time. I quickly lock my legs around his back and wiggle my hips as best I can.

"You like dripping down my balls," he says huskily against my neck.

"Yes," I keen.

He kisses the side of my face and my juices that are soaking his beard wet my skin. "I love you," he breathes. "You're the only woman I've ever loved."

"Oh, God, Owen, I love you too."

"You sure, baby? Cause this motherfucker comes with a lot. You ready for that? You ready for me to make you my old lady, baby girl?" he says in my ear through his labored breath.

His thrusts are mind numbing, so it takes me a few minutes to reply. I nod my head, but he nips my ear, silently letting me know he wants more confirmation than that. "Yes, I'm sure," I moan as he dips his knees and increases his thrusts. "I'm ready."

"That's what I thought," he says against my neck. He sucks my skin into his mouth. I claw my nail across the back of his neck. "Fuck, baby. So damn good. I'm going to be just as good to you as this pussy is to me."

"I don't think anything can be as good as your dick," I purr.

He chuckles and groans. "Damn, you let me come in this pretty little pussy. Now you're having my baby. Do you know how much that turns me on?" he says against my lips.

I shake my head, letting his lips brush mine. "No, please show me."

He takes my mouth hard and starts to move us toward the bed. He pulls me off his length and gently places me on the bed, using my thighs he pulls me to the edge of the mattress. Hovering over me, he enters me again, with my legs over his shoulder.

Yup, he shows me all right. I black out by my third orgasm. If we were supposed to be hiding our relationship, it's no secret by the time Owen finishes serving me love, life, and air. I breathe him for the night.

Owen

I'm going to be a father. I can't stop smiling into the darkness of Eva's bedroom. A part of me knows I've been subconsciously wanting this.

My first taste of Eva was like a drug. I knew then I wouldn't be able to break away from her. Now, I have so many reasons to hold on to her. I love her and she's having my baby.

You would think all that would make me a saner man. Not really, the Lost Soul in me has become thirsty for blood. The blood that will ensure my woman and child's safety.

My smile is, in part, for the death I plan to deal out. I didn't start this, but I plan to finish it. I swear by that. I laugh when Eva puffs her lips out in her sleep. I lean to peck them.

I plan to be the husband and father my old man never was. My mind wonders to Cage. I would love to have a son and be the father he was to so many of us.

I sigh when I think of my brother. I hurt King. That shit ain't sitting right with me. It's one of the reasons I'm still lying here awake after fucking Eva to sleep.

I think of a million ways I could have done this better. None of it counts now. I wronged my brother and I still owe him his right.

I kiss Eva's forehead and slip from her hold. She grumbles in her sleep and makes the cutest face. I lean over the bed to plant one more kiss on her lips.

Tugging my jeans and T-shirt back on, I head over to the door to be a man. If I have a son, I want him to always honor his commitments and his word. So, it all starts with me.

CHAPTER THIRTY-ONE

Brother to Brother

Owen

I knew I would find King here. We know each other well. It looks like Mix knows us both too. As I enter the dank basement room, Mix stands inside against a wall.

"You two are as stubborn as two mules," Mix huffs and shakes his head.

"I respect this brotherhood. I know what I did was wrong," I reply.

King snorts. He stands to his full height from the table he had been leaning against. I stand firm as he stalks over to me and gets right in my face.

King and I are the same height, so we're pretty much evenly matched. He's a bit leaner, where I'm a bit on the brawnier side. Don't let that fool you though, we have gone toe to toe as kids and we both have our wins under our belts as well as our ties.

Only, this time I don't plan to fight back. I owe him this for not coming to him as a man. I hold my hands behind my back as

I stare him in his eyes, letting him know I'll take whatever I have to for my woman.

"That kid has had my heart from the time my old man brought her home. She's tough, but sensitive to the core. If you can't bring her the world, you walk now," King says after a long stare down.

"She's had my heart for just as long. Eva's my world, brother. I've wanted her for a long time. That's the truth, but it's not about some pussy. I love her more than a man should love anything. I'll bring her the world and beyond," I say with conviction.

"If you were anyone else, you would be leaving here in a sling," he says, then punches me in the gut. "You're the closest thing I have to a brother. Never hide shit from me again."

I grunt and nod as I stand upright. He throws a right at my jaw and I eat that too. We stare each other down again. King's hard glare breaks into a broad grin.

"We would have kids at the same time. Little fuckers are going to drive us crazy." He booms with laughter.

I snort. "Shit, we're going to get back everything we've done."

"Yeah." With a nod, King stops laughing and looks at Mix. "All right, old man," King huffs. "What don't we know?"

"This is your daddy's shit you're dancing in," Mix says seriously.

"I'm listening." King nods.

"Rose and Cage weren't in some freak accident. Your daddy called me to let me know he had a tail. He and Rose had been out shopping. Your daddy thought he made out an old friend.

"The plan was for him to ride toward me and I would meet up to cover him and Rose. I didn't make it in time. We were only seconds too late. A pickup rammed Cage from behind out of nowhere. The second cage that followed them pulled to a stop when they saw me and a few brothers rounding the bend.

"Shit got ugly. Spark took down the motherfucker driving the truck and we cleaned house with the others."

"From the truck?" King cuts in.

"Yeah, there were about five of them. We put them all to ground." Mix nods. "Your daddy and Rose were hurt bad. I didn't want to move them, but if we didn't, I knew we would lose them both. We loaded Rose and Cage in the bed of that truck those fuckers were in."

He pauses with a haunted look in his eyes. His face has turned red as he speaks. I can tell he's reliving it all.

He continues. "The other truck... I saw that motherfucker. I saw him with my own two eyes. I should have put him to ground for what he did. That night he beat Jewels to death in front of those babies, I should have killed him then."

"Misty's father?" King says tightly.

Mix nods. "Pop has had a hard-on for your daddy and me for a long time." He takes another pause to shake his head. The sadness surrounding him is palpable.

"Jewels was a wild one. Misty reminds me a lot of her. She cornered Cage the same way Misty did you, King. She was content with taking what she wanted. Rose had been playing hard to get then. So, Cage took the bait.

"When Jewels came to me claiming she was pregnant with Cage's son, I promised I'd protect her. Pop hadn't put two and two together. Jacky had those hazel green eyes, but I've known your daddy since we were in diapers. I knew his mama too. She had those eyes.

"By the time Cage found out, he didn't want Rose to know. She and Jewels locked horns whenever they were around each other. Jewels would press Rose's buttons. And that Rose had a temper." He chuckles.

King furrows his brows. "What are you saying, old man?"

"Jacky is your little brother. Pop eventually figured it out. He blamed me and Cage for his life falling apart and for his beating Jewels like that. Pop was crazy, jealous, and greedy to begin with. Our friendship had long since crumbled. We all came up together, but he didn't show his true colors until your daddy became prez.

"It didn't matter that Cage wasn't the only one Jewels cheated on him with. He had a hard-on for your daddy. All Pop talked about was becoming prez someday. And then it happened for your daddy."

"Wasn't he the club treasurer?" I question.

Mix nods. "Until he started to unravel. Cage wasn't going to let him take the club down with his shit."

"So, are you telling me Pop is the one that's put a price on our heads," King says with narrowed eyes.

Mix gives a nod. "It's been a long time coming. He's been playing the shadow, trying to find the right pockets and support to do it. Some of the brothers who didn't like the changes your daddy made early on left. They're the ones who helped Pop try to take Cage down."

"Un-fucking-believable," King bellows.

"No one thought you would step up to take your daddy's place. They had plans to challenge and overthrow me when I took over. I was too old for that shit. I knew you would handle things. Cage felt the same way."

"Hold on," King and I say in unison.

We look at each other, then turn back to Mix. "You keep talking about my daddy like he survived," King says as he steps toward Mix and tilts his head.

"He and Rose did, for the most part," Mix says as he looks between us both.

"You didn't think they could kill your old man did you?" The sound of a raspy voice comes from behind us.

King and I spin around at the same time. Standing tall in the doorway is a scarred-face Cage. He looks older, but bigger and more sinister than I remember. His golden hair is tied back as if to show his scars with pride.

As I take him in, I notice the slight tumor on his right arm. Cage sees me home in on it and flexes his chest, taking a step forward. "Don't let that bullshit fool you," Cage rumbles. "I've had enough time to build my strength back. Now, are you two boys going to stand there and stare at me like a ghost or are you going to show your old man how much you missed him?"

King is in motion before Cage finishes his words. They wrap each other in a tight bear hug. I'm stunned. I fight back my own emotions as I watch King hold on to his father.

The two can do nothing but embrace for how long, I couldn't tell you. Cage repeatedly pats King on the back, hard, as he begins to tell him how proud he is of him. I thought I couldn't be more shocked than when Eva announced she's pregnant.

Now, I'm just struck speechless. King and Cage release each other, and Cage opens his arms for me. I move into the arms of the man who has been my only real father figure. My heart bled when I thought I lost this man forever.

As I pull back and look at his scarred face, I want to quench my thirst for blood more than ever. It never sat right with me that Cage was in a freak accident. He's one of the best riders I've ever seen. He taught us all.

"Six years," I choke out.

"A long fucking time, son," Cage says gruffly. He grabs me and King by the backs of our necks. "You boys have made me so proud. I'd hoped my shit wouldn't come knocking at your door, but I've been waiting. Getting my strength back and waiting. That son of a bitch has known how to find me.

"I've even played the sitting duck for him to try—posing in a wheel chair and all—but my life won't satisfy him. He wants the club or at least what's left of it after he tries to bring it down."

"That shit's never gonna happen," King grates out.

"You're fucking right, son. My grandkids are going to run this show someday," Cage says with a wide grin.

He kisses first King's forehead then mine, reducing us to the boys we used to be. My heart squeezes, I love this man and we all took losing him hard.

"Damn proud of you boys," Cage chokes out in the raspy sound that has become his voice. "My boys."

CHAPTER THIRTY-TWO

Distraction

Owen

The four of us roar with laughter in the clubhouse basement. It feels damn good. Cage looks like he's been in need of laughter and camaraderie for some time now. From the way he has told us he has been living, I know it to be true.

I think I'm still in shock that Cage is sitting here before me. It feels good though. It feels damn good. I don't think I've stopped smiling since we all pulled up chairs and started to talk.

The trouble brewing has taken a back seat for a few hours. Right now, we're just a few men shooting the shit. Cage has a way of putting a smile on your face. That hasn't changed.

What has changed, is the twinkle that used to dance in his eyes. Cage looks like he has become a harder man than he used to be. Don't get me wrong, Cage Kennedy has always been one bad motherfucker. He just had a way about him that put you at ease in every situation.

Now, I don't think many people would feel too relaxed in a room with him. It's not just the scars or his new raspy voice either. It's like Cage has truly become a lost soul—the shit Squad members are made of.

Suddenly, the air in the room shifts and the laughter dies down. "How are my girls?" Cage asks somberly.

King tosses a thumb over his shoulder. "Well, you already heard this one knocked up Eva. Other than that, I think she's good. Then again, what do I know? Those two have kept me on my fucking toes."

King shakes his head. "Some shit went down with Sal. She won't tell me what and I know not to push her. I've just been hoping it's not as bad as my imagination has made it," King stop to purse his lips. "Seeing her with Gutter is the happiest I've seen Sal in a long time. I hate that shit, but I noticed."

"Boy, you've done the best you could. Rose and I left you in a tight spot. You took care of your sisters and you've run this club." Cage nods. "You've done a fine job of both."

"Now you're back and you can take the gavel back," King says with a broad grin toward his father.

Cage shakes his head. "My days as prez are over. It's time for new blood to take over. You're where you're supposed to be. Now it's time for Brick to take his place," Cage says as he looks me in my eyes.

My green gaze locks with his hard, blue stare. I knit my brows in confusion. "I've been leading the Squad since you've been gone," I say.

"Right where we needed you to get you ready for now. Mix isn't getting any younger. It was always in the plans to groom you two to be prez and VP. Eva is the right fit to take over Soul Deep for you in a year.

"I've had my hands in everything from a distance. You two just thought you were carrying out Mix's suggestions and your own ideas." Cage grins, causing his scars to lift and stretch.

"Wait, you want me to take over as VP?"

"Why not? I don't think there's a brother willing to openly deny you the right," Cage says as he stares me in the eyes.

I sit and look at the old man for a moment. I've never thought about taking any office other than handling my squad. I even passed up enforcer to let Grim step in to fill the spot for me. It has just been easier to straddle both worlds that way.

"How would that work? Being VP would make me more visible to the public as a Lost Soul," I think out loud.

"You already lead the Squad. You've been acting as a VP for years, not realizing it. Grim has settled in as enforcer under your watch. With the direction the club is going, there's no need for the separation any longer. This is where I always saw things going. You are all ready, it's time."

"I think I like the idea of enjoying my grandkids and not wrangling in you knuckleheads." Mix chuckles.

I pull a hand down my beard, lift my brows, blow out a deep breath, and sit back in my chair. I think of Eva helping to run Soul Deep Architecture and Construction, she would be amazing at taking over in a year. I won't have to fully resign, but I would need to be here in South Carolina a lot more.

We could set up a main office here, since the gap between my club affiliation and business would be closed. I think Cage's words over. I have been at King's side whenever he calls over the years. I have noticed Mix fading more and more into the background. I never mentioned it or gave it much thought.

I've always been there for whatever King needed without question. Mix's role was never my concern, unless it compromised King. Mix has never neglected being there for King or any of the other brothers for that matter.

"Looks like we'll be having church. It's time to bring back a ghost and pass a torch." King nods.

"We're good?" I ask King.

"I'm going to want to fuck you up every time I see you with my sister for a while, but if she loves you and you love her, I'm good. Hurt her and I have no brother," he says pointedly.

"I guess we'll be brothers for life."

King nods and grunts. His phone vibrates on the table, pulling him away from our conversation. He looks down at it and his face turns red. I'm on guard right away.

"What is it, son?" Cage asks.

"Son of a bitch." King looks up at me. "There's a fire at one of the warehouses. Laces said I should come down personally. Someone left a message for me."

"Let's go." I stand and pull out my phone to call in my squad.

When I get it out, it buzzes with a message. I read it and growl. "Motherfucker," I spit.

"What?" King demands.

"Fire, worksite you came down to."

"Take Grim and Reap with you. I'll send Sugar to sit on Mags. Fly out and find out what the fuck is going on. Gutter stays put with the girls. I'll take Tracks and Jacky with me. Meanwhile, have Diggs get over there while you guys are in route," King rattles off orders.

"Already on it," I say as I'm in motion.

I was thinking the same thing. Grim can get me there in the chopper and cut down the time while we still have our bikes. I text him to get him in motion.

"Something stinks," Cage mutters. "I'm riding out with you, King."

"I was thinking the same thing, brother," Mix says as he moves to leave with me. "I'm riding with Brick."

It's damn near dawn and not one, but two fires on Lost Souls properties. This shit isn't sitting well with me either. Looks like our friends are ready to rumble.

Eva

I blink my eyes and take in my surroundings. I pout when I realize Owen is gone. I miss his warmth and the comfort of his arms. It takes a second for me to realize that it's my cell phone that has disturbed my sleep.

I reach for my phone to see a number I don't know lighting up the screen. When my eyes flicker to the time, I frown. It's seven in the morning. In the back of my mind, I wonder where Owen has gone off to and hope he hasn't been called out on club business again.

I then wonder who the heck is calling me this time of the morning. I answer the call, but my voice is raw and dry from sleep and the screaming Owen had me doing before I passed out last night. I clear my throat and try again.

"Hello," I push out.

"Hello, I'm looking for an Eva Kennedy," comes the voice on the other line.

"This is she," I say as my brows knit.

"Hello, my name is Nurse Henry. Your name is down as next of kin for Rose Kennedy. You were next on the list. I wasn't able to get in touch with Mr. Kennedy or King Kennedy. However, the file has notes for us to notify the family as soon as Mrs. Kennedy wakes up or in case of any major changes."

"Excuse me," I hiss. "Is this some sick joke?"

I can feel the tears well, one slips over as I wonder who would be this cruel. I swallow past the lump in my throat, ready to curse this woman out. I was devastated when I lost my mom. This isn't funny.

"N-no, ma'am," the nurse stammers nervously. "This is Eva Kennedy, right? Mrs. Kennedy has come out of her coma. It's a miracle after six years, but it has happened, ma'am."

"Wait, what?" I say and sit up in bed. I toss my legs over the side as my chest heaves. I can't believe my ears. My brain tries to process what I'm being told.

"Listen, I'm new. I don't want to lose my job. I was told if there were ever any changes to call the doctor first. Then to call the next of kin, in the order in the book, until I reached someone. Your name was next.

"Wh-where are you calling from?" I almost whisper.

There is a moment of hesitation on the other end. For a moment, I think she has hung up on me. I lick my dry lips when I hear her sigh on the other end.

"I'm at the private residence of Mrs. Kennedy. I'm just one of the private nurses from Loving Arms Home Care," she finally answers on a shaky breath.

"Okay, okay," I say to my own thoughts. If it's possible she's telling the truth, I need to see proof with my own eyes. I need to get to the bottom of this. "I'll be there as soon as I can. Can you give me the address?"

There's another pause. "Listen, lady. You called me to tell me my mother has woken up from a six-year coma. I was sixteen when she went into that coma. Give me the damn address, so I can see my mom," I say heatedly.

My patience is shot. My face and ears are burning. If I could reach through the phone and shake her, I would. She is either one, fucking with me and telling me some complete bullshit in which case I do plan on beating her ass or two, telling me the mother I thought I lost is alive and has woken up from a coma. Which means, right now, this woman is standing between me and my mommy.

I swipe at a mix of scared, angry, and hopeful tears. When she starts to give me the address, I rush to grab a pen and flip to a page in the back of an old journal on my nightstand. I hang up without saying goodbye and tear the page right out.

I'm up off the bed tossing on a T-shirt and a pair of jeans. I shove my feet in a pair of sneakers and grab my purse. I know I have to figure out a way out of here. We're still on lockdown.

I bite my lip as I make the decision to go to King. Mom was like a mom to him too. The woman on the phone said she couldn't reach him, but she had to have had a wrong number or something.

I pass King's office and just as I thought, he isn't in there this early. I head down the corridor where King's bedroom is. He and Misty are probably still in bed. That sounds so weird in my head.

Now that I know they're together, it doesn't seem like a far stretch. I've always known Misty had a thing for King. I just didn't know she took things into her own hands to make good on that crush.

When I get to King's bedroom door, I don't even hesitate to bang on it. When I don't get an answer right away, I bang again. This can't wait.

An annoyed voice sounds through the door. "Hold on a minute. The hell." I recognize Misty's grumble.

She pulls the door open, looking irritated, tired, and as if she might have been in the bathroom blowing chunks again. I peek behind her, looking for King. The room seems to be empty.

"Where's my brother?" I rush my words out.

"He rode out not that long ago. Some fire or something at one of the warehouses," Misty mutters as she props herself against the door. "What's going on? You okay?"

"No, I just got some random call from some woman saying my mom is alive and she just woke up from a six-year coma." I have a hard time hearing my own words out loud.

Misty nearly falls off the door. "What?" she gasps in shock.

"I have to get there and see for myself," I tell her as I turn to head for the garage. With no King here to stop me, there's no way I'm not leaving.

"Eva, wait," Misty calls from behind me.

"No, I have to get there." My back is still to her as I shake my head and keep moving.

"Eva, you can't go alone. Let me get dressed," she says.

I spin around. "You are in no condition to come with me," I protest. "I've got to go."

"Go where?" I turn to find Sal looming in the hallway, looking at me curiously. "I thought we were on lockdown. What's the matter?"

"Oh, God, Sal. I just got the weirdest call. Some lady says she's Mom's nurse and Mom just woke up from a coma," I tell my baby sister.

Sal's face turns pale and she stumbles back. Gutter seems to appear out of nowhere, shirtless, in a pair of low-hanging jeans and barefoot. It's than that I realize the oversized shirt Sal has on must be Gutter's missing shirt.

"What?" puffs out of Sal's mouth as if she's just able to find air.

"You can't go alone," Misty calls from inside the room behind me. She's moving around inside. No doubt trying to get dressed to come with me.

"You're not going anywhere. You three are under my watch until King and Brick get back." Gutter frowns.

"Oh, the hell I am. I need to go find out what the hell is going on," I demand.

"Calm down, Eva. How do you know you can trust this woman? I mean, this just sounds crazy. You can't go running off. Think about the baby," Sal says with worry and shock written on her face.

"What if she's telling the truth?" I stomp my foot in frustration. "I can't not go. It's Mom."

Sal nods at me with tears gathering in her eyes. She turns and looks up at Gutter, which I note is amazing, because my sister is so tall. Gutter looks down at her and his eyes soften. I know my sister is about to wrap him around her finger and get me out of here.

"Pierson, please, babe. She's right, what if it's real? What if my mom is alive somewhere?" Sal says softly.

Gutter closes his eyes and nods. "We all go." He sighs. "I'm not letting the three of you out of my sight."

"Thank you," Sal purrs and hugs him. When she breaks the hug, she turns to me. "I just need to throw on something to wear. Don't run off, we're doing this together."

I nod as more tears surface and spill over. I really didn't want to do this alone. I don't know what I'm going to find. I'm still trying to hold myself together without letting my hopes get too high.

I watch Gutter and Sal move down the hall to Gutter's room. Misty wraps her arms around me from behind in a comforting hug. She places her head on my shoulder and we stand there waiting. Waiting to find out how hard my world is about to be rocked.

CHAPTER THIRTY-THREE

Escape

Magdalena

I never meant to lose my husband. I resent the fact that I have. Of course, I had been in a relationship with Jemma when I met Brick.

She was young, vulnerable, and gullible. I was able to talk her into anything I wanted and needed. What I needed was to escape Miguel.

I couldn't live under his thumb for the rest of my life. I made the foolish mistake of making myself valuable to him, thinking it would keep me out of his and other men's bed's.

It had worked for the most part. Miguel refused to invite me into his bed because he didn't trust me. I don't blame him. He was well within reason not to.

I became a ringer for Miguel. I showed him my beauty could do more for him than make him money in some high-class whorehouse. I showed him I also had a brain. I became a lethal beauty.

I would set his enemies up to spill their secrets or just set them up for death. I've never taken a life directly, but I've been the cause of many demises. A distraction here, a distraction there. Once or twice, I've slipped something into a drink. Okay, more than once or twice.

I did what I needed to survive. Jemma was no different. She looked up to this cousin she had in the States. All she did was talk about him and how he made it out of their terrible life. She had dreams of doing the same. It didn't matter how, she just wanted to live a life like he was living.

I took advantage of that. Miguel didn't see how unhappy I was. He didn't know I was plotting to leave. However, I should have timed things differently.

He'd sent me to get some important information the night I disappeared. It's the reason he's after me. I have the key to millions, and he wants it.

If I can help it. I'd rather die without him ever getting the answers he wants. After all he did to me, it's the perfect revenge. He'll never get his hands on me again.

I didn't lie to Brick. Miguel did used to beat me. It was his way to control me. To keep me in line. To make sure I never got any ideas to turn on him.

The one lie I told Brick was that I didn't care what he did or who with. I fell for him the moment he opened his door to me and Jemma. I'd had feelings for Jemma, but not like the ones I had for Brick.

I was just afraid of those feelings. I didn't think I could ever trust a man. It was the reason I allowed Jemma to talk me into aborting my baby.

Our baby, I was the first to carry his child. I'd been shocked at first. We always used protection. Brick was adamant about it, and Jemma had made me promise.

She was so furious when I told her I was pregnant. Brick knew nothing about it. I cried for weeks after getting rid of my baby. Jemma tried to console me, but it didn't work. I was crushed.

So, imagine how I feel now. That bitch Jemma is keeping her baby. She betrayed me in the worst way. Now, my husband has moved on and some little slut is pregnant with his child.

I thought I was going to hurl when I heard Brick declare his love for her and the spawn she's now carrying. I've lost everything because of Jemma. Now Miguel is coming for me and I'm pretty sure Owen is going to have that bitch Reap try to kill me.

I have to get out of here before they come back. If I'm here when those two psychos Grim and Reap return my life is over. I know it.

I look at Sugar. She's too friendly. If you get her comfortable she talks a lot. I know I can use that to my advantage. So, I put a plan in motion.

"Hey, I'm hungry. Is there something we can do about that?" I ask.

Sugar looks up from her nails and scrunches up her pretty face in thought. She rolls her eyes over me. I know she's trying to calculate how much of a threat I really am.

She has no idea. Eva may have kicked my ass, but she caught me off guard. Besides, I have strength in other ways.

I should never be underestimated. They're all going to learn that. I'm getting out of here and I plan to settle a few scores. Jemma and that fucking Eva are on the top of my list.

Sugar sighs. "Yeah, I'll order something. I'm starving," she replies. "There's a great Chinese place around here. Is that cool?"

"Sure, make sure to get us some sweet teas," I chime. I've spent time around Sugar. I know she loves sweet tea.

Sugar smiles and gives a nod as she pulls out her phone. I listen to her place the order, listening in closely as she gives the address. I'll need that.

Thanks, hon.

She hangs up the phone. I need to keep her busy with conversation as we wait. I'll be out of here soon.

"I need to get my nails done after all this," I say, looking at my nails the way I caught her doing earlier.

She perks up and looks at me. "Yeah, I was thinking the same thing."

"Is it me, or do you feel like you're always looking for a new place because your tech left or the one you like starts to get all careless and whatnot," I say and roll my eyes.

"Oh God, isn't that so annoying? I've changed places three times in the last month and a half. I've been trying to talk one of the brothers into opening a place with me, that way I can hire someone I like and go in anytime I want," she says.

She has totally relaxed now. Just the way I need her to.

See, I'm always prepared for anything. It's the way Miguel made me. Always ready to do his bidding. At any moment, I would need to follow through. So, I'm ready.

The intercom buzzes with our food. Sugar narrows her eyes at me for a moment in warning, but then she relaxes again and stands to answer for our food.

Good.

"I just need to go to the bathroom," I say as I too stand.

Sugar waves me off as she buzzes the delivery guy in. I lucked out. They brought me here to an apartment and not some secluded location. I rush to the bathroom before Sugar can follow or question me.

Now what I'm about to do may gross a few people out, but a girl's got to do what a girl's got to do. Yes, I have been known to carry razor blades in my mouth and right now, I'm in this bathroom dropping my panties to retrieve a little help from my pussy.

Some habits die hard. I've fallen back into a few old ones in the last few months. Carrying my supplies is one of them. I don't know what Jemma told Brick. I saw her talking to him and he hasn't looked at me the same since.

Yes, I tried to set that bitch up. I was pissed at Jemma, but I didn't know it would backfire like this. I was only trying to get David angry enough to force her to have an abortion. That was my plan. I didn't mean for Jemma to be in any danger, at least not then.

As I said, I do love that silly bitch. The fact is, I'm hurt I didn't break things off to try to make things work with my husband. I know I could have made Brick mine. Now that homewrecking bitch is in the way, and I can't trust Jemma.

I grumble to myself as I carefully pull the string on the little latex sash I have inside me. I bust the sack open and retrieve the vile with the capsules inside. I rinse my hands and pocket the other little items I had in my hideaway.

I don't plan to hurt Sugar. I just plan to knock her out for a bit. Well, that and cause a little paralysis. I need to buy as much time as I can.

"Oh, that smells delicious," I say when I return to the living area.

"Dig in."

Sugar has already started eating. I look to see she has a sweet tea open with another right next to it. Good, like I said, I don't plan to hurt her. I would prefer to slip something in her drink when she's not looking. I'm not a total bitch.

From what I overheard. Grim and Reap were on their way to Georgia with Brick. That's where I'm headed.

Yup, I've got a plan. I'm going to settle the score and then I'm going to cash in on the payday Miguel is after me for. I might not get face value, but something is better than nothing now that Brick is done with me. I don't have time to try for the highest bidder.

I sit and pick up the chicken wings closest to me. I start to munch and bide my time. Sugar, just as I expected, starts up a new conversation. I know just how to distract her.

"This place is pretty good, but the one by the shop is my favorite. I think it's the way they season their food," she rambles on.

"I'll have to try them out sometime," I reply.

She gives me an odd look, but shrugs. I know what she's thinking. My days are numbered.

I look her over. Sugar is a mix of Latina, Native American, and Black. The first time I met her, I'd complimented her hair in

Spanish and she responded back shocking me. It was then I learned of her ethnicity.

She's a really pretty girl, but I don't think she knows it. She also doesn't know that two of the brothers are particularly interested in her. I've learned that she thinks she's just one of the guys. Axle and Diggs are only best friends to her.

I've seen the way they are with her. Always bending over backward for her. Diggs has a habit of hovering around Soul Deep's offices when Sugar is in town. I picked up on it right away, when I was with my husband.

Both men have several tattoo's inked by the pretty and strange woman. It's how they engage her. You get Sugar talking about tattoos and you'll have her talking for hours. I've seen her eyes sparkle and face light up numerous times.

"You do any new work for Diggs lately?" I ask in between bites.

Just as I said, her eyes light up. "Oh, God, he asked for something new. I just need to figure out how to work it around the others. I can't wait to show him what I came up with."

Sugar nods her head as if answering her own thoughts. I watch as she looks off into space dreamily.

No doubt she's thinking more of the design than the man. What a shame and a waste. Axle and Diggs are two fine-ass men. I shake my head and focus on my task.

"I was thinking of getting some ink," I say, drawing her attention back to me.

She looks at me with new curiosity. "Really, what are you looking to get?" She places her food back on the table in front of her and gives me her full attention.

I shrug and feign thinking. "I'm not sure yet. I thought maybe a butterfly or something. I've been trying to figure out if I want an open one or one with its wings closed. You know? I think I'll lose the chance for detail if I go with a closed one."

"Well, not really. I mean, you could always add details in the illusion of motion of the wings or vary the size to offer the wings more detail," she says, seeming to be in thought.

"What do you mean?" I ask and hold my breath. I'm counting on her next move.

Just as I hoped, she digs into her boot and pulls out two sharpies. "Come here, I'll show you." She waves me over.

I set the rest of my chicken down and move to sit where I can block her view of her open sweet tea. Sugar taps her chin in thought.

"Take your shirt off. I have an idea for the perfect tat for you," she chirps and the light bulb goes off.

I pull my shirt off and let her start to draw on me with her sharpies. Sugar gets lost in her drawing. I wait until I know she's fully engrossed in her work and slowly snap a capsule open, I subtly move forward toward her sweet tea and drop the powder in.

"Try to stay still," Sugar mutters.

I look over my shoulder, but she is focused, her tongue hanging out the side of her mouth in concentration. I grin, relax, and wait. It doesn't take long.

Sugar absently reaches for the jug of sweet tea and chugs it. She places it back down and continues to work. I know the moment it starts to kick in. Sugar swipes a wrist across her brow and blinks.

"Shit," she mutters, and widens her eyes at the task before her. I see when it dawns on her that she's fucked. "No."

She tries to fight, but her lids are already drooping. I tsk at the surprised look on her face. Reap told her not to trust me. She should have listened.

I grab Sugar's phone and dial my little bitch. "Hey, what's up, Sug," Jemma says sleepily into the phone.

"It's not Sug. It's me. I'll give you half of the money. Just help me get out of here," I say sharply.

"What changed your mind this time? How do I know you'll follow through?" Jemma grumbles.

"He's going to let them kill me. I have no choice. My back is to the wall. Miguel isn't far away. I can feel it and now I don't even have Brick to protect me," I seethe. "You made sure of that.

It doesn't matter if word gets out that I've cashed in. He's already coming."

"I only told Brick the truth," Jemma replies and I swear I hear the smile in her voice.

Fucking bitch.

"Whose truth, Jemma?" I yell.

"Ours, Mags, you tried to fuck me over. You did fuck me over. David is gone. That's what you wanted, right?"

"No, I wanted you to know how I felt. I wanted you to see how much it hurt to give up my baby for you," I say as my chest heaves with anger.

"You're delusional, you know that. You decided to have that abortion. I told you to go to Brick about it."

"Whatever. I said I'll get us the money. So, come and get me. Now!"

I hang up the phone and text her the address to come for me. She'll be able to get away from the clubhouse. No one gives a shit about her but me. Brick tolerates her.

I'll show them all. If I can't have him, no one can. Bitch should have killed me while she had the chance.

Jemma

This is a mistake. I know it is. Brick will never forgive me for this.

He wants Mags gone for good, but if I help her that's not guaranteed. I have a baby to think about. I know Mags has lost it.

Her words prove it. I never forced her to abort that baby. That was her choice. She was afraid of Brick and what he might do. I told her he would never hurt her. I've always made Brick feel like all of this is his fault, but it's mine.

I brought not only my crazy, but Magdalena's crazy into his world. That's why I have to do this. I have to help her and help myself.

I can't ask one more thing of Brick. He has always helped me when he didn't have to. I help Mags, I get my cut of the money, and then I can be off and out of Brick's hair.

I stare at the gun in my hand. If Mags reneges, I'll put a bullet in her trifling head. I'm tired of being led around by her every whim. It stops here.

"I'll fix this, baby," I say to my unborn child.

Shoving the gun in my bag, I put the car I just hotwired into drive. Rodney came through for me again, he was the one to let me out of the gates of the compound. The sooner I get this over with, the better off everyone will be.

I should've killed this bitch when I had the chance.

CHAPTER THIRTY-FOUR

It's Her

Eva

"No, I don't remember," she says in a quiet voice. She looks around at us all, but there's absolutely no recognition.

I try to tell myself it's because I'm older, but deep down I know it's more than that. I fist my hands at my sides fighting back the tears. It's been the same thing for hours.

She has been in and out of sleep. We've tried to jog her memory each time she wakes, hoping she'll remember us. Each time nothing.

"It's me, Mommy, Eva," I try for the hundredth time.

"And I'm Sal," my sister says brokenly.

Mom shakes her head, still looking very confused. "I'm sorry," she whispers.

Through tears, I stare into the same brown eyes I used to look up into when I was a little girl. She's still just as beautiful as the last time I saw her. She and Sal have the same face.

Her skin is still as smooth as the last time I saw her. She still looks as young as I remember. Only, she's thirty-nine now.

She was so young when she had me. Cage was ten years older than she was when they married. Her eyes were more vibrant then, but it was the same face.

She doesn't know me. She doesn't remember any of us. Not her own daughters, and not the girl who had once become like a daughter to her.

It's my mom, she's alive, and she doesn't remember me. I place my hand over my nonexistent bump. I couldn't imagine forgetting my baby or how my baby would feel to be forgotten. I know, in this moment, I'm devastated all over again.

"My head hurts," she whispers as she looks away from me to the doctor who was here when we arrived.

"Yes," Dr. Justice nods and steps forward. "That's to be expected. Maybe we should cut this visit short for now."

"What?" I exhale.

I have so many questions. I know she probably doesn't have answers and at this point we don't know if she ever will. I'm still reeling over the fact that it's really her. It's my mom.

"I'm sorry. This has to be very overwhelming for all parties. However, I do believe with some rest we will be able to relieve stress on everyone's part."

I want to scream that she's already rested. Nothing has changed all day and she's been sleeping off and on. What the hell will rest do to make her remember me? However, I bite the words and my tears back.

"Come on, Eva," Misty says, tugging me from the room.

I move with her, only because I'm in shock. I wrap my arms around my middle. I need Owen's arms around me. He would know how to make me feel better.

He would at least know how to make sense of this. Owen sees what no one else sees. At least at work that's the way it is.

I need that now. I need him to see what we have missed for the last six years. How has my mom been here and we've not known about it?

I stop in my tracks as the nurse's words come back to me. '*I wasn't able to get in touch with Mr. Kennedy or King Kennedy.*' My mind starts to spin. This can't be happening. Why now?

Oh, my God. It's not impossible. I mean, Mom is sitting in that bed. What if Cage is still alive? I turn out of Misty's arms.

"Where is that nurse?" I ask.

"She's downstairs," Gutter offers as he looks at me questioningly.

"What's going on?" Sal asks.

"I have a question for her. I need to talk to her," I say and start for downstairs.

Just then the doctor steps out of the room. I don't want to hear anything else he has to say. He's been saying a bunch of nothing since we got here. He's a nice man, but the answers I want and need are downstairs.

Misty is on my heels. I ignore her and continue down the stairs. When the nurse comes into view, I move faster to approach her.

"I want to see the call sheet," I demand.

"What?" she asks with a look of confusion.

"I want to see the call sheet. The list for the next of kin. Show it to me now."

"Oh, okay," she replies as she wrings her hands.

She scurries over to the den and picks up a paper off the desk. I snatch it from her hand and pull my phone from my pocket. I look down at the page and my heart squeezes.

At the top of the list it says Mr. Kennedy. No first name is given. I know it's not King because his name is second on the list.

I quickly dial the number. It rings twice before the line picks up. My heart aches as the voice on the other end meets my ears. It's not the voice I thought it would be, but I think that hurts more.

"Hello," the person I've known since I was a little girl answers in his deep voice.

"Mix," I sob.

"Eva? Is everything all right?" he asks in concern. "How'd you get this number?"

"My mom just woke up," is all I can say. I'm crushed to find out someone I've trusted so much could keep something like this from me.

"What?" Mix says but I can't.

I pull the phone from my ear and hand it to Misty. "Talk to your dad." I push the phone into her chest and walk off. I need fresh air.

I think I would have rather had been right. I wish it was Cage that answered the phone. To know that Mix has known all this time... it plain hurts.

I stumble out of the front door of the large home my mother has literally been asleep in for six years. I swipe at my tears. They're tears of sadness, anger and so much hurt. I feel like I might crumble in on myself.

I'm so lost in my grief as I stagger from the house I don't take in my surroundings. I keep moving, not sure where I plan to go. I need to breathe.

I stop as a chill runs through me. I realize I haven't brought a jacket out with me.

"Hey, bitch," is whispered in a hiss against my ear right before I feel a prick in my neck.

I don't have time to turn and fight or respond. It happens faster than I can blink. Everything goes black and I do crumble.

CHAPTER THIRTY-FIVE

Lost Souls Squad

Owen

I snap my head up the moment Mix mentions Eva's name. I watch him closely as he asks her if something is wrong. I saw his face when the phone rang.

He grew pale from just looking at the number. Now, he's calling her name frantically.

"Eva, Eva, Eva," Mix calls into the phone. "Misty?"

I move closer as he listens to whatever is said to him on the other end. Mix's eyes widen and he nods as if he can be seen through the phone. He pulls a hand down his face.

"Fuck me," he heaves out. "Shit, baby girl, I didn't want you all to find out like this."

He pauses to listen some more. He places a hand on his head and starts to pace. "So Gutter is there with you all?" Another pause. "Good, is she talking... wow, this is fucking unbelievable. Where's Eva? I can explain all of this." He sighs.

I get closer still as Mix paces. I have an uneasy feeling. We've been dealing with this fire all day. The marshal says it was started by someone. It's the same bullshit going on in South Carolina from the text I received from King. I don't trust any of the shit going on around us.

"What do you mean she's gone?"

"Put it on speaker," I demand.

"Daddy, she's gone. She went out the front door, but I don't see her," Misty says in a panic.

"Go get Gutter, now," I bark.

"Gutter," Misty starts screaming.

I pinch my eyes closed. That's not the smartest way for her to do things. However, when I hear Gutter's gruff voice, I find myself relaxing a bit.

"What's going on?" I overhear Gutter ask.

"Eva's gone," Misty replies.

"Gutter, find my woman. Find her now," I growl.

My phone rings as I'm barking orders. I look to see it's Axle. I pick up right away. He was supposed to be heading over to sit with Sugar as soon as he reached South Carolina from his run.

"That bitch is gone and Sugar's being rushed to the hospital, when I get my hands on her ass she's dead," Axle says into the phone before I can even answer properly.

"Wait, no one knows where Mags is," I bellow.

"No man, and Jemma is missing," Axle replies.

"Reap, did you do what I told you?" I look over at Reap who's looking down at her phone.

"Always." Reap nods. "This is interesting. It looks like their headed this way."

"To Georgia?" I ask with my eyes narrowed. "Both of them?"

"Yeah." Reap nods and looks up.

I had her slip a tracker on Jemma earlier. You live and you learn. I don't trust my cousin completely.

I'd be a fool to. Mags knows how to manipulate her.

Reap is a slick little one. Jemma has this charm bracelet she wears. I'm sure Reap was able to slip the tracker on Jemma with no problem. I also had her slip a tracker on Mags. I always have to think ahead with those two.

"Get on the road, Ax," I say into the phone. "See if you can intercept them."

"Got it," he grunts and hangs up.

I dial my dumbass cousin, because I know she's not crazy enough to harm my woman or baby. The phone rings four times and I think I'm going to voicemail when Mags' voice comes through the phone.

"Brick, Jemma isn't available at the moment," she sings.

"Where is she?"

"She's taking a nap," she cackles.

"What have you done?"

"Nothing yet." She snorts. "I just put her and your precious whore to sleep until I need them. We're on a little road trip, coming to see you, Daddy."

I close my eyes to reel in my temper. When I open them, I signal for Grim to call in every one of the Squad members. This has now become priority.

"I swear to you, Magdalena. If a single hair is out of place on my woman's head. Your death is going to be slow and painful."

"My death has already been slow and painful, husband. I just can't wait to watch you lose everything in front of my eyes," she bites out and the line dies.

"Call who you need. Get a chopper in the air. Find them," I order, through a tight knot in my throat.

I feel like I'm the one dying right now. My woman and my child are in danger and for the first time since Cage saved me as a little boy, I have something to lose. I can't control this and that just might make me lose it forever this time.

Eva

My head is pounding as my brain clears from the darkness. I can't open my eyelids, but I count that as good as Magdalena's voice becomes clear to my fogged-up mind. I need to assess the situation.

"This is crazy. How did you even know they'd be there at that house?"

"You're not the only one with a spy in the ranks," Mags says smugly.

"Where are you taking us?" the other person says.

"We're almost there. You'll find out soon enough." Mags laughs.

"Why are you doing this?" I recognize the voice this time. It's Jemma, Brick's cousin.

Jemma had been keeping her distance from Mags at the compound. She tried talking to me a few times. I'd been polite but short with her. I don't trust anyone who can do what she's done to her own cousin.

"He brought this on himself. If I'm dead to him, so are you and that slut."

"Stop the car. Let us out now and you can just go," Jemma says, but her voice sounds a little funny. Slurred sort of.

Mags doesn't reply. I take a chance and try to open my eyes. This time they open slowly. I can feel my head pressed to the cool glass of the car window. It's like feeling is coming back to my body slowly. I close my eyes again.

I start to pray that whatever she stuck me with doesn't hurt the baby. My pregnancy is so new. I fight back the tears, not wanting them to give me away.

Jemma and Mags don't say much for a long time. It's when I feel lights shining against my lids that I open my eyes again and see downtown Atlanta come into view. It's then when Jemma speaks again. I hold as still as I can to listen.

"You brought us here. You're actually taking us to him." Jemma gives a laugh. "You should have run."

"It will be the end for us all," Mags says emotionlessly.

Panic rises in my chest. My man and my baby are in danger if I don't do something. This bitch is off her rocker.

I flex my fingers and toes. I don't know if I have the strength to fight her, but I think I can run if I need to. Owen's words ring in my head about protecting our baby and not fighting.

I crack my eyes open to look out of the window. My head is still pressed to the cool window. At first nothing looks familiar in this area. In the four years I've been here in Georgia I've rarely explored the city.

I almost gasp out loud when I see the Soul Deep Enterprise Building come into view. It rises up like a beacon of hope. If I can get to that building I can get to help. Security is there around the clock.

I wait for the car to get a few blocks closer to the building. God is on my side, because the light turns red about two blocks over. I can see the building from between the surrounding ones. That's my path.

If Mags wants to follow me, she'll have to do so on foot. I may be a heavier girl, but I'm fast. I had to be if I wanted to run behind King and Brick.

This is it, I think. I slowly move my hand to the lock and the handle, but I freeze when I hear Mags hiss.

"What the fuck do you think you're doing?"

"You're going to let us out of this car," Jemma demands, causing me to sag against the door in relief. Mags wasn't talking to me.

"Where'd that gun come from?"

"You have always treated me like I'm the stupid one. You'd be dead by now if it wasn't for me." Jemma's voice shakes.

"You *are* the stupid one. You think David gives a shit about you. He left us, he wouldn't do shit for you or his unborn baby," Mags says vehemently.

I look into the passenger side-view mirror from the back seat. I can see Jemma through it with the back of her head facing the window. I shift my eyes into the car and see Jemma's arms shaking as she holds out a gun.

Mags is facing the barrel of the gun with her jaw clenched tight. "No, Magdalena, he wouldn't do anything for you. You fuck up everything you touch. I was fucked up when I met you, but you made me into an even more fucked-up person.

"I hate what we do to people. I hate who people think I am because of you. You're crazy Mags, you're so lost in your lies you don't know the truth anymore. I'm tired, this ends now. I can't play crazy with you anymore," Jemma sobs.

Behind us horns start to blare and the atmosphere in the car shifts. It happens so quickly. Mags reaches for the gun and they begin tussling. My good sense tells me to make a run for it now. I'm not waiting around to get shot or to find out the outcome.

Swiftly, I pop the lock and throw the door open. I bolt out of the car. My body feels like lead, but I push with everything I have in me. I tense up when the sound of a shot firing behind me goes off.

Don't look back, keep going, Eva.

I push forward willing my legs not to give. My heart pounds when Mags begins to call my name behind me. I ignore her and plow forward.

My lungs start to burn. I guess it's been a while since I've had to run. I push that aside. My goal is right before me. I can see the front doors of the Soul Deep building straight ahead.

"Stop running, you bitch," Mags huffs. It's clear she's winded. I can also tell she's a pretty good distance behind me.

I call on all my strength and push my burning legs forward, hard. I push clear of the buildings on either side of me and that's when I hear it. A sound that used to scare and excite me when I was a little girl.

The growl of a motorcycle engine. Not one, but multiple. I pray the riders are my family. *My family, my Lost Souls.* I've never felt those words more than I do now.

"Fuck," Mags hollers and that's when shots are fired.

A bullet whizzes right by my ear. I pump my legs harder. Moving toward the sound of the roaring engines. Two things happen at once.

I register the sound of a chopper overhead as its light beams on me and the area around me. Then I see them, I would know them anywhere. I've looked up to them for as long as I can remember. I falter a step because I can't believe what I'm actually seeing.

I know the bikes, but one doesn't make sense. The sight before me doesn't make any sense. King is leading the formation, but right beside him is my daddy, Cage. I don't have to see his face. I know the bike, I know the way he rides, I know his frame on a bike.

Flanking King and Cage are Brick and Mix. Behind them are eleven other bikes. *Squad. Our family came for us, Baby.* I think to my unborn child.

The pink and black bike in the middle of the formation breaks rank and rides around the other bikes. I know right away it's Reap. She puts herself and her bike between me and the gunfire.

I stop in awe as Reap's bike lifts onto the front wheel and her arm comes out holding a gun. I watch as the bike rotates on one wheel and Reap starts to spray bullets.

I turn in time to see Mags' body jerk back once, twice, three times. Mags takes a bullet to each shoulder and her left thigh before she drops backward to the ground. When I look back to Reap, her bike lands back on two wheels with a bounce.

I'm so lost in the action I don't notice Brick has stopped his Harley right behind me until he scoops me up into his strong arms. He buries his face in my neck and inhales deeply. I can feel his body shaking with rage as he holds me tight.

"Are you okay?" he chokes into my hair.

"Yes," I try to speak through my heaving chest.

I turn my head sharply when I hear Mags screaming and cursing in Spanish. Axle is standing on her left leg with the bullet wound. Reap is standing over her as well, with her gun pointed at her head.

"You're gonna die slow, bitch," Axle sneers. "Sug never fucks with nobody. That shit you gave her almost killed her. She had a fucking allergic reaction. I swear, you're gonna pay."

"What the fuck is he talking about?" Diggs says as he swings his leg off his bike and he moves in Axle's direction. He says it with so much venom my skull catches a chill. "What happened to Sugar?"

Oh, this isn't going to go well. Reap snatches Mags up by her hair and whispers something in her ear as Axle and Diggs bend their heads together to talk. Diggs roars into the night when Axle's lips stop moving.

Yeah, this is going to be bad. Even I know about this. Everyone but Sugar knows Diggs and Axle have a thing for her. With them being best friends, neither has tried to make it known to her.

Owen pinches my chin between his fingertips and turns my face toward his. He searches my face with his green eyes. When he seems satisfied, he crushes my lips with his.

"I love you so much," he murmurs against my mouth.

"I love you too."

I'm breathless. He moves his hands to my back where he runs them up and down soothingly. I sag into him as the adrenaline starts to wear off. I inhale him like he did me. Then, I fall apart as everything hits me.

As if knowing I'm crying in part because of him, Cage appears over Owen's shoulder and looks down at me. I look up through my tears into my daddy's eyes. He may not be my real father, but he will always be my daddy.

My heart aches as I see his scarred face. My mother's face has remained smooth and clear, but I didn't miss the scars on her arm. They're not as deep as Cage's and cover less of her skin.

Just looking at him, I know he took the brunt of whatever happened to them. It only makes sense. If you knew how this man loved my mother you would come to the same conclusion.

"You just gonna stare at me, sugar, or you gonna come give me a hug?" Cage asks with a smile.

His eyes sparkle at me, transforming his scarred face. He's still handsome as ever, scars or not. Kennedy men are simply gorgeous, no matter what.

I pull from Owen's embrace and rush into my daddy's open arms. I can't find it in me to be angry with him. Not now, not seeing him in the flesh.

Cage holds me so tight, but it's what I need, because I feel like I might fall apart if he lets me go.

"Shh, darling. Daddy's here now," Cage whispers.

I jump in his embrace when I hear the slamming of car doors. I look around Cage to see Jemma dragging herself from one of the cars. She's soaked in blood and collapses into Track's arms as he rushes to help her.

Misty and my sister catch my eye as they rush from a Soul Deep SUV. Everyone else moves about to get things under wraps before the police arrive. Owen doesn't need this mess in front of his empire.

"Didn't I tell you two to stay at the loft?" Gutter barks.

"Daddy?" Sal questions, ignoring Gutter, sounding like a little girl. Tears roll down her cheeks and her lips tremble.

"Come here, baby girl." Cage holds out an arm for her.

Sal rushes forward and stumbles into our father's arms right beside me. We both cling to him. I still don't think it has hit me that this is real.

Yeah, everyone has a lot of explaining to do.

CHAPTER THIRTY-SIX

Time to Process

Brick

"Thank you," Eva says as I place a glass of water on the island in front of her.

After getting her checked out at the hospital, I brought her back to the warehouse apartment. It wasn't smart to try to return to South Carolina yet. I believe we were all exhausted and overwhelmed by the time Eva was released from the hospital. However, King and Cage did head back early yesterday morning with a few of the Squad members to tend to Rose.

Rose and Cage are still alive.

Two resurrections in one night. I, for one, feel like I'm in the twilight zone and have been since the day before yesterday. Seeing Cage on his old bike tugged at something deep inside of me.

"I'm still trying to wrap my head around all of this," Eva says as if she's reading my thoughts.

"I know what you mean. What are the chances she'd wake now, when Cage decides to return? My mind is so fucking blown," I muse aloud.

"Can we take a bath? I just need to sit and think for a bit."

I wrap my arms around her and place my chin on the top of her head. "We can do anything you want to do."

After sleeping in yesterday and most of today, we're trying to get our bearings. I ordered something to eat to feed her and the baby and now we've been sitting in silence for the most part.

Although I want to get back to South Carolina, I'm not going to rush Eva. I can tell she needs some time.

"Well, in that case, I really want to sit in your arms and breathe for a moment," she says.

I scoop her up from the stool she's on and start for the bedroom. "Then a bath it is," I say and place a kiss on her forehead as she wraps her arms around my neck.

She rests her head on my shoulder as I carry her through the apartment. Once in the bedroom, I head straight into the bathroom. Placing her on her feet, I note the lost look on her face.

So much has changed over the course of one night. I can't blame her for needing a few days to process it all. I've come to learn how much both Cage and Rose mean to Eva in the time we've been together.

"I got that," I say when she starts for the hem of her T-shirt.

I pull the fabric over her head and toss it aside. Needing to have my hands on her to remind myself she and the baby are okay; I place my hands on her hip and draw her closer. With the gesture she comes back to me from wherever her mind has her.

Eva turns her pretty face up and gives a shaky smile. I hope to have a son because if my little girl ever looks up at me with this much hurt in her eyes, I'm going to kill the motherfucker that placed it there.

I'm already standing in a long line of brothers who want to put Pop to ground. The need to sooth Eva's hurt and my own anger consumes me. I dip my head and seize her lips for a tender kiss.

"That has been the best part of this awful week," she says with a catch in her voice as I pull away.

"Come on, let's get this bath going and then I'll get the rest of your clothes off," I say and kiss her forehead.

Once the water is running, I go for her favorite bubble bath. I noted a while ago she favors this one. It's a citrus scent.

I make a note to pick up some more as I turn to her and pull the tie of my sweats she has on. Her belly comes into view. Not firm from the pregnancy yet, but still a reminder of the seed inside of her.

As I tug her panties down her legs, I can't help but get hard at the thought of her carrying my baby. If someone would have told me all of this would have happened when I woke up four days ago, I would have put a bullet in them for being a lying fuck.

"What are you thinking?" Eva says as she runs her fingers through my hair.

I look up from my crouching position. As exhausted as she looks from the events of the last few days, she's still concerned about me. I don't deserve her, but I'm sure as fuck going to cherish her now that I have her.

"The last two days have been the longest and most eventful days of my life," I reply.

Eva gives a small laugh. "You can say that again. I think I've learned more about the club in the last few days than I knew from the time Mom married Cage."

I stand and strip out of my sweats and T-shirt. When I'm naked, I walk Eva over to the bath and cut off the water before helping her in and stepping in behind her. I sit and place my hands on her waist to guide her to straddle my thighs as she sits in my lap.

"This is nice," she says as I pull her against me so we're chest to chest. She gives a small breathless laugh. "We won't be able to do this once my belly starts to pop."

"We'll make do. Nothing can keep me from having my arms around you," I say, tightening my hold and kissing the top of her head.

We're silent for a moment. Our bodies relax in the water. For a moment, I think she's fallen a sleep until she lifts her hand and starts massaging my beard with her fingers.

I take her hand and kiss the palm before I let her return to her massaging. I close my eyes and revel in the feel of just being still and knowing my woman and child are in my arms. They're safe.

"He had her locked away in that house like some precious doll or something. Now that I think about it, it was sort of weird," she says to break the silence.

"She's always been precious to him. So I guess it's not that weird."

I hold back from telling her I'd probably do the same thing Cage did to keep her safe and to hold on to hope. I'd do everything in my power to keep her alive if I had to.

"I want to be angry at him. At both of them, Cage and Mix. While we were at the hospital, a few times I did feel some anger, but then I'd look at Daddy and it all went away. I'd rather the lies than to never be able to see them again. Does that make any sense to you?"

"Yeah, darlin', it does. You have a right to the way you feel," I reply.

"I mean, he stayed. Cage wouldn't leave the hospital until he knew I was okay," she says and sniffles.

I noticed that too. He looked concerned the entire time we waited for Eva to be seen. I could feel the relief come off of him when I let everyone know she and the baby were going to be okay.

I always knew Cage cared for Eva and Sal. However, tonight really showed how much of a father he is to them and how deep his love for them runs.

"Love will do that. I don't think Cage meant for this to go for so long or for you girls to get hurt. Honestly, as far as what Mix told me, they didn't think your mom would wake. At least, everyone but Cage had given up," I say.

"He has never given up on her." Eva chuckles. "You know, she thought he was too old for her. She once told me that was one of the reasons she tried to avoid him and turned him down."

She lifts her head and looks into my eyes. The smile on her lips is the first real smile she's given me in days. I reach to trace her lips.

"What?"

"I guess I got dating older men from her," she teases.

I growl and close the distance between us to take her lips. She wraps her arms around my neck and we get lost in our connection. The kiss turns feverish. It's clear we both need this more than we know.

She breaks the kiss and looks at me through her lashes. "Make love to me," she whispers.

I grab her hip with one hand and palm her breast with the other. "You don't have to ask twice," I say before dipping my head to take her nipple between my lips.

Eva

I cry out, my body aches for him. I had been tired and confused with everything going on but sitting here in his lap has caused my body to come to life. I can no longer ignore his erection that's been twitching against my ass.

"Babe, Owen, yes," I sing for him as he sucks on my breast and fingers me from behind.

I begin to rock my hips, greedy for more of him. For now, I let all of the drama slip away. There's nothing I can do about it now anyway.

What I can do is enjoy the way this man makes me feel. I drop my head back and move my hands to hold on to his strong shoulders. He circles my nipple with his tongue in a teasing manner, causing me to lower my head and look down at him.

He lifts me and lines up with my entrance. I follow the command he gives with his eyes and lower myself onto his throbbing length. The way he fills and stretches me makes me feel like I've come home.

"Thank you," I say in a moment of insanity.

Brick bursts out into laughter and even that feels so good and delicious. I cup his face and place my forehead to his. We breathe each other in as I start to move up and down.

"I'm forever yours," I whisper.

"I'd move heaven and hell for you. Forever, it's not long enough for how long I'll love you."

My heart blooms and I fall apart calling his name. I have hope that in the end we'll all be okay. I have my mom and dad back and I'm having a baby of my own. Most of all, I've fallen soul deep in love.

CHAPTER THIRTY-SEVEN

Gift from Reap

Brick

A few days later...

It's been a long time since I've been at this location. It's an old shack in the woods. It looks abandoned to the rest of the world.

We keep it around for club business such as this. The woods play their part in the end. The wild hogs will provide aid as well.

"You say the word," Reap sings gleefully.

I nod, giving her the go ahead. I want this over. There's more to be done.

We're not even going to fool ourselves into thinking this is all over. Mags had nothing to do with the guys outside my club, the fires, or the attacks on Sal. Those were just warnings.

We still have a problem out there. The sooner we take care of this one the better.

Mags screams as Reap approaches her. "Please. I've told you all I know. Please, no more. I'm sorry. I'm so sorry. I'm so sorry. Please," she cries.

She's been saying sorry for the last two days. Too bad I know she isn't. She's only sorry she failed and got caught.

Her cries fall on deaf ears. Mags looks like she's been through a meat grinder, but I can't find it in me to feel the least bit moved by her appearance or her pleas. Not even with the skin hanging from her face and arms.

Reap tortured the information we need out of her after we had a doctor stitch up her original bullet wounds.

"Now that we have what Miguel wants, we have the leverage we need to bring the pressure," Grim says.

"Exactly." I nod. "If he wants us or that money, he can come at us. We'll be waiting."

"Do you think he will show up once he knows she's gone?"

"Brother, I don't give a damn. He'll be lucky if I don't show up at his door after I handle this other bullshit. You know I believe in just cutting the entire fucking head off the snake whether it's facing me with its hiss or not," I reply.

"True, strike now before it turns and comes for you while you're asleep."

"Exactly."

The distinct sound of a bullet's pressure moving through a silencer grabs our attention. I turn to see Reap with a satisfied smile on her face and Mags slumped to the side.

"That's that," Grim says.

"Sure the fuck is."

And I feel nothing. I should. I was once married to that heap of flesh. However, she killed any feelings I may have still had for her when she tried to kill my woman and child.

Honestly, I won't shed a single tear. Magdalena meant to hurt my woman and family. She got what she deserved.

"Bring Jemma in," I say coldly.

My thoughts are moving quickly. My cousin was released this morning after being treated and monitored for her bullet wound. They wanted to keep an eye on the baby.

As I said, I trust only so much these two have ever told me. I want to confirm Mags' story and then I want the information

Mags left out because despite the torture, I know she held back what she could.

Jemma enters the room and screams.

"She meant to kill you, get over it," I say dryly. "Now, I'm going to ask you some questions. If you don't want to end up like her, you'll answer, and remember, I'm very close to forgetting you're my family."

"Brick, I didn't mean for—"

"Save it. What I know… when it comes down to it, Miguel never wanted any of the Lost Souls. She stole from him and he wanted his shit back. She's been sitting on a fortune all this time because cashing in would have brought Miguel to her door. Now, it's your turn. Tell me what I don't know."

Needless to say, she starts singing like a canary. Smart girl. Maybe I'll help her after this. We'll see.

Reap

"You ready?" Grim asks as we pull up in the jeep in front of Miguel Silva's home.

This little trip to Brazil is all business. I have a message I want this bastard to receive. It's all my pleasure to do this for the prez and boss man.

"Ready," I grin.

"Listen, Erica. This is just a drop. Don't get crazy."

I turn to look at Colin. I place a hand over my heart and feign shock. He rolls his eyes at me.

"When do I ever get crazy?"

He barks out a laugh. "You were born crazy, baby. Now get your ass out there and deliver your gift. It's hot and I want to get back home tonight."

"Fine," I mumble and step out of the car.

I get the box from the back seat and turn to walk to the front gate. My lips turn up as the guys outside the gate are too busy checking me out to realize how close to danger they are. I want it that way. The leather miniskirt and thigh-high boots are doing their job perfectly.

I wink at one of them and lick my lips. His grin grows and he looks around at his friends like a showoff. He poofs his chest out and adjusts himself. I laugh to myself.

I'd eat him alive.

"Hey, boys. You get this to your boss for me. Let him know I'll come back here anytime he wants," I purr in Spanish.

I hand over the box and turn to skip my way back to the Jeep. I'm sure they're watching my tiny skirt bounce as it barely covers my ass. That will give me the distraction I need to get back to the car before they realize what I've given them and I have to end a few lives.

Shame. That would be so much fun.

"Let's go," I say as I half hang out of the car.

Grim takes off as I slam the door shut. Our job is done.

I turn to him and grin. "I hope Miguel likes his head served on a platter." We both burst into laughter.

CHAPTER THIRTY-EIGHT

Forever

Brick

A month and a half later...

I watch Eva as she takes notes on her tablet while we do this walk through. She has no idea this will be our new Soul Deep Architecture and Construction headquarters here in South Carolina. She thinks it's only another site I'll be finishing off.

The original developer lost his funding and had to pull out. I picked it up for a steal. It's still early enough in the project where I can put my own spin on it. Including a nursery for the staff.

I grin as I drop my gaze to Eva's belly. She's still not showing yet. However, I've woken every morning for the last few weeks with my hand pressed to where her little bump will be.

"What do you think?" I ask as she looks up from her tablet, her eyes distant as if she's already redesigning the floor plan.

"It's a great location and with a few tweaks you can totally make the final design your own. I have a few ideas if you want to hear them," she says and bites her lip.

Still shy, but she's grown so much. I think she'll be ready to take over before the year is up. The workers love and respect her already.

"Come show me what you're thinking." I wave her over.

As I thought, she has the plans open on her tablet, already laying out her ideas alongside the list she'd been making for me. I'm going to miss working together like this. It's my hope that I'll get all the club shit settled so I can spend time in the office working with her.

Either way, Eva will do great. She has a mind for detail. With time she'll have the confidence to match.

I point to the tablet. "I like this, but let's move this and I'm thinking about an apartment over our office," I say and look up through my lashes to watch her reaction.

Her mouth forms an O shape, and she furrows her brows. It takes only a few seconds before I see it sink in. She looks around the space and turns in a circle.

"This is the new office," she breathes.

"It's been official since this morning," I say and grin.

"Oh, wow, this place is huge. It's bigger than the Georgia building. Wow."

I wrap my arms around her. "It's going to be all yours. Are you ready for that?"

"Wait, what?"

I chuckle. "We talked about this. You're training to run Soul Deep. You're going to take over for me."

"I was half asleep when you started that conversation, and you were rubbing my feet. I was fully asleep before you got more than two sentences out," she says and gives me a wary look.

"Well, it's all yours."

"Ours," she corrects. "It's our empire. Well, it will be..."

She trails off. Ah, she's leading us right where I'm heading. This ring is burning a hole in my pocket.

I pinch her chin between my fingertips. I've told Eva I plan to marry her, but I don't think she believes me yet. I saw her face during King and Misty's wedding.

"You're right. Our empire. Everything I own belongs to you, darlin'. My heart, my soul, everything," I say and plant a kiss on her lips. "You feel me?"

"I feel you."

I take the tablet from her hand and get down on one knee, placing the tablet on the floor. Her eyes grow wide and she covers her mouth. I pull the ring box from my pocket and open it up.

"Good, because I need to make that shit clear to the world."

"Owen," she drags out.

"Eva," I mock and wink. "I wanted to give King and Misty time to have their moment. Now it's ours."

"O-wen," she sobs.

I laugh. "Reel it in, baby girl. I need to ask you something."

"Yes," she shouts.

I throw my head back and laugh. "I still ain't asked."

"So. You already know my answer. Yes."

I shake my head. "Come here, darlin'."

She moves closer and I slip the ring on her finger. I stand and wrap her in my embrace. I pull back slightly.

"Just so we're clear. This means you'll marry me."

"Yes, I will marry you Owen Brick Mason."

"About damn time," King booms as he and the rest of the Squad appears. They're popping champagne as they enter the space.

"It's only been a few months," Eva says and starts to laugh.

"I'm with King. Too damn long."

Eva shoots me a look and I peck her lips. I've wanted to make her my wife since the night I found out she was carrying my baby. It killed me to wait this long to make it official.

Misty, Sal, and Reap rush over to tug Eva from my arms to wrap her in a group hug. My brothers and soon to be father-in-law all gather me in a hug as well.

"We got some celebrating to do," Cage croons.

Eva

I'm still in shock. I thought we were just coming to walk through a new project. I had no idea we'd be walking through our new offices or that Owen had planned to propose.

I was actually counting down the days until I have the baby and I can get Brick's brand on me. I'd thought about a wedding as I watched Misty get married, but never once had I stopped to consider Owen would propose.

"Hey, Eva."

For the first time today, I frown. I turn to see Troy looking around at all of my family celebrating our engagement in our new office. I draw my brows in, wondering what the heck Troy's doing here.

"Hey, Troy," I say warily.

"Looks like quite the party," he says like a goofball.

"What brings you here?"

Before he can answer, Misty and Reap come over. "Eva, you have to come hear this," they say in unison and laugh.

"Hold on," Troy says. "I wanted to talk to you."

"About?" I lift a brow. Something in his tone gets my attention.

He moves in closer, seeming to try to close Reap and Misty out of the conversation. I notice right away that the gesture gets Reap's attention. She leans to whisper something to Misty before she walks off.

"Well, your school sent the forms to be filled out for your evaluation," Troy says, bringing my attention back to him.

"O-kay. Someone fills that out so I can get my grade, right?"

"Yeah." He licks his lips and lets his gaze roll over me. "You see. I thought it might be a conflict of interest for Mr. Mason to fill it out. If your school found out about your intimate relationship…"

He allows his words to trail off like the sleezy, sly bastard he is. Right at that moment, Owen stops behind him. Troy has no idea that my fiancé is now only a foot away with his arms folded across his chest, his ears red, and his nostrils flaring.

Now, I've seen Owen angry, but this is next level. I don't think I can even call him Owen at the moment. All I can think is Brick.

I decide to play along with Troy and see how far he plans to take this. "I'm not sure where you're going with this," I say innocently.

"I'll be happy to fill the form out myself. That is if you'll have that lunch date with me," he says and gives me that annoyingly unattractive smile.

"Wait, let me get this straight. You do know that I'm involved with Owen?"

"Yes, but I'm sure completing your internship and graduating are of some consequence to you. This fling you have going with him can't be worth losing all of that," he replies.

I place my ringless hand on my nonexistent bump and lift the other to reveal my engagement ring that this smug dumbass hasn't taken the time to look at. It's much too big for him to have missed if he weren't such a pompous dickhead. His eyes nearly pop out of his head.

"Does this look like a fling?" I question.

Behind Troy, Reap hands Brick a crowbar. Before I can think to move out of the way, Brick swings the thing right at Troy's knees. I yelp in surprise.

"Party's over, ladies," Reap sings as she grabs me and Misty by the arm. I glance at the door to see Gutter pushing Sal into Daddy's arms and out the door.

"You've disrespected me repeatedly," Brick snarls. "I let your ass slide and you come here with this shit? All you had to do was your fucking job. Drop the docs off and leave with your life."

"Oh God," I gasp as I look over my shoulder to find Brick choking the shit out of Troy.

"Honey, that's your man. The Squad captain, a Lost Soul for real. And in about thirty minutes it will be as if that shit never happened," Reap says before she laughs her ass off.

More to Come

Eva

I look around at all the brothers and their old ladies as I sit at the raised reception table in the clubhouse's main hall. Do they all have stories like ours? There are so many smiling faces around the room.

I've never felt the love as much as I do now. I went to college to get away from all of this, thinking I would reinvent myself. The funny thing is, I never tried and I'm glad I didn't.

Instead, I found my way back home. I beam as I come to that realization. The Lost Souls are my home.

"Hey, Mason," Misty says as she comes to sit beside me and laugh at herself.

"What's up, Kennedy?"

Her cheeks glow. It's not just the baby. King wasn't playing about her being his for life. Their wedding was in true Lost Souls fashion, right here at the compound.

Owen and I chose a church wedding, but the reception had to be here. King insisted and Owen looked as if he would have been disappointed if I wanted to do anything else. Honestly, this was the only thing that felt right.

"God, that sounds so crazy," she says.

"I know, right?"

Becoming the prez's old lady looks good on Misty. I'm happy for her and King. My brother will have a son soon and I plan to spoil my nephew.

"We just became sisters and now you're changing your name." She pouts and reaches to play with the wedding rings on my swollen finger. "I wish I could still wear my rings on my hand."

"*Ha*. Mine are on there just barely," I say with a laugh. "Besides, we'll still be sisters. I'm changing my last name, not my family."

She reaches for her wedding rings on the chain around her neck and smiles. "Yeah, I guess you're right. I never thought this would be where we'd all end up. Married and having children with the prez and VP."

I place my hand on my undeniable bump and smile. "Would you rather have it any other way?"

"No, not at all."

"Come on, let's get a dance in before they move the party outside and our feet are too swollen for us to move," I say.

She smiles and nods. I laugh as she pushes up from her seat and waddles ahead of me. I'm big, but not that big yet.

King and Owen appear as soon as we get on the dance floor, as if we'll hurt ourselves out here or something. These two are going to be a mess when these babies get here.

Owen pulls me into a tight hug and rocks me from side to side and kisses the top of my head. I wrap my arms around him as much as my protruding belly will allow. A song starts and the swaying becomes a part of the music.

At five months it's becoming a challenge to get as close to Owen as I'd like. The fact that there are two little ones in there might account for most of that. I smile when I think about them.

"You look beautiful, Mrs. Mason," Owen says in my ear.

I laugh. "Is everyone going to call me that today?"

"They better," he growls, his eyes sparkling as he looks down at me.

"I love the way it sounds."

"I do too."

"Now, this is how you celebrate," King croons as he holds Misty in his embrace beside us. "We've got a clubhouse full of bikers showing some real love."

"Couldn't have asked for more," Owen says with a gorgeous smile on his lips.

"I can. This little boy is demanding I eat again," Misty says.

I laugh. I was thinking the same thing not even a second ago. As soon as we started to dance I got hungry. However, I didn't want to ruin the moment.

"Let's feed my boy then," King says. "You want something, sis?"

"Please, the fruit was so good. I can eat that and still dance."

"We don't have to dance if you're hungry," Owen says as his brows pinch with concern.

"No, I'm not ready for this to end."

"I've got you," King says and pats Owen on the back.

I can't stop smiling as I watch King and Misty walk toward the food tables. Cage catches my eye and lifts his beer at us. I beam at him and then look up to see Owen smiling his way as well.

However, there's something else in his expression. I slide my hands to his chest, drawing his attention. The look I caught is still there.

"What's wrong?"

"Nothing," he says.

I frown. "Then what's with the long face?"

"Memories. Cage has been a father to me since the day he walked into my life," he says, pain showing in his expression.

I sway in his arms thoughtfully. I've never asked him how their relationship came to be. He was already with Cage when we moved in.

"He means a lot to you. How'd you become one of his kids?"

A cloud grows over his face. "He saved me from hell," he says.

"What?"

At first, I don't think he's going to answer me. We continue to dance, but he's stiff and his gaze is hard. I try to think of something to change the subject and lighten the mood. This is our wedding reception after all.

"I was seven. My real father had been beating on me for over a year. He hated that I was alive, but my mama wasn't and he was stuck with me.

"One night he beat me to within an inch of my life and left me to die. For two days, I laid on that trailer floor in my own body fluids with broken ribs, a broken leg, and a broken arm."

He gives a snort of disgust. "My daddy came in and out with whores to fuck, stepping right over my small body. It was the one who came to feed me after my pop passed out who called Cage and had him come get me."

"Oh my God, babe. I—"

"No, I want you to know," he says in a detached voice and continues. "It's how I became a Lost Soul."

"Okay." I nod.

"He picked up my broken body after he beat the shit out of my pop—ending that sorry son of a bitch's memorable life—and took me to get care. He asked me if I'd like to be his son and have a safe place to grow up and I was his boy from that day," he says.

"Wow."

It's lame, but I don't know what else to say. I cup his face and his smile comes back. I love this man so much.

"For as long as I can remember, this clubhouse has been my home. Now you know where the darkness comes from. Cage got to me before it was all too late."

"And then he managed to bring us together without even knowing," I say.

"Yeah, I think from that first summer home, somehow, in my heart, I knew you were my destiny."

His words bring a huge smile to my face. I lift up on my tiptoes and Owen bends to close the distance. I kiss my husband to show him how much he's loved.

He might be a lost soul, but he's my lost soul.

***

"Eva," King calls as I make my way across the clubhouse headed for the back door that leads out to the yard.

I turn and smile at him. He tilts his head toward his office. I nod and go to follow him inside. I think this is that talk that's been coming for some time now.

Taking a deep breath before I walk inside, I hope I can keep from crying. I've been so emotional lately, but it's time to face the music. Brick and I were wrong in the beginning.

I find King sitting on the couch in his office with his long legs stretched out in front of him and his arms stretched across the back. He pats the seat beside him.

I walk over and sit in the place he gestured to. He wraps an arm around me and gives me a little squeeze. I snuggle into him the way I used to when I was little and we'd watch scary movies with Misty tucked into his other side.

"I remember when my father moved you guys in. He took me to the side and told me it was my job to watch over you girls. I was a big brother. If you girls got hurt, it hurt us all. I took that shit seriously." He pauses and blows out a breath.

"I tried my best after we thought we lost them. I know I fucked up somewhere with Sal. That shit has eaten at me because I didn't know how. Then you both go and fall in love with brothers." He snorts and shakes his head.

"Not just any brothers. Squad members," I tease.

"Exactly." He draws a hand down his face. "We're the worst kind of motherfuckers. I fought my feelings for Misty for so long because I know she can do so much better, but I'll be damned if anyone else ever puts a hand on her.

"What I'm trying to say is. Look around you, Eva. We're not normal. I wanted you to have normal. This ain't it." He frowns.

I tilt my head back and look up at him. "What's normal? Would any of us know what that looked like if we saw it?"

"Probably not," he says and laughs. He gets serious again and his blue eyes soften. "I want you to know, I was dealing with my own shit when it came to you and Brick. It had nothing to do with the two of you. Same with Sal."

"Yeah, I figured that." I lift a shoulder.

"I failed by not going to Mix with our shit and that caused my head to be all fucked up—"

"King, for as long as I've known you, you have come running to protect me and make sure I'm all right. Owen and I knew what we were doing. We knew you would be upset," I say.

"But love is a motherfucker and none of that mattered." He chuckles. "Owen. He'd knock the rest of our heads off for calling him that."

"Yup. Makes me feel special."

"You are special. If you can get his crazy ass to fall in love, you're more than special."

"Yeah, um, I didn't know what I was really dealing with until Troy," I say and bite my lip.

King roars with laughter. He gives me a gentle squeeze. "Yeah, well, you know that was minor."

I groan. "But I still love him, so I'll take it."

King laughs louder and harder. I can't help smiling. This talk wasn't so bad. I love my brother for always being there for me. I can't be mad at him for it.

Owen

"We've come a long way in such a short time," Eva muses aloud as I rub circles on her belly.

"Yeah, a hell of a long way. I swear, you would think you could read my mind. I was just thinking the same thing."

"Great mind," she sings with a smile in for voice.

We've been sitting in the back of the clubhouse on a lounger for the last hour. The party hasn't even begun to die down. She's nestled between my legs with her back to my front. I can't bring myself to move an inch. I'm beyond content.

It's been a long day. We're married. I keep saying it, but it's still surreal.

"It felt good to get away from the bullshit for a day," I mutter into her neck as I nuzzle her skin.

She reaches back to massage my beard. "Yeah, you're right."

I think over the day and my heart swells. King stood beside me as we took our vows. I wouldn't have wanted anyone else to be my best man.

Although, I think it was the look on Cage's face when he walked Eva down the aisle that made the ceremony for me. I saw with my own eyes how much love he has for his girls, the club, and his wife. I've seen it before, but something about it was different today.

I think I saw the peace he made with his sacrifices. I admire him for all he's been through. With Cage's return and Rose waking up, a lot is going on around the Lost Souls family.

Word in the streets says Miguel has backed off. I'm sure Reap's message had something to do with it. I smile at that thought.

Eva tips her head toward the yard. "Do you think Jemma will be okay?"

I look out and find my cousin with her son in her arms. They've been staying here at the clubhouse. Lord knows there have been a few interesting developments there.

Some better than others, but only time will tell if Jemma is better for them. So far so good. I think my cousin may finally find peace.

"I think they'll be fine," I reply.

Jemma doesn't have to look over her shoulder now that Mags is out of the picture. I'll still be keeping my eyes and ears open, though. However, Miguel is a problem we can deal with in the future.

For now, we have a bigger problem. Pop has been putting in work to get some weight behind him. Mags and Miguel were only a nice distraction for him to make a move.

With those two out of the way, Pop is going to have to come at us head-on. He hasn't made a move yet, but we're ready. Especially now.

Misty is due any day now and Eva is getting larger still. Sal, well, she and Gutter are happy and finding their way. That's something we couldn't say about either of them five months ago.

"Daddy looks miserable," Eva pouts.

I turn my gaze on Cage. He does. You can see it in his face every single day. Rose still doesn't remember him and she's skittish as fuck when it comes to him.

"She'll come around just like she has with you guys," I reassure Eva.

"I guess so."

Rose doesn't remember much about anyone, but she's excited about the babies. She's been more than willing to get to know the girls. Eva and Sal, even Misty, have clung to Rose since she's come home.

Home, we're all in South Carolina for now. The longer we're here the more right it feels.

"Their busy in there," I murmur against Eva's neck. The twins are moving around in her protruding belly beneath my hands. I just started to be able to feel them a few weeks ago and it made this all so real for me. Eva's making me a father.

I can't help the smile on my face. We don't want to know what we're having, but I'm hoping for two boys.

Her musical giggle fills the air. "Yeah, it's been an exciting day."

"The fucking best," I say with a smile.

Things may not be perfect, but we have each other and our Lost Soul family. Eva has come out of her shell since being kidnapped. I don't know whether I should be alarmed or not. She spends most of her time with the Squad. I know my brothers would never put Eva in danger, but they're a batshit crazy bunch for her to become locked in with.

Honestly, I think it's just a testament to the fact that Eva is a true Lost Soul. She's seen her fair share of hurt to earn her place. Her place, right at my side. *Property of Brick*, Lost Souls, VP, the Lost Souls Squad Captain.

Lost Souls Series

⭐Forever: Book 1-Brick
⭐Never: Book 2 -Gutter
⭐Always: Books 3-King
Again: Book 4-Cage
Before 4.5- Thor
Sometimes: Book 5-Jackie
Lifetime: Book 6-Grim
Still: Book 7-Kevlar
Once: Book 8-Diggs, Axle, and Sugar
Now: Book 9 -Tracks
When: Book 10-Holden

BLUESAFFIRE.COM

ACKNOWLEDGMENTS

Thank you so much for reading this one, whether for the first time or if you're reading it as the new version. I loved this book the first time around, but I've learned so much and was happy I could rewrite and expend this one.

I've fallen in love with this book all over again. I think I love it more. Thank you for coming on this journey with me. There are eight more Lost Souls to go and I know we're going to have a blast getting to know them. I swear, each one gets more raw than the last.

Thank you so much for your support. I love what I do and I'm grateful to have all of you to share this with. Last year was tough and I had to make a lot of tough decisions. In the end you guys have shown tremendous support and love. You have no idea how much that means to me. The messages, the emails, comments and posts all gave me life when I needed it. Again, thank you.

I would be so wrong not to thank my husband who has shared his wisdom with me repeatedly, even when I had a hard head and had to bump it to learn to listen. Thank you for hanging in there with my crazy. Thank you to my team, you are a family I didn't know I was looking for.

Now we know I'm going to thank God, my source, because He has been my guidance and to Him all the glory goes. It's one think to say you have faith and another to demonstrate it. I give praises because I know what it's like to walk on water. Thank you, Lord.

Next! Gutter! Get your tissues. It gets deep.

ABOUT THE AUTHOR

Blue Saffire, award-winning, bestselling author of over thirty contemporary romance novels and novellas, writes with the intention to touch the heart and the mind. Blue hooks, weaves, and loops multiple series, keeping you engaged in her worlds. Blue is a hybrid author, writing for Sourcebooks and for her own publishing company Perceptive Illusions as Blue Saffire as well as Royal Blue.

Blue and her husband live in a house filled with laughter and creativity, in Long Island, NY. Both working hard to build the Blue brand and cultivate their love for the artists. Creative is their family affair.

Blue holds an MBA in Marketing and Project Management, as well as a MED in Instructional Technology and Curriculum Design. She is also an NLP Master Practitioner.

Wait, there is more to come! You can stay updated with my latest releases, learn more about me, the author, and be a part of contests by subscribing to my newsletter at
www.BlueSaffire.com
If you enjoyed Forever, I'd love to hear
your thoughts and please feel free to leave a
review. And when you do, please let me
know by emailing me at TheBlueSaffire@gmail.com
or leave a comment on Facebook
https://www.facebook.com/BlueSaffireDiaries or Twitter
@TheBlueSaffire

Other books by Blue Saffire
Placed in Best Reading Order
Also available....
Legally Bound

Legally Bound 2: Against the Law

Legally Bound 3: His Law

Perfect for Me

Hush 1: Family Secrets

Ballers: His Game

Brothers Black1: Wyatt the Heartbreaker

Legally Bound 4: Allegations of Love

Hush 2: Slow Burn

Legally Bound 5.0: Sam

Wicked Prince Charmings**

Brothers Black 6: Ryan the Joker

Brothers Black 7: Johnathan the Fixer

Forever Book 1: The Lost Souls MC Series**

Title from Blue Saffire and Sourcebooks**
The Blackhart Brothers Series***
Calling on Quinn
In Deep

Coming Soon…
A**holes Club Series (Book 1 Pit)**
A**holes Club Series (Book 6 Kelex)**
Never

**Blue Saffire Exclusive on the
BlueSaffire.com Site****
The A Million to Blow Series
A Million to Blow
A Million to Stay
A Million Blown Coming 2022

His Miracle Baby**

**Other books from Evei Lattimore Collection Books by Blue
Saffire**

Black Bella 1**

Destiny 1: Life Decisions**

Destiny 2: Decisions of the Next Generation**
Destiny 3: coming Winter 2020/Spring 2021**

Star**

***Book not connected to the Legally Bound Spinoffs.*
****Books published by Sourcebooks*